# SURVIVING HAL

First published in 2018
Published by Puncher and Wattmann
PO Box 441
Glebe NSW 2037
http://www.puncherandwattmann.com
puncherandwattmann@bigpond.com

National Library of Australia
Cataloguing-in-Publication entry:
Flanagan, Penny
Surviving Hal

ISBN 9781925780000
I. Surviving Hal.
A823.4

Cover design by Miranda Douglas
Text design and typesetting by Christine Bruderlin

This project has been assisted by the Australian Government through the Australia Council, its arts funding and advisory body.

# SURVIVING HAL

Penny Flanagan

Puncher & Wattmann

*For my parents:*

*Dad, who leads by example, Mum, who never doubts.*

# I
# Holy Matrimony

# 1.

At the baggage carousel in Bangkok Airport the girl beside us spoke in an abrasive nasal drawl that physically repulsed me.

"I'm goin' straight to a bar an' get pissed, it's heaps cheap here, ay?"

I nudged Andy. He 'tched' in unspoken empathy and my agitation abated somewhat. We were here together, just the two of us. We'd left our kids behind for the first time in ten years. We were free and easy; untethered and set adrift.

I stayed close to Andy as he pushed our luggage-laden trolley down the concourse. Usually I am an independent sort of a woman, but here I felt some cloying need to grasp his arm and hold on for dear life. I was thirty-eight, he was not much older, but I imagined the two of us as an elderly couple, holding to each other in the face of a fast-moving and increasingly unfamiliar world.

The terminal was a deceptive bubble of airconditioning. Every now and then a door shifted open and the real world blasted in; a fog of hot, putrid air from a city rotten with the spoils of urban excess.

As we walked down the arrivals concourse there were eager crowds on either side of us. Everyone was expecting someone. We were expecting Tom.

A familiar-looking Thai woman caught my eye. I was just thinking to myself, *Gee that stout little Thai woman looks just like Hal's wife,* when her eyes widened with recognition and she started squawking,

"Hal! Hal!"

She was waving her finger in our direction, no doubt grasping for the English words to say, "Your estranged son is here! And his pasty, uptight wife!"

Hal sprang out of the crowd like a demented jack-in-the-box. He seemed as surprised as us, then the realisation hit him; we were trying to slip into the country without him knowing. A resigned, 'poor me' look fell over his face. He thrust his hands into his pockets and hung his head morosely, the victim. I looked at Andy and could tell that it had started already. He felt torn between a deeply ingrained impulse to care for his father and, at the same time, to keep him at an arm's length.

Nostalgia won out. Andy's face brightened with a smile, then his shoulders folded around his father in an embrace. A split second of father-son dynamic unspoiled by history.

"Hey! Good to see you, you reeker." Andy glossed over the betrayal with some family jargon.

Hal directed Andy towards Phan, pushing them together for an embrace. "Say hello to your stepmum," he said, and even I had to laugh.

Andy gave her a kiss on the cheek and then everyone looked at me. I held up my hand in a 'how' gesture designed to keep everyone away from me. It worked for a while, then when I was distracted—sizing up the Thai woman lurking behind Phan and wondering who she was—Hal seized the moment, sidling up beside me and clamping his arm around me, claiming me as part of his *farang* clan in front of all these Thai nationals.

At that point, both Andy and I were thinking the same thing; Tom had sent Hal for us instead of meeting us himself. What a dirty thing to do.

It turned out Hal was there to meet his friends, Greg, Jean and Ivan, and take them all to Pattaya for a couple of days before the wedding.

It was awkward. We hadn't seen Hal for twelve months. Andy doesn't exactly stay in regular contact.

The odd flurry of disjointed sentences spat onto an email arrives in our inbox from Hal every couple of months. Usually he wants something like mail forwarded from his PO box, that sort of thing. The last series of communications, increasingly solicitous, were to procure a long, specific list of 'essentials' from Australia, Andy to bring them. I thought the Savlon cream was fair enough, the Bushells tea ('no bags, leaves only'), the specialised toothpaste, Vegemite ('tubes only, no jars'). But manila folders? Do they not have stationery in Thailand?

We all stood around attempting conversation; awkward bursts of familiar sounding words that went nowhere. We tried to pretend it was normal that a son wouldn't be in contact with his father regularly enough to prevent an entirely coincidental meeting at an international airport. I made small talk with Jean for a while. She seemed friendly enough. She had a crinkly smile and an honest face that I trusted. I wasn't sure where Ivan fitted in but I assumed he was an old family friend. He was a short, stocky guy with a goatee and wrong-for-the-climate polyester pants. Andy said later, "Did you see his shiny pants? Weird." And they weren't just 'travel pants', either. He continued to wear them religiously over the next week or so, through the humidity and the stifling heat, in remote village and city alike.

Now, I'm not just saying this because of what I know now, but there was something about him that unsettled me: he was the sort of man who locks eyes with you and stands too close.

The woman loitering on the edges was Phan's sister, Jeng, an identically stout woman all dolled up in lipstick and clicky heels. She was plaintive in both her expression and posture; hopeful and nervous but not entirely optimistic about whatever it was she was anticipating.

She was introduced to me by Phan almost as an afterthought and met my eyes only momentarily; either I was of no consequence to her, or she had decided that she was of none to me. It was all hideously awkward. I longed to be beamed up and removed instantaneously without explanation.

Just as things were getting dire, Tom appeared, pushing through the crowds, waving his hand above his head in a full-arm movement like an air traffic controller. Hal saw Tom and calculated the facts quickly. Tom had kept our arrival time from him. We all stood around a bit more. The air was loaded with subterfuge from all parties.

Finally, Tom herded us off, the awkward goodbyes of the 'I won't see you again' variety were assuaged by the promise of reunion at the engagement dinner later in the week.

"Who's that guy, Ivan?"

"Some mate of Hal's," Tom replied, seemingly resigned to this, a person he didn't know at his own wedding.

"Is he an old family friend?" I asked, looking from Andy to Tom.

It was a leading question. The subtext: *if not, what's he doing here?*

Andy shrugged. "Never heard of him."

"Hal's invited him along to hook up with Jeng," Tom said, taking charge of our luggage trolley. "Phan said she wouldn't come to the wedding unless Hal bought her some gold and set her sister up with some white cock."

He said this last part in a suitably pornographic sort of voice. *White cyooock!* Andy and I guffawed with horrified laughter. I bent over double and had to stop walking for a second or two.

My heart raced. We were here and it was on. There was something exhilarating about it, if you put the reality of it aside and viewed it from a distance. A great story for the telling later. Welcome to Thailand.

"They're all off for some sex touristing," Tom said, matter-of-factly. "Although I'm not sure what Jean and Greg are doing. I don't think they realise what they're in for."

Then Tom stopped walking and turned to Andy, looking slightly stricken. "I'm gunna need you to keep Hal under control."

"Sure," Andy said. "No worries, mate." Andy slapped him on the shoulder in a big-brotherly way.

"He knows," Tom said. "He knows he's in serious if he fucks up my wedding."

He resumed walking, pushing our luggage trolley for us, through sliding doors, along the white-tiled floors. His posture was the image of Hal's; hunched shoulders, long loping arms, neck retracted into his collarbone in a slightly furtive, watchful way.

"Sunisa's father is a policeman," Tom continued. "I've told Hal he'll end up in a cell if he shames her family."

We all snickered with delight at the thought of Hal being bundled into a cell and locked there for the duration of the two-day wedding ceremony.

"That'd be great wouldn't it?" I said. Andy gave me one of his cautioning looks that said, *Go easy, that's my dad you're talking about.*

Tom flicked a quick look around, then said in a low conspiratorial voice, "Seriously, Sunisa's father has 'disappeared' about seven people. They're buried in the fields somewhere on the outskirts of the village."

I laughed incredulously, because I didn't know what else to do. It was cartoonishly evil. Tom snickered too, his shoulders shook and he sniffed out his sneaky laugh. Tom and I had this affinity. We always ended up snickering longer than anyone else.

Outside the terminal, the air was thick as cotton wool and slightly rotten smelling. It bathed us. Tom lit up a fag without missing a beat on the pushing of the trolley or the leading of the way up through the levels of the car park. I was disappointed by the familiarity of its concrete tiers: we could have been in any Western city.

"Here we are," Tom said. The lights on a Mercedes convertible flashed.

"What?" Andy gasped.

We were both surprised by Tom's sudden, apparent affluence. Tom, who had landed broke on our doorstep more than a few times in the last ten years. Who hoovered our fridge, our wallets, our goodwill and then disappeared back to whatever city he was living in. Who hadn't had a landline since the '90s because he had burnt Telstra that many times in unpaid bills (and had run out of slightly off-kilter pseudonyms of his name to set up accounts under—Thom Saw, Todd Slaw, etc.). Tom, who probably owed Andy the price of the Mercedes in a lifetime of unpaid loans. A Mercedes convertible? Tom was an English teacher, earning Thai baht. We all know Thailand is cheap as chips, but I'm pretty sure foreign luxury cars come in at the same price point.

"Did you rob a bank, mate?" Andy said, pointedly.

Tom wore it. He sort of flicked his chin to it, his mouth stayed clamped shut, his eyes shifted. "Get in."

We edged out of the car park and onto the open freeway. Tom put the top down and the air came rushing in. We were raised above the earth, on a great arcing roadway that stretched towards the high-rise jumble of the city in the distance. Freeways sprouted in all directions: great tentacles of curved concrete reaching across the landscape. Roads were not built on the ground, they were raised up in the sky, travelling unhindered over the streetscape, a method of A-to-B, urban convenience, nothing more.

The whole city—the sky, the buildings, the air—was the colour of a bruise, and with the fading light, the thick smog that blurred it to softness, it was strangely beautiful. The smell, damp and fuggy. Just a sly edge of shit. I decided not to take a set against it. I decided to embrace it: the modern ugliness, the crazy Asian urban jungle, the confronting detritus of a city's underbelly exposed all over the streets as we ran the gauntlet between glossy high rises and half finished ghost buildings. Rubbish, rubble, sewerage, rats, mangy limping dogs.

I was here without my kids, *What's not to like?* I convinced myself as I batted away the growing monologue about the state of the modern world, the dangers of pollution and open sewers, Hep A, Typhoid, Cholera, the poisonous consequences of mass population that emerge when a Western sense of order breaks down. I sank back into the leather seat and let my judgmental voice leak right out of me. It was liberating.

Tom smoked most of the way, and as is the law of smoking (she who is most bothered by cigarette smoke shall always find herself downwind), his stale smoke blew back towards me and wrapped around my face like a blow-away scarf. I didn't complain, it was his car. (Or was it?) Who was I to tell him what to do? *What does it matter?* I told myself cheerily. *You're on holiday. Relax. Relaaaaax!*

The sky darkened and lights came on. The traffic slowed to a peak hour crawl. Andy took a drag on Tom's cigarette. I swallowed my inner fishwife and tried not to think about all the money he'd spent on hypnotherapy two years ago. I tried not to think of him as slipping out of my grasp.

Then Andy turned to me in the back seat and raised his eyebrows. I knew exactly what he was thinking. *What's with the car?* The wordless communications of a ten-year marriage.

We still had it.

## 2.

Andy Straw was the sort of man who looked right into your eyes when he shook hands with you. When I first met him this gave me a thrill. I shook his hand and felt the corny old zap of attraction that you read about in romance novels. He was the sort of handsome that some women do and some women don't. As it happened, I was in the 'do' category. He appealed to me physically. His face was just on the right side of handsome without being too blandly perfect. It seemed friendly.

He was also the sort of man who liked to make an impression. When we were told a representative from Sydney Council was coming to meet with us, we expected the usual humourless bureaucrat in a brown suit. Then Andy swept in wearing his fitted Jack London number. He had Rhonda the receptionist tittering like a schoolgirl. I heard the commotion and looked up from my computer to see him there, leaning over reception with his elbow cocked on the upper lip of the front desk. He was invading her space and she was enjoying every minute of it. Clearly, she was in the 'some women do' category, just like me.

Andy was doing what I now call his 'Fake Salesman Laugh'.

It goes: huh-huh- HAAAA! Two short, one long and is always disproportionate to the joke. He can do it on cue and often does it AT me because he knows I am onto him. But Rhonda, a woman who fancied herself a fun sort of lady when the lights were low, was chuckling into her chins the way middle-aged women do when young men flirt with them. She was a soft target if ever there was one. I went out to meet him and he looked up at me and said "Hello," as though my sudden appearance was the most enormous pleasure he'd had all day.

"Andrew Straw?" I asked.

He extended his hand and did that thing where he looked right into my eyes. "I'm the garbage guy," he said without shame. "And you must be . . . ?"

"Nell, the bus shelter girl. Well, there's a few of us and I'm one of them."

"The Bus Shelter Girls, sounds like a band."

"Or a community dance troupe."

Then he did something else that endeared him to me. He sang a doo-doo-doo version of "do the bus stop" and did the bus stop disco moves. Right there in reception, with our austere modern logo as his backdrop.

*Who is this fool?* One side of my brain was thinking, while the other romantic, idiotic side found it stupidly attractive. Which just goes to show, there's no formula for human attraction. What you *say* you find attractive, is actually not what your heart has in mind at all.

Rhonda of course, was HOOTING with laughter. Then she ruined it by yelling, "Medic!"

A look passed between Andy and I; conspiratorial. "Well," I said, ushering him away from Rhonda's gaze, lest she get too distracted to answer the phones, "This way, garbage guy."

The meeting went like all meetings go; a lot of people talking and no one saying much of anything that couldn't have been put in a bullet-pointed email and sent in place of Andrew Straw the Garbage Guy.

But being an all-female design team of three, we appreciated the testosterone in the room, if nothing else. Andy was the kind of man who oozed testosterone. Even my mentoring senior partner, Ellen Thomas, was not immune to his charm. After she'd appraised his notes on the brief with her glasses on and asked a few very pointed questions about how things aligned and why so many recycling bins were needed in that particular spot, he even broke her cool exterior by saying, "I'm guessing you're the captain of the bus shelter girls?"

To which I snickered and Ellen see-sawed forward in the way she does when something really makes her laugh. Then she busied herself making notes on her brief and said casually, "We'll be down at The Duck and Swan later this arvo, Andy—team drinks—if you want to join us."

As though she wasn't up to anything, anything at all.

I was ordering the second round at The Duck and Swan when Andy appeared across the other side of the bar. His eyes widened and he pointed at me as if to say, 'There you are!' which I also found endearing; he wasn't playing it cool at all. He was totally up front about the fact that he was looking for me. To a twenty-seven-year-old woman, who was used to men being all coy and elusive about their intentions, this was a revelation.

He made his way around the crowded bar and gave me a peck on the cheek.

"Hello, hello," he said.

"You made it."

"I never turn down a beer invitation." This much still holds true, although from a wife's perspective, not so attractive.

Ellen was happy to see him, too. She was playing matchmaker, it turned out, which was another of her favourite things to do, although I'm not necessarily saying she has a flair for it.

In the past she had attempted to set me up with a 'dear old friend' of hers, a lovely guy who had mysteriously never had a serious relationship with a woman.

"But Tony's a lovely guy," she promised. "You'll really like him."

Turned out I did like Tony, mostly because he was gay and I love gay men. I knew it as soon as my 'date' turned up brandishing a classy bottle of pinot grigio, which he simply 'raved' about. He also talked a lot about his mum.

On the night of that attempted match, Ellen kept pulling me aside and whispering excitedly, "How's it going? Do you think there's chemistry?"

To which I could only say, "Ellen, we'll talk about this later."

Back at the Duck and Swan, Ellen ushered Andy to sit and then instructed me to sit beside Andy. She 'scootched' us together so our thighs were touching. For all her attempts, this would be her crowning triumph as a matchmaker and she has never let us forget it. She's the sort of person who still likes to mail a card or send a thank you note. Every year on our anniversary we get the obligatory card from Ellen, a thoughtful note written in her impeccable architect's hand.

Her self-appointed role on the night was to interview us both, like the middle chair host on a panel show.

"Andy, Nell is one of our most talented designers. I was her tutor at university and I handpicked her for this project."

"Andy, do you have any brothers or sisters?"

"Nell has one older sister who lives in San Francisco, tell him about your sister, Nell."

"So, Andy, have you done any travelling? Nell has been to the US to visit her sister, but never to Europe, can you imagine? She's twenty-seven and never been to Europe!"

Sometimes Ellen gets so invested in her role as matchmaker she forgets when to withdraw her presence. And so, for another two rounds, Andy and I played end-chair guests on Ellen's matchmaking chat show. She was right, however, there was chemistry, she just needed to get out of the damn way.

Which was why I eventually did something very forward that was somewhat out of character. Generally I am the sort of person who sits back. But every now and then, when I see something I like, I just step forward and elbow everyone else out of the way.

I excused myself and went to the bathroom. On my way back, I stood at a distance from the table where Ellen and our group were sitting. I waited for Andy to look up. Then I gave him a 'Let's get out of here' gesture and exited stage left. It was a flick of my head and a raised eyebrow, which he says he's never forgotten. And his instant recognition of it proved, beyond a doubt, that we were simpatico.

Still, he took his time about it. I stood on the quiet inner-city street, wondering if maybe I'd been too confident. I'm not a striking beauty, after all. I'm not hideous, but I don't stop traffic, let's put it that way. What had made me think I could just flick my head and some handsome guy in a hipster suit would follow? I was just about to concede defeat (for me and Ellen both) when Andy swept out of the pub into the street.

He took my hand, led me up to the main street and hailed a cab for us both.

# 3.

Truth be told, Andy was what I would call 'an overlapper'. That night when he took my hand and led me into a cab, he was still entangled in the dying throes of his previous relationship. To be clear, lest you think I'm obfuscating, the relationship was not over, but Andy, emotionally speaking, was done with it.

"I should probably tell you something." He turned toward me in the cab and put a hand lightly on my knee, which to be honest, thrilled me.

"Are you really a woman?" I asked. He laughed, short and hollow, nervous, self-effacing. I could see the effect I was having on him, it made me like him more. He wasn't so confident after all.

"I'm assuming . . . " he began, then took his hand off my leg.

"Whatever you're assuming," I said, "is right."

There was something about him that made me bold with my feelings.

"My last relationship has not quite ended. It's over, but . . . "

"Has it ended or not?"

"For me it has . . . "

"Has it ended for her?"

"Well, we're . . . you know, it's inevitable, I just haven't . . . "

"So, you have a . . . girlfriend?" I ventured, hoping he wouldn't upgrade that to 'wife'.

"Yes. But it's over."

"If she's your girlfriend, it's not over."

He laughed nervously. I could see I had him on the back foot now. Something about that, the power of it, made me giddy.

"Shall we get a drink?" he said, changing the subject. "I know a great place on the water, down near Pier One."

Without waiting for my reply, he directed the cabbie to his little waterside haunt. A hole in the wall music joint that happened to be built into the lower level of one of Sydney's old piers. This was back when the area was a ragged fringe edge of the city. Rows of abandoned wharf buildings in the ominous shadow of the Harbour Bridge. He knew the girl on the door, she greeted him with a squeal and stood up to receive a kiss on the cheek. It was too loud inside to speak so we were spared the small talk. She stamped our wrists and we walked into a room full of sweaty bodies dancing to a live funk band. The bass physically pummelled my chest and I considered for a split second abandoning this whole idea of stealing some other poor woman's boyfriend and just going home. My life could go on as it was, without this increasingly complicated entanglement.

Then, as though he sensed me about to scarper, he took my hand and led me through the dark, noisy room to the waterside platform on the outside of the building. The dark harbour sloshed around the pier piles beneath us and the outside bar area was haphazardly dotted with moulded table and chair ensembles, the kind that are prefabbed in one piece out of fibreglass. He settled me at a table and then went quickly to the bar. He brought back two cold beers, set one down in front of me and took a long swig of his before he spoke.

He was still living with her. The relationship was volatile. She once threw a phone at his head and nearly knocked him out. He showed me the small scar up near his hairline, where his head had been stitched back together. Her name was Lindy and they'd been together for five years. She was a heavy drinker, on her way to being labelled an alcoholic, as it turned out. But back then, everyone just characterised her as a party girl, a hell-raiser, a girl who liked a drink or two, or ten, before passing out on the bathroom floor.

"When she met my father for the first time," he said, "she wore a Lycra cat suit."

"As a dress up?" I asked, confused.

"No," he laughed. "It was a full body cat suit, really low cut and I couldn't believe it."

"A cat suit?" I couldn't believe it either. I was trying to picture a cat suit in my head and where one might buy it.

"If you knew my father, you'd know how totally wrong that was," he laughed.

"It's wrong regardless of that," I said, missing the clue about his dad. "How did you meet her?"

"We worked together."

"Do you still work together?"

"No."

He grabbed my hand across the table.

"But anyway . . . "

"Anyway, nothing," I said, but I left my hand in his.

"I'm moving out," he said to the table, not meeting my eyes. "Soon."

I sat back, eyed him and took a big gulp of my beer. I set it down. Then I picked it up again and drank the rest. I stood up, a bit unsteady as the beer rushed to my head. "Call me when you're out," I said.

I walked back through the funk and the bodies to the roadside of the pier. I got in a cab and went home.

A few weeks later, he called me. Like most men, he needed something to jump to before he jumped: an overlapper. He jumped to me. I was his next landing point. I was his final landing point, as it turned out. An anomaly in a history of damaged, broken women.

He chose me and now I know why.

When Andy and I started going out, Hal's name was mentioned in dark, comical asides. I recall more than once, one or other of Andy's friends asking me ominously, "So, have you met Hal yet?"

The question carried in it some bleak joke that seemed to amuse them. This led me to believe that Hal was merely someone to be suffered and largely a source of amusement. Indeed the very mention of his name seemed to plant a wry, knowing smile on all of Andy's friend's faces. It also led me to believe that Hal was harmless.

What I should have been paying attention to was the sense of remove between Andy and his father. The very fact that he called him 'Hal' and not 'Dad' should have been a red flag that there was more to Hal than a potentially insufferable in-law. I should have noticed the change in temperature that came over Andy when Hal's name was mentioned. The frozen smile, the far-off look. The way he said, "Now, now," as a way of shutting friends down on this topic as soon as it was raised. What I don't get is why his friends thought Hal was an amusing topic.

There really was nothing funny about Hal.

# 4.

Most Fridays we went to Tom and Anita's house for beer, takeaway and cards. They lived in Glebe then, in a terrace that Anita's father owned. Still in their early twenties, Anita and Tom were both eternal students and living that scratchy, minimalist existence where there's never enough cutlery for the takeaway and none of the plates match. If we drank wine, we drank it out of middy glasses pinched from the local pub.

Anita was a sweet-faced pixie of a girl with a beautiful round face and the kind of short-cropped haircut that only certain women can get away with. She smoked elegantly, along with the boys, but was more considerate about blowing her smoke away from me. She spoke the Straw family lingo—this and that was 'reeking', said 'balls!' instead of bullshit, 'base' instead of bum, 'you larries'—but her soft girlish voice made it all the more endearing. She held her own and she shuddered helplessly when she giggled, which I loved.

If my affection for Anita is somewhat magnified it is because she and Tom, high school sweethearts, eventually petered out before reaching that point where they should have married. We all miss her terribly, especially when you consider the way things turned out.

Anita's brother lived in the other room but he was something of a Boo Radley character; we never saw him and if we did, he was lurking in the shadows of the hall with his spooky eyes and then gone before we could ask him to join us.

The first time I went there and met Tom, I was confused. Firstly, he was so much younger; eight years. Plus, they did not look like brothers at all. Tom was blonde—the proper white-blonde that stays until adulthood—and fair-skinned. Andy, on the other hand, was so cohesively olive-skinned, brown-eyed and dark-haired that people often mistook him for a Greek. But when they opened their mouths and spoke, the family tongue was unmistakable.

The house was typical of Glebe terraces back in the '90s. It was dank. Attached on one side to its sibling terrace, the freestanding side then smacked up against a rock wall that absorbed moisture like a sponge. We sat in the kitchen at a formica table with the doors open to the courtyard on a hot summer night. The kitchen was updated, but not in any practical way; just a galley along one wall, with trendy down lights that left us sitting in semi-darkness in the no-man's land between the kitchen bench and the wall. The smell of damp stalked us intermittently throughout the evening.

Anita was an art student and the entry hall was an eclectic gallery: her art; old framed photos from her childhood; a photo of her and Tom as teenagers and an old black and white of Hal and Corky.

When I first saw it, I thought the blonde teenager in the photo was Tom, but the era wasn't right. It was clearly taken in the '50s or '60s. It had that deliberate and meticulous artistry about it that old black and whites have: a perfectly plain-lit backdrop; a beautifully art directed paling fence; Hal as a fresh-faced teen grinning on one side and Corky the aggressively upbeat puppet on the other.

"Jesus," I said, peering closer when I first saw it. "I could've sworn that was you, Tom."

"Spooky," Tom agreed.

"He was quite the larry," Andy said, a hint of pride. Larry, in

Straw-speak, meant larrikin.

"And who's this guy?" I asked, pointing to the puppet with its manic red-lipped grin.

"Corky, the puppet." Tom sniggered. Then, both of them announced in unison, "*The Bubble Up Children's Happy Hour*!"

"Never heard of it," I said.

"Dad used to do quite a bit of improvising," Tom said, adding air quotes over the improvising.

"Quite good sport," Andy chuckled.

"Have you seen it?" I asked.

"Oh, Dad's got his whole back catalogue on video tape."

"It's pretty funny," Tom said.

"What are they talking about?" I asked, looking at the Tom-clone who was actually Hal and the slightly 'Chucky' ventriloquist's dummy apparently named Corky.

"Girl troubles," said Tom. "That was the segment, he'd talk about his girl troubles with the puppet."

Andy and Tom were swaying between being proud and being dismissive of Hal. They couldn't quite decide.

"And . . . then he joined the police force?" I said, confused. Next along the hall was a photo of Hal Straw as a young man, in a perfectly pressed police uniform.

"Ah, Constable Kershaw," Andy said. "*Magpie Creek*."

"The TV show," Anita said, then when I looked at her puzzled, she shrugged in solidarity, *I've never seen it either.*

"Poor old Constable Kershaw, he met with a very unfortunate end."

"Decapitated in a car accident," Andy said, like it didn't delight him at all. "So violent."

"People bombarded the ABC with complaints," Tom said proudly.

"Did you ever see the show?" I asked Andy.

"Not when it went to air, but Hal's got every episode he was ever in stored on video tapes somewhere. He used to make us watch them before bedtime."

"It's quite stiff . . . the acting," Tom giggled. "You know, it's very, 'I say, Constable!' But when we were kids, we loved it."

Andy regarded the old photos again. "He was a handsome prick," he said, with begrudging admiration.

As it happened, Hal lived around the corner from Tom and Anita, in a three-storey terrace that had once been the boys' family home. But they no longer went there to visit. According to the boys, Hal's second wife, Helen, was 'a reeker'; their own invented noun from the descriptive word 'reeking'.

"Sometimes he walks by at night, down the lane," Tom said, "and we're lying in bed when we hear this voice coming out of the darkness, 'No humping!'."

Tom and Andy snickered at this, then Andy patted his pockets for the car keys.

"Shit!" He jumped up. "I parked my car right outside."

He rushed out to move the car, not prepared to alert Hal to his presence.

After he'd gone, Tom looked at me and said, "You're not quite ready for that, Nelly-girl."

"For what?"

"For Hal," Anita said warningly. Anita was an old hand with the family Straw.

"Who dealt this tripe?" Tom said, back to the hand of cards.

I eyed Anita across the table. We were playing together, as usual. Andy and I had resolved, for the good of our relationship, to never play 500 again after a particular incident early on in our courtship, about which we no longer speak. But suffice to say, when you play cards with the Straw boys, you need to keep your wits about you.

*They* learned by playing with Hal that mistakes, even at age eight, could result in you being called a little cunt.

They were very particular about the formalities, it was almost a bit OCD. The table had to be immaculately clean, the cards cut always to the person on your right and table talk of any kind was not tolerated.

"Six hearts?" I said hopefully. Anita's eyes went immediately to the hand of cards in front of her. A small smile twitched at the corners of her mouth and I knew then she had the left bower, possibly the joker.

Andy came back inside and lobbed his car keys into my bag. "Whose call?" Then as he sat down beside me, "Breast! Breast! Breast your cards, Nell."

I pressed my cards against my chest instinctively.

"Breast!" Tom shouted, just for the hell of it and we all snickered like teenagers.

"These two reekers are table talking again," Tom said matter-of-factly to Andy as he fanned out his cards in his hand. "Your bid."

"I never," I said.

"Six hearts?" Tom did an exaggerated impression of me, the upwards inflection much more obvious. "Then she . . . " he pointed at Anita, ". . . smiled."

"I NEVER!" Anita said with exaggerated offence. See what I mean? They didn't miss a trick. Their instincts were tuned way up; survival at all costs.

"Come on, then," Andy said, "We'll whoop your arses anyway." Then, ever so casually like he hadn't done it a million times before, he said: "Misère."

We all groaned, even Tom.

## 5.

Three months later I was deemed ready. I was introduced to Hal over lunch at a trendy café in the eastern suburbs of Sydney. It was BYO and Andy brought four bottles of wine, which he clutched in a plastic shopping bag like giant worry dolls.

"Four bottles? Are you sure?" I asked.

"Trust me," Andy said, ripping the cigarette in and out of his mouth with a one-last-request desperation as we walked along the beachfront towards the restaurant, "we'll need them."

Hal was waiting at an outside table. I recognised him immediately from the Shrine to Hal wall in Tom and Anita's hallway. Still the same foppish hair, but white now instead of blonde, his face was a melted version of the young guy in the headshots.

When we were introduced Hal uttered, "Yes, lovely, lovely. Nell Wylie." He said my name as though to confirm the identity of the object in front of him. Then he lunged forward with wet lips. I was nimble. I faked left then right, so he caught me awkwardly on the ear. But he grabbed me in a tight embrace all the same, pressing his spongy old body against me. Then he held me at arms length for an intense visual examination with his pale, watery eyes.

It does seem especially odd now, that Andy would not simply shield me from Hal for as long as possible, but, looking back, I think relationships, sexual conquests, held currency with Hal. Despite his better judgment, Andy still wanted to impress his father and to do so, he had to deal in Hal's currency.

I needn't have worried about what sort of impression I was going to make on Hal. In fact, I needn't have stayed beyond the first meet-and-greet impressions. About ten minutes into the lunch, bored with the polite get-to-know-me chit-chat, he stopped communicating with me directly and proceeded to conduct entire tracts of conversation about me while I was still sitting there.

"You like them thin, don't you son? Yes, very thin."

"Isn't she gorgeous?" Andy redirected him, grinned at me, kissed my cheek firmly and put a protective arm around my shoulders.

"She can talk too," I smiled.

Andy laughed. Hal didn't notice.

"Bit of an improvement on the drug addict," Hal said, casually rearranging his cutlery.

"Dad, she wasn't a drug addict."

"Well, a heavy drinker."

Hal turned to me, just to make sure I was clear that we were now discussing Andy's ex-girlfriend. "His last girlfriend, very heavy drinker. It really takes a physical toll on women, the drinking. You can see it in their face, the skin."

I'd actually seen photos of Lindy by that stage. Contrary to Hal's inference that she was some sort of scaly-skinned alcoholic, she was in fact a dark-eyed beauty with a mane of glossy black hair. I'd have been intimidated if I didn't know the phone-throwing story.

"Anyway . . . " Andy tried to move him on.

"Remember the whippet?" Hal said.

"Not now, Dad."

"She was so thin, we nicknamed her the whippet." He chucked back a half a glass of Andy's chardonnay and held out his glass for a refill.

Andy topped him up, a strained smile on his face.

"But you were quite taken with her, weren't you? Very taken."

"Yes, I was," Andy said, his voice tight.

I took the opportunity to look out at the surf, sip my wine and wonder deeply when the entrées would arrive.

"But rough. She was a bit rough, wasn't she?" Hal continued.

"You thought she was."

"A Westie," Hal said, keeping his eyes on Andy as he knocked back another glass.

"Now, now." Andy kept his voice light.

"You were furious when I threw her out of the house," he hooted at the memory. "Furious!"

"I was furious because you called her a slut," Andy said in a tone of voice so light and congenial that I almost mistook it for something like, 'didn't we have some fun times'.

"Fair's fair mate. You were humping under our roof."

"I was eighteen."

I felt an urgent need to go to the bathroom and excused myself.

When I returned, the entrées had arrived. Hal was attacking a plate of prawns. Caught without a finger bowl he began to bark orders at passing waiters.

"Finger bowl!" he demanded. "Here. Quickly. I smell like a whore."

Did he really say that?

"Dad!" Andy cautioned.

"I'm up to my balls in prawns here," Hal cackled like a naughty school boy, chastised but secretly pleased with himself.

Andy motioned politely to a waiter and with much practised

charm procured a finger bowl for Hal who continued to rip the heads and legs off his prawns before devouring them.

"So you're in love, son?"

"I am. Very happy," Andy glowed at me. The open admission to being in love caught me off guard. I didn't think we were up to that yet and for the briefest of seconds I felt cornered. But Andy didn't do things by halves, he didn't hesitate or weigh up options, he just followed his heart and went barrelling into love and commitment. This, from a man, was a novel concept to me. And despite my instinctive sense of reservation, that inner voice that said 'Careful!', I was completely smitten.

"Oh, he likes the ladies," Hal sing-songed to his plate of prawns. "And family? You've met them?"

Was he talking about my family?

"No, I haven't met them yet," Andy said.

"Know anything about them?"

Why didn't he just ask me about my family?

"Nell?" Andy brought me into the conversation.

"Yes?" I was beginning to tire of this whole weird thing, where I was at the table but no one would speak to me directly.

"Would you like to tell Dad about your family?"

"Would you like to *ask* me something about my family?" I said, looking Hal in the eye with what I hoped was a steely 'don't mess with me, you old fucker' gaze.

Hal chuckled.

"Ooh look out, she's waxy." He fussed around with the last of his prawns, sucking the juice out of the heads. His hands feathered around nervously. He realigned his plate, his glass, the salt shaker.

Andy refilled my glass. "Have some of this chardonnay darling, I think you'll like it."

"So, your parents, where do they live, darling?" Hal asked. He settled his napkin back into his lap, clasped his hands in front of him, then leaned forward towards me, and gave me his full attention in a forced, unnatural way. Had he forgotten my name already?

"In Manly, on the northern beaches."

"Big house?" Hal said. "Near the beach?"

"Not . . . particularly," I said, a bit bewildered, looking to Andy for direction.

"Nell's dad is Paul Wylie," Andy said hoping to score points with my father's (obscure) fame as a residential architect.

"Oh?" Hals' face drew a blank but he stayed attentive, sensing there was something in this worth knowing.

"He's a famous architect," Andy said proudly. "He's won all sorts of awards. There's a walking tour you can go on in Willis Cove that takes you past all the houses he's designed."

"Not all his," I corrected.

Andy took a lot of license with this sort of information. The truth was, Dad had been part of a collective group of architects who had been commissioned in the '70s to design homes for a new bushland suburb on the (then) fringes of the northern suburbs. At the time, everyone thought them a bunch of crazy arty-farty hippies and the project was widely dismissed as a waste of taxpayers' money.

Gradually though, the mood had turned and now, the suburb and its eco-friendly, Lloyd Wright-esque homes were being hailed as progressive modern classics, houses returned to their original glory by the upper-middle-class families who clamoured to buy them. Hence the walking tour.

"Oh yes, those hippy places on the north shore. Very impressive," Hal crooned. "So that's how you got your job then?" He was looking at me again.

"What?"

"Dad got you in."

"Got me in?" I repeated, not quite believing he would go this way so blatantly.

"Andy says you're also an architect." So he did listen. To things that might be of use when he wanted to bring me down a peg or two.

"Yes," I said, visibly irritated. "But Dad didn't *give* me a job." This was my Achilles heel. He'd hit it perfectly within an hour of meeting me. The precision was frightening. Underneath all that mad professor blathering that he was doing, his mind was trapping facts and stashing them away for later.

"Nell works for an entirely different firm," Andy clarified.

"But Dad must have some influence," Hal said innocently, as though it was a perfectly acceptable thing to imply. "You said he's pretty influential, very accomplished. He probably opened some doors for Nell. You know, proud dad, his golden daughter."

"He didn't open any doors for me," I said evenly. My heart was racing with fight or flight. *Come on, you old fucker!* I thought. *Bring it on!*

"But it's that sort of industry. Everyone would know he's your dad." Hal was all sincerity. Unfortunately for all my bravado, I was gobsmacked. Rendered speechless. Fuming but speechless.

"Nell's very good at what she does," Andy said in that same congenial voice. It was as though we were all just having a nice conversation. As if someone wasn't implying my whole career was owed to nepotism.

"Oh! You're very proud," Hal said, as though it was a surprise that Andy would be proud of me and what I did.

"She's just won a big design competition."

"Gee!" Hal crooned. "Very impressive, a house design was it?"

"No, it was an urban design competition," I mumbled, knowing already where this would go.

I'd been through this a number of times since winning. It never came out sounding as impressive once you drilled down on the detail.

"Urban," he repeated, as though the word were foreign.

"It was . . . " I was searching for a way to put it that wouldn't sound lame. Unfortunately Andy got there before me.

". . . for a bus shelter."

"A bus shelter," Hal repeated.

I knocked back my wine. Andy refilled it and gave me a 'be nice' smile. The waiter cleared the plates. One course down, two to go. Hal looked like he was still processing something about me, my bus shelter perhaps. I prepared my comeback based on the fact that it was a large interchange in a busy part of town. It wasn't just some bus shelter, it was a massive structure that housed four or five major city bus routes. But Hal went in a completely different direction.

"Dad didn't help?" Hal said to me innocently.

"What?"

"Dad, just drop it," Andy said, his composure slipping momentarily.

"So you don't get Dad to help out. Just thought he might give you advice, sort of work with you on things."

"Ah, no." It was all I could manage.

"So you're not that close?" Hal kept on. "To your dad?"

"Yes. We are very close."

"But you don't discuss work?"

"Sometimes we do."

I believe the expression is painted into a corner.

"Nell's very talented, Dad," Andy broke the rhythm.

"So she's on the big money then?" Hal said.

"She's doing fine," said Andy deflecting the reality that architects don't actually earn as much as people think.

"But it's a pretty prestigious title, award-winning architect," Hal was drilling down. "Sort of more prestigious than garbage coordinator."

Andy chuckled, it was a brittle noise that had no air in it. Andy worked for the city, overseeing the waste management program that covered the entire central business district. He was not a garbage coordinator. He worked at Town Hall for Christ's sake, with the Lord Mayor himself.

"She's quite ambitious," Hal said, as though narrating Andy's thoughts for him. "That can be a bit emasculating."

All this was said in a light, bantery way. Not in a nasty tone of voice. If you weren't listening properly, it would have sounded like we were all having a nice conversation over lunch.

"I'm very proud of her, Dad," Andy said with a forced smile.

"Oh, he's very taken," Hal crooned, now talking about Andy as though he wasn't here. "Look at him, he's done his balls."

Things went downhill from there. After the mains, he started on Maude. Andy had warned me about this.

"He'll start calling Mum names," he'd said.

"Why?"

"Because he thinks he's been hard done by."

I'd tuned out by that stage. I'd realised it was actually easier to let Andy and Hal conduct their conversation around me. Whenever I got drawn into it, Hal said something that made me want to punch him in the face. And apparently, I wasn't allowed to do that.

So I didn't notice it happening at first. He said it in the same sort of voice that you'd say, 'Your mother forgot to collect my dry-cleaning.'

"Of course, your mother took all my money."

"No, she didn't Dad."

"And gave it to that fat cunt."

"Hey, settle!"

"You know, she assured me I wouldn't need any super, because she had this inheritance. Then she just nicked off with it, leaving me nothing."

"She left you the house."

"Well, all my super, you know, I'm in pretty dire straits."

All the while he guzzled as much of Andy's wine that could possibly be consumed within the time frame.

"How's Helen?" Andy redirected, referring to Hal's second wife.

I tuned out again after that. I looked at the ocean, I looked at the specials board, I looked at the people opposite us, having a normal time. They were laughing occasionally with real, unguarded happy faces. I wished I was at their table where you didn't have to enter the conversation with your dukes up defensively, ready to jab and duck.

I heard Hal and Andy talking, occasionally I heard Andy say, 'settle,' or 'now, now'. But I didn't listen. Certain words floated across to me and I sort of batted them away like flies: 'humpers' and various forms of the verb 'to hump', 'bitch', 'your mother', 'my money'. It went on. I screened it out. What else was there? Except to come across all stitched up, like a school teacher, saying things like, 'Here, here, I will not stand for such vulgarities.'

But it must have been bad. Because after we'd bade Hal a false fond farewell, after he and I had done our 'fake to the right, to the left dance' where he tried to plant a big wet kiss on my lips and I offered only my right ear, Andy took my hand and led me across to the beach.

"Feel like a swim?" he said, breathing fast like he'd just done a workout.

I looked around me. The sun had gone behind thick grey clouds by then and there was a big coastal wind whipping off the ocean. It was cold. The water was dark and violently rippled by a gusting wind. It wasn't swimming weather.

"Ah . . . no," I said, with a very clear 'I'd rather stick toothpicks in my eyeballs' inflection.

Andy kept walking and led me down to the sand. He removed his shoes.

"What are you doing?" I asked.

"Going for a swim." He was drunk and completely wired. "Come on!" His eyes were like spinning tops. He laughed in a mad, 'I'm completely off my rocker and if we were on a cliff I'd jump off it', sort of a way. I felt myself pulling back from him. After months of unguarded intimacy in the flush of new romance, I suddenly pulled back and realised I hardly knew this person standing in front of me. This person who was now disrobing at an alarming rate.

He dropped his jeans. He didn't even have swimmers on. Just a pair of boxers. He pulled his shirt over his head and, leaving his clothes in a pile at my feet like shed skin, took off to the water's edge. He bolted for the waves, which were dumping violently right on the shoreline.

I winced as he took two steps into the water, arched up and took a great leaping dive into the grey churn. He disappeared. Then his head popped up again and he shot upwards into the air, like a rocket, arced and then head-firsted into the next wave, and the next and the next.

Was it just me, or was that a bit odd?

# 6.

From a parent's perspective, Andy was a pleasing prospect. He had a good job, he didn't say 'youse' and he didn't wear thongs to dinner. But my mother has a sixth sense for people's peccadillos.

"He's very handsome," she said to me later, in a way that spoke of caution. My mother didn't trust 'handsome'. I think it was the overlapping thing she was picking up on.

Around that time my parents were three years into living without an oven, because the one in the kitchen was broken and my father had grand plans to redesign the whole house around a new one. While it's true that if you live with an architect you will live in your dream home, it is often a long wait. Perfectionism and grand visions go hand in hand with indecision and procrastination.

Luckily, Dad had no less than three barbecues to choose from and was currently firing up his small Weber (with retro-fitted rotisserie) out the back. He also had a full five-burner Beefeater on the front balcony plus a flat top built-in barbecue hotplate in the courtyard. The last one had come with the house five years ago and he couldn't bear to part with it.

"It's handy for a few dozen sausages," he'd say, when Mum would suggest moving it on.

The house was a difficult puzzle for an architect to fix. A Federation house on a steep block with the water view out the front and a terraced garden at the back. It had been 'fixed up' by its previous owners in the style of a faux Spanish hacienda, complete with stucco on the walls, scotia cornices and kitschy archways with exposed brick keystones between the dining and living rooms. In other words, an architect's visual living nightmare. (My EYES!)

Along with the problem of the faux Spanish melange, the layout was problematic. The balcony with the modest view of Little Manly beach was out the front with the kitchen marooned at the back. The living and dining were merely the incidental space between the balcony—where everyone wanted to be—and kitchen—the other place everyone always wanted to be. The dilemma was how to join one to the other without sacrificing access to the garden or the view. Dad's plan was to completely rebuild, but how much of the original structure to retain?

"Double brick," he'd say to me, slapping the walls with awe. "You'd be crazy to get rid of it."

I agreed, although I also felt Mum's pain. She was pretty much ready to hire a wrecking ball and drive it up to the house herself with the ball swinging. Decision made.

As is the way of Australian gatherings, Andy went straight out to the barbecue, and stood by it as at an altar with his bottle of beer rested just at his hip. That way he and Dad could stare at the chicken slowly turning and not make eye contact as they talked. I sat at the kitchen bench and ate all the chips while Mum made a salad.

"When are you going up north?" she asked.

"Week after next."

"And you're staying with Andy's mum?"

"Yes."

Mum made a face. My mother hates house guests. We are not a bunking-in kind of family.

"First time meeting her? That'll be . . . interesting," she said, making another of her judgemental faces.

"It's a big house."

"And the father, where's he?"

"He lives in Sydney."

"What's he like?"

"Completely mental." Mum wasn't expecting that. She guffawed and held her hand to her chest.

"Oh Nell! What do you mean?" She was scandalised but loving it.

"I met him over lunch about a month ago."

"What did he do?"

"Are you talking about my father?" Andy had re-entered the kitchen for more beers. He came and stood behind me with his hands on my shoulders.

"I was just telling Mum about our lunch with Hal."

"Quite appalling," Andy said. "Nell handled it very well."

He kissed me on the cheek.

"Why?" Mum was loving this. "What did he do?"

"Drank too much," Andy said, effectively shutting down any further discussion of it. Mum looked at me. She knew there was more. Then Dad started barking orders from the barbecue.

"Plate! Lynn!" He was shouting; like something was on fire and he needed to put it out. To be clear, nothing was on fire. He was just full of the urgent righteousness of he who is barbecuing.

Mum looked at me, raised her eyebrows.

"Lynn! I need a plate!" he shouted again.

"Alright!" Mum called back to him, then just to us. "No need to shout." She handed Andy a clean plate with a sardonic flourish. "Take that out to Lord of the Barbecue, would you?"

"It's very important work, barbecuing," Andy said, walking out to deliver the plate. "I don't think you womenfolk understand."

Mum laughed. Then as soon as he was gone she asked, "Seriously, what did his father do?"

She knew there was something Andy didn't want her to know.

# 7.

If Hal was the initial hazing, Andy's mum, Maude, was the skills-driven obstacle course that followed. To sweeten the deal, Maude and her second husband, Stan, lived in a resort town just north of Brisbane. In later years she would describe its distance from Sydney as 'too far to make in one trip'. Like everything Maude did in the years following The Great Marital Walk-out, it was a calculated move that had Hal's tendency toward the unpredictable in mind.

After a meandering three-day road trip north, we arrived at an ocean-side suburb called Sunshine. It was late on a Friday and the sun was in flattering uplight mode. The rows of brash, modern, moneyed beachside houses, that would normally offend me in hard daylight, seemed almost quaint in their inappropriate-for-the-climate design. When we rounded an escarpment reinforced with a honeycombed wall of grey concrete block, I couldn't help but 'tsk'.

"Not enjoying the scenery, my love?" Andy asked knowingly.

"Just . . . why?" Sometimes it was all I could say.

Andy's mum's house was stand alone at the end of a cul de sac and not visible from the street; just a double garage and gate at the entry.

No sooner had we pulled up than a jolly face appeared on high, from over the terrace railing.

"Hey ho!" yelled a booming voice. "It's Andy!"

The figure waved his arms like a traffic controller; two arms criss-crossing back and forth, heralding our homecoming. Stan Logan was in his late fifties, white hair, stocky footballer's build, Maude's second husband and Andy's stepfather of four years. He reappeared at the lower gate and ushered us inside. To my relief, the house was not brick veneer with a salmon-coloured render and a grand timber-veneer feature door at the entry, but constructed entirely from rustic, recycled chunks of timber. Set high on the steep hill, its large terrace and living areas looked straight out to the ocean.

"You must be Nell." He leaned in and pecked me on the cheek. "Great to see you! Great to see you!" His enthusiasm surprised me.

Maude, while polite and welcoming, was less effusive at first. Not that she wasn't pleasant, I just sensed her reticence. I could feel her sitting behind her eyes, keeping her options open before judging me to be suitable. With Andy's eclectic romantic history of crazy women, it wasn't surprising.

Conversely, her country-bred upbringing made her the perfect hostess, no matter how she felt inside. And after our initial eyeing of each other from opposite sides of the open-plan living space, she broke ranks and swept towards me, a Judy Dench vision in white and taupe linen.

"How lovely to finally meet you," she said, pulling me into a pillowy hug. Then she stepped back from me and did that thing Andy does, where he looks you right in the eye.

She held me at arm's length and appraised me, gauging my reaction to her. My score for the first challenge—'how long will you let me look you in the eye before you glance away'—was low. The second test came soon after we had thrown our bags into the guest room. I call this test, 'Can you guess what I really want you to do even if I tell you to do the opposite?'

Andy suggested we head out the door for a quick ale at the surf club where we could watch the sunset from the deck. Stan looked delighted. Maude not so.

"Now don't be upset . . . " she said to Andy, "but I've got Beverley coming for a quick drink," she tapped her watch, "in about fifteen minutes."

"Mu-um!" Andy whined like a kid who's just been told to wash his face.

Maude looked suitably chastened for devising this ambush. She placed an elegant hand upon her bronzed décolletage, "She's *desperate* to see you, Andy." Then to me, "She's my oldest, dearest friend and she just loves the boys. She heard you were coming and I just couldn't say no. She's like family."

Stan looked torn. Andy had him at 'quick ale at the club'. He was halfway out the door when Maude threw the Beverley-in-fifteen curveball at us. He stood now, frozen, astride the threshold of the sliding glass door, one foot in, one foot out, waiting for the outcome of this Maude v. Andy stand off.

"Well, I've been driving all day, I'm going to the club," Andy said testily. "Just a quick drink, I'll be back in an hour."

"Alright, then. Just be back in time to say a quick hello," Maude said easily, clearly happy enough with that compromise. Then she clocked Stan, half in half out, too afraid to move lest he incur her wrath.

"Oh, look at you, you silly man!" she hooted. "Off you go!" A wave of her well-manicured hand and Stan was given a leave pass. I got the sense that if nothing else, Maude was pleased that Andy and Stan were keen to spend time together. That left me.

"Quick Nell!" Stan stage whispered to me, "Save yourself! It's not too late."

I looked to Maude for guidance on this men v. women stand off.

"You suit yourself, Nell, I don't mind," she said, busying herself at the kitchen bench, "I'm easy." But she wasn't looking at me when she said this. Andy was no help, he was already opening the gate and on his way down the stairs to the street.

I weighed it up; a relatively easy intro to Stan with Andy playing interference, or a complete baptism of fire with my new boyfriend's mother flanked by her oldest friend?

In a split second of travel-weary tiredness I chose the former. I wanted to see the sunset from the deck, and the easy company of men and a cold beer seemed the sensible option.

"I think I'll . . . " I indicated Stan and Andy outside, waiting.

"Of course!" Maude said. "I'm easy, Nell, you suit yourself while you're here." Then she gave me a big smile that didn't quite reach her eyes.

As we walked down the hill toward the club, Andy took my hand and said, "You know, Mum wanted you to stay with her, so she could show you off to Beverley."

"What?" I stopped walking. Stan walked on ahead of us, keeping a cracking pace in his eagerness to get to a nice cold one overlooking the surf.

"She said, I should suit myself."

"Yes," Andy said. "But what she wanted you to do was to stay and meet Beverley."

"Well . . . " I threw my hands in the air. "People should say what they mean!"

"Get used to it."

"Should I go back?"

"It's up to you, my sweet."

"Andy, should I go back?"

"Yes, you probably should. Massive points score for comparatively little effort." I looked at him then and realised I loved him. In that moment, I just wanted to do what would make him happy.

"Alright," I said. "I'm going in." He held onto my hand and pulled me back to him. Kissed me.

"Thank you."

"Whatever." I stomped back up the hill in my boots, I felt him watching me.

"Nice arse," I heard him call out. I gave him the finger and kept walking.

When I arrived back at the house, dusk had fallen and the living room was a yellow-lit interior scene. Two women sat at either end of the couch, each furnished with a flute of champagne. They were talking their heads off. I watched them for a while, feeling mild trepidation at finding a place within this intimate twosome, then I slid the glass door open and stepped inside.

"Oh!" Maude's face broke into a real smile. "You came back!"

She stood up immediately, as did Beverley.

"Andy said you had champagne."

"Always," Maude confirmed as she moved across to the kitchen purposefully.

"Oh, she's *always* got champagne," Beverley seconded.

A flute of frosted bubbly had appeared in my hand. Maude was a magician that way, she could furnish you with a glass of bubbly without you even realising it had happened. She introduced me to Beverley. There was a hint of propriety in her voice and I sensed I was already 'hers'. I also realised that Andy had been right, massive points had been scored just for making the effort. I was now being welcomed inside rather than being viewed from a distance, with the onus on me to impress.

From there it was easy. They showered me with their attention and every answer I gave to their questions seemed to please them; what I did for a living, where I lived, my family background, where I'd gone to school.

Maude seemed to know a lot about me already. Clearly she and Andy had spoken at length on the phone in the early months of our courtship. She filled in the gaps for Beverley, making it seem as though her loyalty was just as much with me as it was with Beverley. She shifted easily between her alliance with Beverley as her oldest friend and an alliance with me as someone who would soon be part of the family.

By the time darkness had fully fallen outside, I was pretty tipsy. Which was when talk turned to Hal. It was Beverley who started it.

"So, Nell, have you met Hal yet?"

"Oh! Andy said he was appalling!" Maude jumped in, referring to our infamous restaurant luncheon meeting. "Just. Appalling."

"He's quite . . . " I eyed them both, they were waiting, wondering what I would say, "evil." It was as much the champagne talking as anything and as soon as I said it I thought, *too far*. They hesitated a minute before reacting. Beverley's hand flew to cover her mouth.

"Oh!" Her eyes widened with the relish of my brutal honesty.

Maude's reaction was more measured. She looked a bit sad.

"Oh, he's gone mad," she said. "He's gotten worse over the years. He wasn't like that when I married him."

"He used to be so exciting," Bev assured her. "And quite handsome."

"He was an actor," said Maude. "I mean, I was this girl from the country and he was so . . . so dashing, wasn't he?" She threw it back to Beverley, who caught it deftly and passed it on.

"He was on that show everyone was watching, he played the . . . the . . . " Beverley grasped for it.

". . . the older brother character."

"Yes, until he got shipped off to war." Beverley mimed shipped off with a cursory thumb gesture that suggested there was more to that than just plot development.

"And came back as another actor five episodes later. That was unfortunate," Maude said.

Beverley whispered to me, "He was just too unreliable."

"Hopeless!" The frankness went up a notch. "Never learned his lines, didn't turn up on time. Just . . . blew it."

"Then after you got married . . . what was that show called?" Beverley put her hand on her forehead as though trying to pinch the memory directly out of her brain.

"*Magpie Creek*," said Maude. Her memory of these events was obviously as fresh as yesterday. They were crucial to the way her life had turned out.

"*Magpie Creek!*" Beverley grasped for the year, to clarify . . . "196– ?"

"Seventy-two, Andy was two." They both looked at me, expectantly. I'd been through this with Andy already. I had never heard of a TV series called *Magpie Creek*. It was before my time. This glorious glow from Hal's past was entirely non-existent to me. He had no shimmer.

"It was a little fifteen minute thing they used to put on before the news on the ABC."

"Oh but it was so popular."

"And when they killed him off . . . "

"He played the young constable character, you know, meant to be the heart throb."

"The howls of outrage from the audience."

"He's never gotten over it," Maude said quietly. "He was just so taken aback that they'd . . . " She did the slitting throat mime.

"Oh, but what could they do?"

"It was so violent though, I mean . . . "

"Decapitated," Beverley clarified for me. "In a car crash."

"He was so shocked when he got the script," Maude laughed. "He was just . . . so crestfallen. It was a terrible time."

"You reap what you sow," Beverley said and took a pointed sip of her champagne.

"He had no idea. I mean, his mother used to dote on him." Maude then did a little impression of Hal's elderly mother. "'Oh, isn't he a larrikin' she used to say when he was running round the neighbourhood putting bungers in people's letterboxes."

Beverley clocked my blank look. "Bungers, you know, they were little firecrackers. It's a wonder no one was hurt."

"And then the police would ring up Mrs Straw and she'd just . . . " Maude affected a wide-eyed dotty old lady smile, "'Oh, they're just boys having some fun.' I don't think she was quite right in the head, to be honest. And she'd trot him around to all the radio talent quests. I mean, he couldn't sing or anything. He was just . . . bold."

"Anyway, after the *Magpie Creek* thing, he landed on his feet in the real estate business."

"Yes, the Bingham and Straw thing."

"Greg was good to go in with him," Maude said vaguely. "And they did well for a while."

"What was the slogan?" Beverley said.

"Oh yes: *Call Hal he's your real estate pal*!" Maude could barely hide her smirk. I guffawed.

"Well he was still quite well known, so there he was in his suit. He was very handsome."

"How did you meet?" I asked Maude, who pointed an accusatory finger at Beverley.

"He was a friend of my brother," Beverley said with a tinge of guilt.

"Bev's brother was in radio."

"He was always having these big parties."

"And Hal would strut in, you know, the big TV star . . . " Maude rolled her eyes. "I was just . . . " she looked at Beverley. "We were just so young." There was a pause, a brief regret. Then it passed. "He was a wonderful father," Maude said, reassuring herself again. "You know, just always so good with the boys." She looked to Beverley again, who did not dispute this. "It was just when they started to talk back that he . . . "

"You couldn't have stayed," said Beverley.

"Oh, for my own health, I know," said Maude. They seemed now to be on a tangent of their own. I had become a mere spectator.

"The real estate thing went under. It was just so stressful."

"Then you had Tom."

"Yes, but Tom was so wanted, so loved," Maude protested. "I always tell him that, he wasn't a mistake, I was just thrilled when I found out I was pregnant."

This was intriguing. I kept out of it hoping for more information.

"Eight years was a big age gap."

"Yes but they're so close, Andy and Tom," said Beverley.

Then they remembered me sitting there. Maude turned to me. "And what about Helen?" she asked with affected nonchalance. "Have you met her yet?"

I got the sense this was another skills-based test. Beverley sat to attention, at the ready for any titbit of goss they could garner from me on this topic. It seemed of particular interest to both of them. And I chose my words carefully.

"Yes," I said. "I've met her."

After our initial meeting, Hal had been relentless in pursuit of more contact. Perhaps to get the jump on Maude. Everything was a competitition to Hal, even knowing more about Andy's new girlfriend was a way to score points. We'd had dinner at the Glebe terrace, the former family home. There was no trace of Maude there, just the ill-fitting clutter of the woman brought in to replace her. In the presence of his second wife, Hal had been more subdued. It was a stilted evening where everyone had struggled to hold their real selves inside.

Knowing this meeting had taken place, I could see Maude struggling to stay neutral, but desperate for more information.

"Oh? Is she a nice woman?" she asked, popping a biscuit with brie into her mouth.

In truth, it was hard to say whether or not Hal's second wife, Helen, was a nice woman. All I could think whenever I saw her was, *Why on earth did you marry this man?* I couldn't say that to Maude though, because the same question could be put to her.

"I haven't warmed to her," I said carefully. Beverley snorted. Maude decided to dig a little more.

"Tom says she's very odd." She picked at the snacks' plate as if that was of more interest to her than my opinion on Helen.

"She is," I confirmed.

"In what way?" Maude ventured.

"It's like . . . she's not really there. She's kind of like a Stepford wife."

Maude kept her poker face on and dug a bit more. "Is she a good looking woman? I mean, I've seen photos but . . . "

"Um . . . she's not unpleasant . . . " I confirmed diplomatically.

The last time we'd seen Helen, Andy had remarked later at the inappropriateness of her sheer white linen pants, through which her large white underpants could be seen.

"I mean, I don't need to see THAT," he had remarked as though she had turned up sans pants. Personally, I thought it was the lesser of two evils.

Maude was still waiting.

"She's sort of got a waxy visage," I said thoughtfully, warming to my topic.

Beverley snorted into her champagne gleefully, which encouraged me.

"And a face like this . . . " I affected the big fake smile we got from Helen when we had arrived, as though behind her smile she was plotting how she would quietly murder us both and chop our bodies into tiny pieces before storing them in the freezer.

"Oh dear," Maude said, barely able to disguise her delight. "And they're still in Glebe?"

"Yes."

"And how does the house look?" Maude said, fishing for evidence of either slovenly housekeeping or a poor sense of interior decorating.

"Cluttered," I answered immediately. "There's *shit* everywhere."

I regretted the 'shit' as soon as I said it, but the frankness of it seemed to please Maude.

"Do you think he's *happy*?" she asked. "I just want him to be settled. Do you think they're a good match?"

"Yes," I said. "I do."

"Good," Maude said sincerely. "It's just easier if he's settled . . . Oh, here they are!"

She seemed caught off guard by the sudden appearance of Stan, her present husband, while she'd been so absorbed in her past. He was behind the glass, almost lost in the reflection until he slid the door aside and stepped back into existence. He clapped his hands together and said, "Beverley!"

Beverley rushed to greet him, the hero's welcome. And in that instant, Hal Straw was back where he belonged—in the past.

# 8.

Three months after our meet-the-parents weekend, and I tell you this in confidence, I had an epiphany.

We were sitting in a restaurant overlooking the water and I looked at Andy and suddenly realised the thought of spending the rest of my life with him did not make me feel nauseous. (Admittedly, I had consumed half a bottle of chardonnay over lunch.) Quite the opposite, the thought of spending the rest of my life with Andy actually made me feel light and buzzy. I looked at him and saw that he was my future. It was unfortunate that I then opened my mouth and let my thoughts travel, unedited, to my tongue. Unfortunate because he has never let me forget it.

"Why don't we get married." I said out of the blue.

"What?" His eyes nearly popped out of his head.

"Nothing." I had that feeling where I wished that words were on a string and you could just reel them back in.

"Did you just ask me to marry you?" he coughed with laughter.

I didn't take that as a good sign.

"No," I said. Then I pointed across the table at him, something I do when I want to show that I am deadly serious and that now annoys the hell out of him after ten years of being pointed at. "If you ever tell anyone," I said, pointing gravely, "I will deny it wholeheartedly."

"I'm telling everyone," he laughed.

"Oh, go right ahead," I said, sitting back so the waiter could set my dessert in front of me. Then I gave him a 'consider the gauntlet thrown' sort of a look.

He did tell everyone. He continues to tell everyone. And I continue to deny it. And because I'm considered the more reliable half of the whole, everyone believes me and he has been left looking the deluded fool on more than one occasion. But now you know.

About a month later *he* proposed by accident, (full of drink the night before he had planned to do it properly) took it back, then proposed properly over lunch the next day at the same restaurant. This time it was my turn to laugh.

"Are you serious?" I spluttered, even though I had been tipped off the night before by him saying, "I'm going to propose to you tomorrow. Oops, now I've gone and ruined the surprise."

"Yes, I am," he smiled. "What's your answer?"

All I could do was laugh hysterically. Now that it was *his* idea and more of a reality, I was terrified. I didn't know this person. What made me think I could spend the rest of my life with this person? The sun went behind a cloud and the sky went ominous grey. Then something shifted. Some intangible thing cracked my feelings into the right place.

"Yes," I said.

He then produced a ring. I slipped it on and was admiring it from all angles, just about to shed a tear of joy when I heard the scrape back of his chair. He was standing up, glass in hand.

"No!" I pointed at him. "Please . . . no."

"Everybody . . . " he announced to the restaurant at large. "I have just asked this beautiful woman to marry me."

"Shut up!" I hissed from my seat. "Just sit down and shut up, will you?" Everyone was looking at me. Andy was laughing, really enjoying himself.

"And she has said yes."

He raised his glass to the ceiling and the whole room erupted into cheers. It was the first of many ways he has devised to embarrass me. It never ceases to amuse him.

Hal gave us seven years.

Meaning, he didn't think we'd last longer than that. Meaning, the marriage would be in trouble and all over, bar the shouting, within that time frame. If I recall accurately, the reason he gave was because Andy, like his father, was 'a humper'. Translation: he wouldn't be able to keep it in his pants long enough to keep me. I was torn as to whether this was an insult or a compliment. Either I was a ball-busting, no-nonsense woman who wouldn't stand for it, or I was not woman enough to keep him interested. Perhaps it was both with both meant as an insult.

He told this to Tom, who of course passed it onto Andy (a sibling's loyalty after all is to his sibling) and then Andy passed it onto me, which was oddly unstrategic of him. Time has proven that it is better for everyone if Tom and Andy don't tell me the things Hal has said. I get so angry. I want to take him on. My mother always encouraged outspokenness.

*Go on, say something,* her voice harangues me from inside my head.

Andy talks me down.

"Do not, under any circumstances, take him on," he says. "You'll be sorry."

At first I didn't understand. I thought it was a warning from him. "Hang on," I said, needing clarification. "I'll be sorry because you'll make me sorry?"

"No, because he will hurt you," Andy said, slowly and deliberately.

"How?"

"He'll lash out at you." He looked distant. "You'll never recover."

"So, what should I do?"

"Just try to get along with him."

Getting married involves bringing two families together, physically and figuratively. In our case, it wasn't so much the families Straw and Wylie as it was the fractured factions of the family Straw that posed the problem. Above all, it was the physical reality of Maude being in the same room as Hal for the first time since she'd absconded with her suitcase.

Putting Maude, Stan and Hal in a room together was the perfect recipe for some sort of 'incident'.

Admittedly, the room would be a very large Golf Club reception room, the largest and grandest on Sydney's northern beaches, with a balloon arch at the entry way, a parquetry dance floor in the centre, a Moby Disc turntable by the hall that lead to the toilets and a series of carefully planned tables around the edges. But a room, nonetheless, with Maude and Hal and all their combustible history contained therein.

Back then, the anticipation of an incident was near hysterical, right down to the wording on the invitation and how it might offend. In the end, in an attempt to keep things neutrally traditional, I managed to offend everyone. And we hadn't even stepped inside the church.

My mother and I ineptly planned this big event, with our mutual lack of enthusiasm for anything resembling organisation. If I had my way again, I would have taken the very heavy hints Maude was dropping all over the place like giant flour bombs and handed the entire function over to her very capable and willing-to-plan-everything-right-down-to-the-ribbons-on-the-church-pews hands.

As it was, Mum and I left the flowers until the last minute (honestly, who cares?), picked alternate red meat and chicken mains because it was generically easier (vegetarians, get stuffed) and in a random show of enthusiasm went for the optional extra of the white balloon archway, through which Andy and I would make our entrance as Mr and Mrs Straw. (Or Mr Straw and Ms Wylie, to be more accurate.)

There were so many decisions to make that just didn't interest me one way or the other: the bridal waltz, the entry music, the exit music, the wedding cake, the shape of the bridal table, the size *and* shape of the bridal cake, the size, shape, colour *and* vintage of the car that would take us there, the dessert or the cheese plate. Chair covers, ribbons on pews, flowers in church, flowers on tables, flowers in hair, flowers on lapels and who would remove the flowers from the church once the ceremony was over. Did we want them at the reception? If so, where? On the bridal table? At the entry? Would we need vases for that? Big or small? Freestanding or on a table? Hair up or down? White or off-white? Black tie or lounge suit? How to keep Maude and Hal on separate sides of the room all night.

For that last one, Andy worded up two of his brawniest mates to physically remove Hal from the premises at the first sign of trouble.

As it had turned out, it wasn't Hal who needed to be handled but Stan. Heavy-headed with drink, Stan swivelled on the dance floor while doing his best *Boogie Fever* and found himself face to face with Hal. Stan blinked. Hal licked his lips. The music stopped for a millisecond between songs. Andy caught his brawny mate's eye and the guys moved forward. Stan, drunk, stumbled back then righted himself. His right shoulder shifted ever so slightly as he prepared to take a swing.

Then, instead of his arm moving forward through the air and cracking Hal Straw on the jaw as he had so often and so satisfyingly imagined, his arm was taken hold of gently and used to steer him back to his table.

Stan was moved off the dance floor just as *Eye of the Tiger* pulsed to life, as the silver disco ball spun into action twirling white spots of light across the dance floor. Hal found his nerve and uttered these parting words to Stan's broad retreating back, just loud enough for those around him to hear, but not loud enough to have him escorted from the premises as prearranged, "Go on, you fat fuck."

The crowd of jerking, gyrating wedding dancers folded around Hal and he shimmied in triumph, leering at my then-workmate Jessica, who was wearing a tight black minidress and was drunk enough to smile back and egg him on with a shoulder shaking, forward-bending, breast-jiggling dance move. Ever the opportunist, Hal made sure to put his hands out just in time to accidentally cup her ample assets as she shimmied toward him.

Meanwhile, Stan was sat back in his seat, furnished with a large glass of water and was heard to mumble something about wanting to kill Hal Straw.

After the panic leading up to the wedding, the hysterical expectation that Hal would cause trouble, it was strangely disappointing when he didn't. We would have to wait another ten years before the prophecy was finally fulfilled.

# 9.

After Hal had surprised everyone by behaving so impeccably at our wedding, Andy softened towards him a little and made an effort to see him more regularly. The most vivid memory is the time he took us to the Tattersall's Club for our birthdays, which were conveniently two days apart. The venue was his choice because he was a member and got some sort of discount on the meal. It was a tired old place in a dormant part of town, a pain in the arse to get to. Anyway, we went. If only because it would keep Hal off our backs for a while.

Helen was out of town on business and so we were expecting just Hal. Looking back, this fact was probably more significant than we realised. Their marriage, which was always so carefully presented to us by Hal as his happy coda to the harrowing event of Maude's leaving him, was ever so steadily decaying from within. It was only a matter of time before the brittle veneer of it shattered and revealed them both. In hindsight, it was a shame their marriage ended.

If Hal had stayed married to Helen, there is no doubt that things would have turned out differently and I would not be carrying this small deceit, holding it covered in my hands, carefully carrying it through every ensuing day, nursing it to my grave.

That night we were just racking up our second game of billiards when Hal breezed into the billiards bar with some other slapper and introduced her to us like it was all very normal.

No one around me reacted, so I followed their lead and shook her hand, claimed it was nice meeting her. She then attached herself to me like a limpet for the duration of the meal and seemed utterly determined to make a deep connection with me.

Tom and Anita were there too and everyone got more and more drunk, while I became more and more sober. I was three months pregnant with Daniel, our first child, and so I was denied the anaesthetising effects of alcohol. Things became sharper and sharper as the night wore on, the blurred morality more acute, the audacity of Hal bringing his mistress to our birthday dinner more and more offensive. *Why should I care?* I kept asking myself. *I don't even like Helen, so why should I care?*

She had a pug-like face that had probably been attractive for about five years in her early twenties, bottle-blonde hair arranged into a cut and wave, a leathery décolletage and a snappy little figure that she flaunted in a short flippy skirt that I considered inappropriate for her age. As the night wore on, her face sort of melted and became sloppy with drink, her speech slurred and slowed like she was underwater, her hands wandered to my forearm, which she alternately patted and gripped. One of her eyes turned in.

Perhaps because I was pregnant with my first child this woman's presence offended me beyond what it normally would. That and the way she and Hal carried on like randy teenagers at the table, then slipped off to the dance floor with gropes and giggles as though we should all be happy for them. There was a galling sense of smugness about it all. Flaunting it in our faces like that while we all sat impassively and pretended it was perfectly acceptable. In a way, Hal had snookered us. He knew we had no fond feelings for Helen, so how and on what grounds could we possibly object?

As the night wore on, I felt this sordid liaison degrading my unborn child via association. I was feeling extremely righteous and pious, full of the self-importance of any first-time mother-to-be. Suddenly, my life had a purpose beyond my day-to-day existence, a purpose as pure as creating life. I couldn't look at her. She was plying me with questions about the baby, mouthing off with her theory of how ultrasounds can cause an unborn foetus irreparable damage (just as Andy had recounted our first ultrasound anecdote). She was mouthing off generally. Telling me about her son as though being mothers would make us both the same.

She had plonked herself down next to me and was trying to look deeply into my eyes in that way drunk people do. At one point, when I'd had enough of her slurring babble and was trying to pretend that the light fitting directly above my head was enthralling me, she demanded of me,

"Why won't you look me in the eye?" She then shouted to Hal across the table. "She won't look at me. Why? Why won't she look me in the eye?"

Hal guffawed nervously. Andy gave me the look he gave me when he thought I was upsetting the apple cart. That was the crux of it. *Don't cause an upset.* I guess Andy's seen enough upsets to last him a lifetime. But out of everything, that was the thing that I found the most difficult to take. The stretched tension, the hideously misshapen bubble of normality as Hal pushed the boundaries and the rest of us struggled not to react.

It was shortly after this birthday dinner that I began to excuse myself from attending as many Hal-associated social occasions as possible. No longer concerned about what impression I was making, I became more concerned with trying to maintain an optimistic view of my husband and the gene pool that he may be passing onto our children.

Above all, it was the feeling of being gagged and silenced in the face of Hal's always awful behaviour that I found so frustrating. According to Andy, I had to let Hal do what he did and I was not to challenge him. Because Andy, normally such a bull-headed and forthright person, always chose to work around him instead of confronting him head on.

In the early stages of our relationship, I made the mistake of thinking less of Andy because of this. Then one day it dawned on me that somewhere in the past there had been a confrontation that had resulted in this curious Straw family dynamic; where no one challenged Hal and the way he behaved.

I realised then that it only has to happen once. From then on, just the threat of it is enough to keep everyone in line.

# 10.

In the early stages of our marriage, Andy presented his dysfunctional family background as some sort of emotional obstacle course that he had successfully completed.

"I survived it," he'd say brightly when talk got too morose about his father. "Look at me, I'm fine."

Over ten years of marriage, however, the various bruises have come up dark and in places he keeps hidden from everyone else's view but mine.

Andy is for all intents an amenable person—friendly, affable, charming and able to get along with others. But there are times when the façade slips and I see that thing that he tries so hard and so valiantly to contain; the part of him that chimes with the resonance of his father. It's a blind, implacable rage and by blind I mean he cannot see sense when he's in it. It's not literally physical, but its vitriol, its outward waves of contempt and disgust, have felt physical to me at times. And because he is unable to face this part of himself, to admit it is there, he is unable to apologise for it, or even acknowledge it, after it has revealed itself to us.

I first encountered it when I was six months pregnant with Daniel. Andy was working late (if you call drinks with the mayor 'working') and he called to tell me not to wait up. No big deal, I enjoyed the time to myself and the release from an obligation to cook red meat. Now I could eat vegetables and watch some dumb old rom-com. I hung up the phone and it rang again.

"What are you doing?" a familiar voice asked.

"Not much," I replied.

There was no need to say who it was. Marty was that sort of friend. We had gone through uni together, been friends, more than friends, then settled finally on friends again after realising that we weren't suited romantically. So yes, I'm obfuscating here; Marty was, technically an old boyfriend.

But if I may clarify, an *old* boyfriend. So old and so long past that we had settled long ago into a completely platonic and without-any-sexual-tension-whatsoever friendship. Andy, as you have probably already guessed, would define Marty forever-and-ever-Amen as my 'ex-boyfriend'.

In fact, in subsequent discussions of this incident (and there have been many more than the incident itself deserved), Andy has often thrown forth the defence of, "I wouldn't do that to you!". Which is a moot point, given that, were he on fire, none of Andy's ex-girlfriends would cross the road to spit on him, let alone meet up for a nice casual catch-up dinner. Is it my fault he can't stay friends with his exes?

When Marty called that night, it seemed too dramatic for me to say, "I can't see you any more." That sort of response seemed to be giving our friendship more credit for romantic tension than it actually possessed. But it also didn't seem completely the right thing for me to go out somewhere with Marty. That seemed too much like 'a date'.

Anyway, to cut a long story short, Marty came over for dinner. I can see now it was a sort of 'goodbye' dinner. We would probably be seeing less of each other in the future than we had when I was single. This 'goodbyeness', however, was entirely unattended to. Marty (unlike Andy) was a man of vast unspoken undercurrents. Which was why it was so difficult to be his girlfriend but so easy to be his friend. We talked about everything *but* our feelings. We sat at the formica table in the kitchen of the apartment Andy and I were renting. I made some pasta and showed Marty the plans for the student accommodation modules that I was working on for the university. We rolled them out onto the kitchen table and pored over them in an entirely unromantic way. He gave me some good feedback, even pointing out a 'staircase to nowhere' that I hadn't noticed. I was grateful he had seen it before Ellen.

When I served the dinner, because the overhead light was fluorescent and unpleasant to sit beneath, I got some candles and pushed them into two wine bottles. I lit them. Two hours later when Marty was gone, the candles had melted in an incriminatingly sensual way, all down the sides of the bottles. I hadn't meant them to look so aesthetically pleasing.

It was these candles in the wine bottles that really did it. When Andy came home I hadn't cleared away the evidence. And the reason I hadn't cleared away the evidence was a pointed gesture towards transparency—I had nothing to hide.

This was my mistake, a typical rookie error of the newly betrothed. In hindsight, what I should have done was cleared the table and disposed of the evidence. Then maybe I could have off-handedly mentioned that Marty came round without the (apparently) inflammatory candlelit dinner scene. (Who am I kidding? As if, in hindsight, I would mention it at all.)

I was sitting on the couch, watching the late movie, when Andy came home. He said hello then made a beeline for the balcony for a smoke but then stopped short at the kitchen door. He froze in the doorway as though someone was in there pointing a gun at him.

"Who's been here?"

"Oh, Marty came round," I said, trying to sound airy and innocent. "He called just after you did."

"How convenient." His voice was cold.

"We just had some pasta," I said, my heart was suddenly thumping with fight or flight adrenaline.

"Good. Did you enjoy yourself?" he asked sarcastically.

I could tell he was drunk. His eyes were slightly unfocused and dreamy-looking.

"He just helped me with my . . . designs."

"Sounds cosy."

"It was nothing." I was beginning to get irritated.

"Did you have fun shagging your ex-boyfriend while I was out working?" he spat.

"Oh, for fuck's sake!" I rose up to it. "We had some pasta and you were NOT working. You were boozing on with your boss."

"DON'T YOU SWEAR AT ME!" He shouted and then, this was the clincher, "AND DON'T YOU DARE SHOUT AT ME!"

I looked at him, puzzled. Was I shouting? He was shouting, wasn't he? The room around us stretched and warped like time pushing against itself but it was logic and reason that was pushing against itself.

"I'm not shouting," I said, retreating behind my eyes to view him from a safe distance.

"YES YOU ARE!" He bellowed. "And get that look off your face!"

"What look?"

He then affected a very unkind impression of what my face looked like to him in that moment, which I thought was most unnecessary. If he had been his normal self, it would have been something we would both crack up about and the fight would have been over.

But that was the thing, it was as though the Andy I knew wasn't actually there any more. His eyes were glazed and vacant; he was somewhere behind that mask of rage, unreachable. No matter what I said, I was 'shouting' at him and guilty of adultery whilst carrying his unborn child.

At this point, I realised that there were unknown emotional depths to my new husband that I had not yet fathomed. I felt that falling sensation in the pit of my stomach, as if I had plunged into deep water without knowing when my feet would touch the bottom.

Andy lit up a cigarette and instead of going out onto the balcony, as was my 'no smoking in the apartment' rule, he went straight into the spare room. He slammed the door so hard that it seemed to shake the entire building in its sandstone foundations. I stood outside the door waiting. I'd never seen such a raw display of blind rage before, and in response to something so essentially benign. I'd expected a reaction of sorts, but this was so completely off the chart and I had no reference for how I should react to it. My mother's response to anyone raising their voice even mildly in an aggressive way is, "Tone! Tone!" as in 'watch your tone'. The mere sight of her eyes widening in response to a loss of temper is enough to chasten all of us to silence, my father included. This had gone way beyond 'tone' and straight to volume. I simply did not have a frame of reference for such an immediate escalation of conflict.

I heard some commotion in there: things falling or being thrown, a tumble of papers. I braced myself for the sound of tearing, then, from within the spare room, music began to vibrate the walls. He was playing Tegan and Sarah's version of *When You Were Mine* at an ear-shattering volume. It was 11pm on a Thursday. I worried about the neighbours. I knocked on the door. He didn't answer. I pushed the door open and looked in. He was sitting on the floor, an explosion of drawing pens strewn across the carpet in front of him. He was ashing his cigarette into my pen holder having ejected my expensive drafting pens from their home with a violence intended to display his complete disregard for their importance to me. He had dragged the portable music player off my desk without unplugging it first and the cord had knocked my current drawings flying. They lay unfurled, half on the floor and half on the spare bed like the rubbish he clearly perceived them to be.

The music player was on the floor in front of him and he was staring at it intently as the song rang out its overwrought 'you're going with another guy' narrative. I waited for it to end, thinking we could broach some sort of conversation about me not meaning to upset him and perhaps this was over the top. But when the song ended he pressed 'repeat' and it started up again. I stood there for another verse and a chorus and then, repelled by his hostile silence, I left the room.

I waited in the living room for two hours while he played the same song over and over and smoked. At 1am, with the same song still playing on a loop, I went to bed, grateful for the blank hours of sleep that stood between me and making some decision about how I would respond to this revelatory performance from my new husband.

Standing outside that spare room I had felt like Alice falling down the rabbit hole: tumbling down into an unfamiliar new world where up was down and down was up; where this odd and violent reaction to a slight was something I would just accept as the 'new normal' of our marriage.

And there was a pivotal moment, I felt it for the briefest second, where my feet nearly, nearly started walking out the door; the merest twitch in the arch of my foot, ready to propel me out the door and never to return.

*Can I go on with this?* I asked myself.

*Yes,* answered my heart, catapulting me forward into the rest of my life with Andy.

The following morning, Andy was hung-over but, curiously, not sorry. Apparently, I was still the one who should be sorry. And because my heart had answered me so surely the night before, I chose to take one for the team. (What team? The little guy who was now forming in my belly.) So I apologised and we moved on. Well, I moved on. Andy, on the other hand, has never ever let me forget it. Over ten years have passed and he still brings it up.

"Well at least I don't have ex-girlfriends around for romantic candlelit dinners while you're out working."

Because of this and other similar incidents, I have come to behave toward Andy the way Andy behaves towards his father. I choose to minimise the conflict by backing down. I have chosen many times over the course of our ten-year marriage to avoid an incident rather than endure it. So when you ask, as so many do, why did they put up with Hal, why they manoeuvred around him and let him behave the way he did, you could well ask me the same question.

Because I am complicit now, in their little world of domestic deceit.

# 11.

Eventually Andy decided it was best for everyone if Hal and I were kept in separate compartments of his life. Which suited me fine. But you are probably now wondering why Andy didn't just cut his father out of his life altogether. From what I have observed of Andy and Tom (and even Maude), being Hal's family was like being part of a cult and at this point none of them had been fully deprogrammed. They still spoke in raptured awe of the way he was, the funny things he did, the outrageous anecdotes that made up their family history.

And contrary to the feeling that the boys should just turn their faces away from the past and move forward without looking back, they seemed all the more wedded to it. They relived it over and over. They frequented old family haunts, retold stories like religious parables and generally reframed the past so that Hal could remain in place not so much on a pedestal as a plinth; his best angles frozen in time under the most flattering light.

*But he's such a character.* This was always the fall-back position. And it was only when he appeared in person that their carefully moulded family shape became dangerously misshapen.

While it suited me fine to be kept separate from Hal in the early years of our marriage, Andy still came home to me after these (always dreadful) encounters. And there's only so much you can observe, before you want to weigh in.

After Daniel was born, I was given a reprieve of sorts from the birthday dinners. I had to mind the baby. On the first birthday dinner after Daniel was born, I stayed home while Andy met Hal at a swanky beachfront restaurant. Hal had two for one discount vouchers and because it was Andy's birthday (but more importantly because Hal had the vouchers), dinner was on Hal.

At the end of the evening, Hal presented his vouchers to the waiter only to be told they were out of date. Hal absorbed that information without grace and after the waiter retreated from the table (leaving them to contemplate the full-priced bill), Hal simply got up and walked out. This left Andy still seated with the bill in front of him. Andy stayed seated for about two seconds as he considered his empty wallet and our maxed out credit card. (We were on one income and skint.) He got up and followed Hal out thinking he might be able to talk him around, drag him back inside and make him pay.

But when he got outside Hal was a trail of dust; he'd already taken off down the street, leaving Andy with no doubt that they were now doing a runner.

Meanwhile a small but growing ruckus broke out inside the restaurant as the staff realised what was going on. Spurred by his fight or flight adrenaline, Andy bolted. He and Hal ran around the block and came up at the end of the next adjoining street. There were restaurant staff, including the chef brandishing a large carving knife, standing at the top of the street looking for them. They bolted back the other way and up to the main road where Hal hailed a cab, jumped in and slammed the door. The cab took off leaving Andy standing there. He jogged the thirty minutes home from Maroubra to Coogee, never quite sure that he wasn't being shadowed by the angry chef with the carving knife.

Happy Birthday, son.

I was awake when Andy came in. He was panting and wide-eyed with disbelief. 'You won't believe what just happened,' he said.

I listened grim-faced. It wasn't even funny in an outrageous larrikin behaviour sort of way. One of the worst parts of it was we used to go to that café for breakfast. They had a great breakfast menu. No more corn fritters with crispy bacon and relish for me. But on top of that, it made me hate Hal even more. What kind of father does that to his son?

The kind of father who would say to your mother in the heat of an argument, "I'll fuck you with a sharp knife." My god. I know. I should have issued a warning before that phrase. But like you, I was blindsided by it when Andy uttered it, not *at* me, but in what was intended as a comic impersonation of a man in a rage.

"What the hell kind of a thing is that to say?" I asked.

"I know," Andy said, his face clouding over now, as though coming out of a trance.

"Where on earth did you hear that?"

"Dad said it to Mum once."

I was rendered speechless. I felt physically ill.

"I was eight," he added.

Jesus.

Over ten years of marriage, snippets like this have made their way to me. Trickled through Andy, but also Tom and Maude. They are jagged pieces of an ugly puzzle. Like the story of the chicken bones. According to Andy, Hal once went to feed the dog the leftover chicken bones from dinner, something everyone knows you don't do. Maude, worried for the dog's safety, shouted in a panicked way for him to stop. It was unusual of her to challenge him like this, but the dog held a special place in hers and Andy's hearts.

"Shut up, bitch!" he'd shouted wildly. When he continued to scrape the bones into the dog's bowl, Maude lunged forward to grab the plate from his hands. He snapped his fist sharply backwards and connected; a blunt cracking jab to the bridge of her nose that made her eyes swell and water, leaving an angry grey-yellow bruise that was difficult to explain.

Andy elbowed his mother out of the way and got between them. Hal threw a punch. Andy landed one on his jaw and ended it. This is Andy's seminal memory, as it marks the point in time when he was finally big enough to fight back. He was fourteen.

All three of them will recount the story of the milk bottle smashed on the ceiling one morning at breakfast. The details differ slightly depending on who you talk to. Maude says it was because there were no Weeties and Hal liked Weeties for breakfast. Andy claims it was because the milk was out of date and Hal had already poured the milk on his cereal and taken a spoonful. Tom doesn't remember why, just the sound of the glass bottle smashing on the ceiling as it was thrust upwards, the milk dripping down on Hal as Maude silently commenced the clean up. Tom sometimes tells this as though it is a funny story, depending on his mood.

Maude's seminal memory (and one that isn't as often recounted as the others) is the point when she realised she could no longer stay. She can't remember how it started, but she had possibly raised her voice or asserted herself in some confrontational way. He took long strides across the living room towards her, spitting foul language, making ugly threats that he may or may not have followed through. Not willing to take the chance, she picked up the poker from beside the fireplace and held it poised like a baseball bat.

"Come on then!" she heard herself shout. "I dare you!"

And then, as though in an out-of-body experience she saw herself, poised to strike her own husband with an iron poker.

What madness is this, she thought.

But the epiphany itself would never have been enough without another significant event. Around the same time her father died, a bittersweet affair because his death granted Maude her freedom: an inheritance.

A short time later she packed her suitcase and left.

# 12.

About seven years and two children into our marriage, Andy received a phone call that sent our life hurtling back onto a collision course with Hal. The phone call came at eight o' clock in the evening. For two hours we laughed and rocked with a jubilant, and I have to say, unseemly sense of Schadenfreude. But by ten pm (I can't remember who it dawned on first) we were no longer laughing. By ten-thirty I had a sick feeling in the pit of my stomach and we were arguing hot-headedly as we climbed into bed. By morning we were no longer speaking, in that way that married couples don't speak; we spoke on a 'needs to know' basis, with a sharp sliver of 'you're not considering my feelings' emotional distance. A sliver that would widen into a veritable chasm if we didn't reach across to each other and sort things out. Over the ensuing weeks, it yawned wider and I felt the fabric of us stretched to breaking point around the topic of Hal.

At that point we had been, like most other young Sydney families, squeezed out of the glorious coastal edge of the eastern suburbs and deposited unceremoniously in the cheaper seats of the city's western urban edge. Out west, the summers were stifling and the winters, inside those sun-denying, unrenovated rooms of Federation era homes, were bone chilling. We both missed the ocean but when you're chasing the great Australian dream of a giant backyard to play cricket in, something's gotta give.

With the property market booming beyond anyone's control, we were trapped in the renting and saving-to-buy quagmire. Every month the market shifted upward and we needed $5k more to secure that ten per cent deposit. On the upside, we had been lucky enough to find a relatively cheap free-standing Federation house on a large block in the only-just-inner-west suburb of Concord West. The rent was cheap because it had, unbeknownst to us until the night we moved in, a granny flat attached to its western wall. In our defence, the flat was not visible from the street, it was set back and lurking behind hedging to the right of the house. How we missed it there on the inspection day I'll never know. But if you've never rented in Sydney, you don't know the true meaning of, 'Quick, just sign the lease before someone else gets it!'. It also had a damp problem, slow plumbing and tangled vertical blinds that didn't quite cover the windows. By Sydney standards it was a real find; mostly unrenovated so cheapish, a large backyard for the kids, a small study off the kitchen and double-sized bedrooms with turn-of-the-century ceilings that could comfortably take a set of bunks.

The granny flat had hosted a revolving door of tenants in the years we had been there. Presently it was home to a particularly humourless single professional woman and her two unneutered Great Danes. Their giant black balls were at eye-level to our children and Elizabeth, four years old, was fascinated by them. Incidentally, I never complained about her dogs' gonads nor the way the dogs lunged at my children whenever we tried to get from the car to the front door, but she continually complained about the noise our kids made in the early evenings. If we were unsure as to her true feelings about us, she made it perfectly clear by pointedly trimming the hedge out front to the exact point where she perceived our property ended and hers began. We rarely trimmed our section of the hedge and so the half-done topiary reflected clearly our differences in lifestyle priorities.

The phone call had come from Tom, who was by then living in Melbourne. In the existential crisis that was the aftermath of his break-up with Anita, he had applied for and been accepted into a prestigious acting academy. It was an odd and sudden change in life direction, as though somehow being untethered from Anita made him drift closer toward some essence of Hal-ness. Once there, he'd quickly found a girlfriend who conveniently lived in a house provided by her parents. He moved in with her and some other acting students. We had met her a few times, she was nice enough, but in truth we weren't quite over losing Anita.

Tom seemed to find new purpose in the acting thing. Just like Hal, he was a natural, although Tom was more determined to apply himself to the discipline and craft of it. He became a yoga advocate (for its mentally centring benefits) and like most young actors, was entranced by the whole Stanislavsky method thing.

Down in Melbourne, with the safety of geographical distance, he kept in more regular phone contact with Hal than we did. Which is why he heard it first. Hal and Helen had broken up.

"Turns out Helen's wealth was not as liquid as Hal thought," Tom told Andy.

When Hal married Helen, she had apparent independent wealth stashed in properties all over Sydney. I can't say for sure that this was part of the attraction for Hal, but it certainly would have sweetened the deal. However, now that Hal and Helen were no more, the apparent independent wealth had quickly vanished in a puff of 'mortgaged to the eyeballs' and negative gearing that had now left them both wrestling with their plummeting credit rating. In addition to this debt soup, they were also having the usual tussle over who would get what of the things they did actually own.

It was a particularly sweet victory for me. I don't know if you remember this (I will never forget it) but when we first married, Hal gave us seven years. Irony? I'm not sure if that's strictly correct, but there was certainly a satisfying quirk of fate to it that tickled us pink for two hours.

Then it crept up on us. Without Helen to absorb Hal's attentions and with Tom (conveniently) interstate, we were it.

"Well, I guess we'll be seeing a lot more of Hal from now on," Andy said.

My response was swift and reactive. "What? How do you figure that?"

"He'll be lonely."

"Like I care."

"We'll have to have him over for dinner every week, to make sure he gets a good meal."

"Are you on crack?" Seriously, was he winding me up or what?

"Nell, he's my father."

This was Andy's trump card. What could you say to that? He was right. A son did have certain obligations to his father and the bottom line was Andy did not want to be like his father. So, in order to *not* be like his father he had to act in a compassionate and completely unvengeful manner. He had to extend to him some unconditional love.

Over the next few weeks the fight for the spoils between Helen and Hal became downright shameful. Both parties went wild (in a calculated manner) with their joint credit card. Knowing that the other would be forced to cough up at least half, they each resolved to spend the lion's share of the total so as to make a profit. Helen bought a new car. Hal responded in kind by purchasing a ticket to Thailand for that coming winter. In the meantime, Hal came to dinner once a week and sat at our table bemoaning the ancient trigger for his life's misery; when Maude left him.

By this stage, we had Daniel, six, Elizabeth, four and a third (as yet unborn baby Albert) was over halfway grown inside me. I was the picture of a life halted by reproduction; bloated and carelessly stained, lumbering around after children. Everything about me screamed, *there are more pressing issues right now than my appearance!* My hair was yanked hastily back into an unflattering bun, my face was blotchy and entirely untended, my clothes were loose and practical, my swelling feet most often were in Ugg boots. I hated Hal seeing me like this; my powers dulled, my reflexes fogged by a lack of sleep and the million things I needed to remember to make a day run smoothly. Whenever he was around I was immediately on the defensive to offset any attack that may or may not be coming my way.

One night Elizabeth was still in the bath when he arrived. I heard the doorbell and for some reason felt an urgent need to get her out of the bath and into her pyjamas before he could enter the house. It wasn't so much a need of organisation, of getting everyone ready, as a need to not have her sitting naked in a bathtub with the door open (as it would be while I tended to dinner) and Hal wandering past at will. Something about that scenario sparked a flash of danger within me. It flared and was gone before I could look directly at it and rationalise it. But the instinct would not be pushed aside and I found myself quickly yanking her out of the hot, bubbly water without warning, which made her furious. I wrapped her in a towel while she howled her protests and behaved like a wild animal.

"I wanna stay in the bath!"

"Time to get out."

"Why? I'm cold!"

"Yeah why, Mum. She's only been in for a minute." Daniel was standing leaning in the doorway, all of six and full with the crusade of the weak—his little sister.

She took the opportunity to make her move. I had her by the elbow, but she twisted free and splooped back into the bath, triumphant, then submerged herself fully so that the water rendered her deaf to my usual threats. She lay under the water like the lady in the lake, small mercurial bubbles of air escaping from her nostrils to taunt me.

"Elizabeth! Out! Now! I'm going to count to three!"

"Why does she have to get out?" Daniel was increasingly intrigued by my urgency, my desperation.

"Hal's here."

"So?" He sat himself on the toilet lid. "I can watch her."

I looked at Daniel. Was he fishing for it? Did he sense the answer and just want it confirmed by me?

"I just want her out," I said, exasperated by his uncanny ability to sense when questions shouldn't be asked and then ask them. "Elizabeth, I'm counting to three. One! Two! . . ."

"For god's sake, stop shouting!" Andy hissed at me as he went to get the door. "You sound like a banshee."

Out of desperation I pulled my trump card. I reached into the murky hot water and pulled the plug. Elizabeth lay looking up at me, unawares until the watery world around her began to subside and she realised what was happening.

She went from smug to terrified in a split second. It was a cruel trick; she had a deep-seated fear of the plughole sucking her down and always asked me to wait until she was well clear before I pulled the plug.

I yanked her out as she scrambled for safety. She was furious and humiliated and she flailed around as I tried to contain her angry, frightened tantrum and wrap it inside a towel. One hand escaped and scraped its sharp fingernails down the side of my face. The pain was sudden and unexpectedly eye-watering.

"Ow! Fuck!" I shouted and before I could stop myself I retaliated by smacking her bare bottom so hard the lower half of her flew forward while the upper half stayed behind. Her eyes were wide with shock. As were mine.

"Nell!" Andy's voice; deep and primal, king of the castle.

I looked up and saw Hal and Andy standing outside the bathroom door, staring in at this textbook scene of bad mothering. There was a terrible pause. Then like an air raid siren, Elizabeth started low before whirring upward into terrified wailing. Andy seized Elizabeth from me righteously and wrapped her in her towel. She buried her face gratefully in his neck. Daniel looked askance at me as he soothingly rubbed his sister's back.

"Why couldn't you just leave her in there?" he said accusingly.

"Uh-oh, the witching hour," Hal sing-songed unhelpfully.

Andy made a show of comforting Elizabeth, who was now dobbing me in for pulling the plug while she was still in the bath. He carried her into her room to get her pyjamas. I stayed where I was, kneeling on the bathroom floor, shamed and outcast; the family pariah.

"Hello Nell," Hal said, his tone lightly weary as though defeated already by my hatred of him. Then he moved away and ensconced himself upon a comfy chair in the living room. It was from there I heard his cry: "Drink! Someone! Can I get a drink, *sheh-sheh, merci beaucoup*?"

# 13.

Later that night, Andy and I climbed into bed hissing at each other.

"What's gotten into you?" Andy said.

"I don't want him here," I spat back.

"It's only one night. Come on, Nell, he's my father."

"I just . . . " I couldn't even articulate all the reasons why I didn't want Hal in our house with our children. "Why can't he get a cab home?"

"He's broke."

"Well he shouldn't have drunk so much, then he could've driven home," I said.

"Nell, he's in a bad way."

"Entirely of his own making," I said primly.

"He's painted himself into a corner."

"How much has he got?"

"$200,000." Andy and I stared at each other.

"And he's only doing auction work here and there. So no real income."

"What happened? I thought they had four properties."

"They negative geared themselves into oblivion. They've been borrowing against borrowed money for about five years."

"So he's got $200,000—does that count what's in the house?"

"That's all he's got. That's what's left when they sell the house and divide it up."

"What about his house, your family home? Didn't your mum leave him that?"

"He sold that remember, they sunk the money into shared property."

Some years before, Hal had made the classic second marriage error of selling his own well-priced, inner west asset to invest with Helen in an expensive, overpriced townhouse in the prestigious Sydney suburb of Vaucluse. The shift from west to east never goes well for Sydneysiders. It's like exchanging Australian dollars for US greenbacks; you never quite get your money's worth. Plus Andy and I couldn't believe Hal had merged his solid, bricks and mortar guaranteed cash cow with Helen's dodgy 'pea under cup' investment property portfolio.

"Why?"

"Because he's an idiot," Andy said. "Meanwhile, she's been re-mortgaging against any equity they had, so he doesn't even have what he went into the marriage with. He's fucked."

"What's his plan?"

"Funny you should ask," Andy said. He had a weird look on his face. A look I didn't much care for. He paused and took a deep breath. "He's suggested that we buy a place together, all of us, with a granny flat out the back for him. He'll throw in his $200,000."

Was he serious? I didn't say anything. My ears were boiling with rage.

"Nell," Andy said soothingly, "I think we should consider it. We could get something really nice with the extra $200,000."

"You cannot. Be serious," I said.

"I think we'd be foolish not to take the opportunity," he said.

I looked at Andy. He looked back at me sincerely and all of sudden I began channelling Linda Blair in *The Exorcist.*

"You've got to be fucking kidding me," I spat. Even I was surprised by how my voice sounded when it came out of my mouth. I had wanted it to sound strident and forceful but it got tangled in my throat and came out all twisted.

That was it. Andy's face crumpled, he doubled over, wheezing with laughter.

"Oh—oh . . . " He was trying to speak but he was laughing too hard. "Oh, my love, you should see your face," he wheezed.

"It's a joke, isn't it," I said hopefully. "You *were* joking."

He wheezed himself into a coughing fit. "Of course I was joking," he said finally. "As if."

"That was not funny," I said.

"Yes it was. You should've heard yourself. *You've got to be fucking kidding me."* He was red in the face from lack of air, given he was in spasms of laughter. "I thought you were going to start spewing out green stuff."

We creased ourselves until tears of relief poured down my face. For a split second I had considered him on the other side of a massive divide. It seemed we were still on the same side. For now.

"Imagine that," I said.

"I have," he said. "It's never going to happen."

"It will never happen, will it?"

"Darling," Andy sobered up suddenly, "You have my word."

"You mean Hal . . . living with us?" I thought it was important to clarify whether he meant just the granny flat thing or a blanket denial that Hal would ever live in our house.

"Yes."

He turned off the bedside light and I curled into him. After a silence I said, "I was so desperate to get Elizabeth out of the bath . . . "

"I know," he said.

It was too horrible to articulate, but we both knew exactly why. It was a suspicion completely without any merit: unfounded and unprecedented by anything remotely related. There was nothing in their family history to suggest such a thing. But still we both held it in the dark recesses of our minds. And neither wanted to voice it out loud. We just let it sit between us without either of us laying claim to it.

"I know," he said again.

## 14.

Six months later we got an alarming phone call of another kind. It was on our landline voicemail one Saturday morning. We had just come home from a garage sale crawl. We bundled in the door with our boxes and bags full of junk, the satisfied flush of consumerism still upon us. I took baby Albert straight into his cot to put him down while Andy listened to the messages. He was still holding a boxful of junk that I had begged him not to buy (a breadmaker, an orange crock pot and a giant plastic thing with a fan that purported to repel mosquitoes and flies via special magnetic field technology).

Elizabeth helped me fuss over Albert, force-feeding him his dummy like it was some sort of peg-in-the-hole game and telling him in an inappropriately authoritarian voice that it was time to 'GO TO SLEEP NOW, OWBERT' as though he were a misbehaving toddler, not a four-month-old baby with hardly any consciousness for deviousness. (She thrived on having someone smaller to boss around, even if he was a dribbling blob of compliance.) We quickly exited before he could figure out what was going on and bless him, he was a lovely little bugger, he just smiled and stared blankly at the ceiling.

When we returned to the living room, Andy simply handed me the phone with the message replaying for my edification. I took it, assuming it was my mother but was confronted instead by Hal's voice delivered straight to my ear. His manically upbeat tone, like a recurring nightmare, buzzed across oceans, through a hissing line from Thailand.

"Hi there! Hal here. Oops, I did it again! (nervous laughter.) I'm in love! Getting married. Third time lucky! Coming in on the 14th, Qantas Flight Q543, at 10am, that's a Wednesday—Wednesday the 14th, Andy, Q543 10am—Wednesday—so hopefully you can pick me up from the airport, need some confirmation of that, so I'll try you again later. Over."

I looked at Andy. "Did he just say, he's getting married?"

"I believe so."

"Who's getting married?" Daniel sensed that things were getting interesting and decided to tune in with both ears flapping.

"No one," I said quickly.

"Poppa Hal," Andy said.

"Getting married?" Daniel appeared confused. "I thought he was married to Helen."

"They got divorced," Andy said.

I hadn't bothered trawling through the ins and outs of Poppa Hal's sordid marriage breakdown with the kids, they hadn't asked where Helen was so I hadn't said anything. Unlike Andy who bandies about his belief in speaking frankly to the children and just answering their questions truthfully, I favour more of a 'needs to know' and 'white lies of omission' parenting style. There are already too many questions about things as mundane as why we don't speak to the woman next door and have to quickly rush in the door if we see her coming down the street with her ball-swinging dogs as we're arriving home, or why Daniel has to go to the women's toilets with me instead of going into the men's by himself when we go to big shopping malls.

Opening up the Hal and Helen can of worms would have led to them thinking about the fact that at some point in history, Maude and Hal, who they knew were Andy's parents, must have been married and now no longer were. This chain of events was yet to occur to them and I preferred to keep them in ignorant bliss of the idea that people who were married sometimes (often) didn't stay married. I wanted them to have the simplicity of absolutes for a while longer.

"When?" Daniel asked.

"Last year sometime."

"Why?"

"Who's Helen?" Elizabeth piped up from her Barbie pile on the floor.

"Hal's wife," I said to keep things simple.

"Ex-wife," Andy corrected in the interests of complete transparency.

"What's an axe wife?" Elizabeth asked.

Andy laughed. "Axe wife!" he chuckled. "That's quite good."

Daniel laughed too, then thought about it some more. "Why is that quite good?" Daniel asked.

Little did I know, the future held something even more complicated to explain to small children.

Hal's Thai fiancée, Phan, was younger than me. This is not an unusual scenario but for the children, something about it did not fit their idea of what grandparents do. Especially when Hal introduced her to Andy thus: "Say hello to your future step-mum. Give her a kiss."

This led to Elizabeth looking from Phan to Andy, to Hal, to me, to Phan, to me again and trying to figure out what it was that didn't sit quite right for her. I could see the wheels turning in her head, formulating questions for later, or even for now if there was a lull in conversation. I could see her watching my face for cues on how to react. I tried to keep my face as neutral as possible, which probably meant I had a bit of a lemon-lipped look about me. To add to Elizabeth's confusion, Phan seemed (like most Asian women) ageless. She could have been anywhere between twenty and fifty years old. At present, her face had broken out with the change in climate and this gave her the look of a pubescent teenager, marked by an angry rash of hormones all across her cheeks.

She wasn't entirely what we were expecting. She was more homely than we had been led to believe. A stocky barrel of a woman with a large square, you might say 'determined' face framed by short, practical layered hair. Hers was a handsome face rather than a pretty one. As she came in, she started doling out gifts from a large duty free bag. To Andy, a carton of duty free cigarettes (terrific). To me, she offered a floor length, gold wraparound skirt made of Thai silk, which Elizabeth demanded that I wear, right now.

"Put it on Mum, go on. It looks like a princess skirt. Put it on, Mu-um, put it on now. It's really pretty, I wish I had one. Did you bring one for me too?"

I tried to pretend I wasn't listening to her, so engaged was I in the stilted cross-language conversation I was having with Phan. Elizabeth was having none of it. She tore open the plastic packaging and held it up to try to figure out how to put me inside it this instant. Phan took the cue and helped her, commanding me to stand still while the two of them walked around me in circles, wrapping me in gold Thai silk like an Egyptian mummy. When they were finished I was bound up like a geisha and had to shuffle forward in small steps. Phan put her palms together and bowed to me.

"Very beautiful," she concluded.

"Can you wear that tomorrow when you pick me up from kindy?" Elizabeth asked eagerly.

"Oh maybe," I said non-committally because if I said yes, she would hold me to it and saying no would lead to further interrogation regarding why I wouldn't want to shuffle around in a gold silk bandage in front of all the other inner-west mums at pick up time.

"Go on, you should. It's sooo pretty."

Phan then produced an identical one for Elizabeth and helped her put it on the same way, wrapping it around her like a bandage. Elizabeth was won over; cheap little tart she was. All it took was a 30 baht skirt from a Thai market to put Phan in favour.

Daniel was characteristically circumspect. An antenna for family tensions, he sensed my discomfort and had noted Andy's brittle mood. He sat quietly, careful not to draw attention to himself so that he might pick up signals from me or from Andy about how to react to seeing his grandfather with a young foreign woman in tow.

Hal picked up on this and acted. He swooped on Phan's bag of gifts and produced something for Daniel, a remote-control dune buggy that climbed walls, did a somersault and bumped itself back onto its wheels. He demonstrated it for Daniel. Flashing lights, noise, remote control; the trifecta of fun for any little boy. It was a masterstroke. They drove the car up the wall together, whooping and shouting when it landed back on its wheels every time.

Meanwhile, Phan spied baby Albert, all fat cheeks and smiles, lying in the bouncer in the corner, where, as the third child, he spent most of his days as a willing audience to the rest of the family. In all the excitement, I'd forgotten he was there.

She made a cooing noise and walked over to him. He smiled encouragingly and flapped his limbs, bouncing himself with delight.

She crouched down beside him and stroked his cheek, then turned to me, her eyes bright with longing.

"Can I? Pick up?"

"Sure," I said. "He loves a cuddle."

Phan lifted him out of his bassinet gingerly, all the while her eyes connected to Albert's. She raised him up in front of her, widened her eyes. He giggled. She kissed his big puffy cheek.

"Getting clucky, darling!" Hal sing-songed from the other side of the room. "She wants *farang* baby," Hal said to Andy. "Thai people love white babies, it's a status thing you see."

Hal looked at me and reiterated again at the top of his voice. "It's very prestigious to have a white baby."

I nodded, somewhat bewildered by this observation spoken so clearly and without cultural discretion in front of Phan. She either wasn't listening or didn't have the English skills to follow background conversations.

She hugged Albert's big, plump body to her own and kissed his head. Elizabeth was there in a flash, proffering assistance.

"He wants his dummy," she said with authority. Her ongoing daily objective was to plug Albert's mouth with his dummy. Whether he needed it or not. She was impressively single-minded about it.

"I want baby like this," Phan said with open longing.

"Oh!" I said, trying to make my voice convey 'how lovely' when what I was really thinking was, 'my god how alarming, Hal and this young woman procreating'.

"She's quite desperate," Hal laughed. "Nagging me for a baby all the time."

"Dad," Andy said quietly, "are you up for a baby at your age?"

"Sure, you just flick pass them onto the grandparents," Hal said without a hint of shame. He even mimed a football pass in illustration of what they would do with a baby if they were to have one. “Phan already has a four-year-old boy. Her parents look after him,” he continued. “It’d be pretty low impact on me.”

“You flick pass them?” I repeated, disbelieving.

“It’s part of the deal.” Hal was talking to Andy. “If you marry a Thai woman, you have to give them *farang* baby, big status for family. So I guess it’s on the cards, God willing.”

God willing? What the hell did god have to do with any of this?

Later on, over dinner, we got to know more than we needed to about Phan. She was, according to Hal, ‘a very successful businesswoman’. She had her own business selling herbs.

“Oh,” I said. “What kind of herbs?”

“Herb to tighten . . . ” she looked to Hal for the word, “to tighten . . . ” she was making gestures towards her lap, “for women . . . ”

“To tighten?” I said, still not getting it. I looked at Andy. He was as flummoxed as me.

“To tighten flab?” Andy proffered. “To make you skinnier?” He made astringent faces as though losing weight and then shouted, “MAKE YOU SKINNIER.”

There was no denying, Andy had been very welcoming to Phan from the moment she stepped in the door. More welcoming than me. But I had already taken him aside twice and told him to stop shouting at her. She was Thai, not deaf.

“No,” Phan shook her head then looked to Hal again, hoping he could help out with the word she was grasping for. Hal chuckled like a naughty school boy and she giggled, whacking him playfully on the arm with the back of her hand. She said something in Thai.

Andy laughed too, in an ‘I don’t know why we’re laughing but this is getting awkward’ way.

"To tighten vagina," Phan said finally, matter of factly and without a hint of modesty

"To what?" Andy coughed.

Did she just say, vagina at my dinner table?

"For sexual pleasure," Hal said with some authority. "It's a special herb that tightens . . . the passage, you know."

"Very popular," Phan assured us, thinking we were judging her business acumen.

She giggled again, in cahoots with Hal. Then in typical Hal fashion, he chose that moment to dump Phan right in it. Without apology, he got up and left the table to go to the bathroom. When he was gone, Phan looked from me to Andy with plaintive eyes.

"I look after your father," she pledged, sensing this dinner was some kind of test of her intentions.

"That's good," Andy said, not meeting her gaze and patting the table in front of him. "Thank you."

She looked at me, her face all wide-eyed with simple country girl honesty. "I look after him," she said again, more insistently.

I stared blankly at her, trying not to give away what I was really thinking, which was, *Do what you like with him lady, just don't send him back here when you're finished.*

My lack of response unnerved her and I think she mistook it for some sort of concern, on my part, for Hal's future and suspicion of her real intentions. She must have flagged me then, as a possible obstacle to her plans because later, much later, I looked across and caught her looking at me in a completely different way.

She was sizing me up. Her face was hard and calculating, her eyes narrowed in focus, her mouth and chin set forward in concentration. She was undeniably, uncategorically, trying to get my measure.

# 15.

Two months later, Hal was back at our dinner table alone. Some of the puff had gone out of him and there were no gifts on arrival. Tom had come up from Melbourne, at Andy's request. It was to be an intervention of sorts, a two-pronged attack from both his sons.

Hal sat now with his head hanging down between his shoulders, thinking deeply on what Andy and Tom were telling him, as they took turns to deliver stabs of advice and instruction. When they were finished talking, he looked up from one to the other and said, "She loves me," with an insistent upward inflection; an unusually plaintive plea seeking reassurance.

"I'm just saying, don't give her any more money," Andy said firmly.

"Well, just enough to get her started up with her businesses," Hal said. "Then she'll look after me, see, in my dotage."

He seemed an old toothless tiger. In his desperation to take Phan for a ride, (thinking her a simple Thai woman who would submit to his every demand) he had been blinded to the fact that he was, *au contraire,* on a ride entirely of her design. He had been well and truly had, like many others before him. Led by one last desperate lunge for everlasting virility, he had followed his primal urges into male paradise—a warm, balmy place where women did as they were told and opened their legs on cue—and realised too late ($120,000 later) that the dream was merely a mirage. It was poetic, really. Despite that, Andy had warned me to hold my tongue.

"Be kind," he said.

Our mission that evening, for which we had recruited the additional services of Tom, was to ensure that Hal did not change his mind about moving to Thailand. Currently, it was a daily pendulum swing between a rock and a hard place.

Phan had returned to Thailand and gotten busy with Hal's money. Hal had responded in kind, scorching the earth behind him in a reckless flurry to be back in male paradise (with sex on call) as soon as possible: a focused and relentless pursuit of the easy lay. In eight weeks, Hal went from the crowing cock with his young Thai bride-to-be blushing submissively at his side, to a man with ever-narrowing options for retirement.

He had sold up everything he owned, outstayed the settlement period on his sold townhouse and was now living on borrowed time, in a limbo of indecision.

Meanwhile, back in Thailand, Phan was currently buying up more businesses to add to her portfolio and calling Hal day and night to demand more money in order that she establish said 'businesses' in preparation for his future dotage. His future dotage, the way Hal told it (inspired perhaps by the way she told it to him), was a place where she would be waiting on him hand and foot (which perhaps included giving him unlimited head jobs).

By all accounts she was quite forceful in her demands for money. In the three times she had called that evening, we had seen him remove the phone from his ear and hold it out, presumably while she screamed at him. Her trump card was threatening to call off the marriage. After the third call, Andy and Tom suggested that perhaps that was not such a bad idea.

"How about this, Dad?" Andy began. "Don't marry Phan. By all means, go to Thailand, but just keep your options open for a while."

"I'm an old bloke," Hal said. "She'll look after me."

"How much money have you given her?" Tom said.

"Just 120 for the businesses she's setting up, she needs the start up then once they get going, we'll have an income, see."

"120,000?" Andy said.

"Yes. Yes," Hal laughed sheepishly.

"Dad, what did I tell you?" Andy said, as though speaking to a toddler.

"She loves me, son. She loves me." Andy and Tom stayed respectfully silent on this. So Hal elaborated, "I'm a good bloke, a larry. She loves the rumpy pumpy with the big white organ."

I told myself that I didn't hear that.

"Tell her you have no more money," Andy said. "You've got 80 grand left, you can live on that in Thailand if you're careful. Just don't marry this woman."

It was a complex game of coercion into which I had been strictly instructed not to wade. If he sensed we wanted him gone, he could turn ugly. Or worse, he might turn around and decide to stay.

"So you're saying I should just hump around, play the field a bit," Hal said earnestly.

*Play the field.* As if he were some handsome playboy cutting a swathe through the eligible ladies of Thailand, when the reality was he would be frequenting ping pong bars and picking up hookers. I was standing at the sink with my back to them, but I let out an involuntary scoff.

"Yes," said Tom, allowing Hal's fantastical version of his future to stand. "And do not give this woman any more money." His voice bristled with anger and frustration. "Do you hear me? Put your money in an account here, where she can't get to it."

Hal stayed silent. He nodded his head obediently, pressed at crumbs scattered around the table top with his fingertip and then flicked them idly off into the ether. (Presumably, for me to sweep up later.)

"Yes, but see," he began slowly, as though it were painful to say, "if I don't give her money, she might leave me."

I turned around then, the force of my frustration spun me on my heels. Andy caught me and shot me a look that said, 'shut it'. But I'd been quiet for three hours. I'd bitten my tongue through the talk of 'rumpy pumpy' and the stomach-turning discussion on genital waxing and its benefits (all within earshot of the children). I'd reached my limit.

"Hang on," I said. "You're saying she loves you for who you are, not your money? And yet, you're admitting that if you don't give her any more money, she will leave you?" I smacked my palm on my forehead in frustration. "What does that tell you?"

Hal sat bolt upright and reeled back as though shot. He blinked his watery old eyes.

"Cruel," he said, drawing the word out—*crew-ell.*

A loaded silence. Andy glared at me. Tom shook his head. Hal's phone rang. It skipped across the table top with the force of Phan's determination.

"Don't answer it," Andy commanded. Hal laughed sheepishly. Some part of him was thrilled that his sons were paying so much attention to his wellbeing. He snatched up the phone and started walking towards the back door via the kitchen.

"Hal here. Yes darling. Hello." He came closer, eyeing me off, a sitting duck by the sink with my arms wrist-deep in suds. He locked eyes with me and in that instant I knew what he was about to do. I backed away but it was too late.

"Nell's here, she wants to say hello." He thrust the phone to my ear. "Say hello, Nell," he said cheerily. "It's Phan."

She was still shouting in Thai when he put the phone to my ear. I had to hand it to him, it was a masterstroke of revenge. I had an excruciatingly strained and polite stop-start conversation with Phan and then handed the phone back to Hal. He moved out the back door to the garden shouting into the phone, "No, no more money. Me no more money!"

I turned around to see Tom and Andy looking at me.

"Nice chat?" Tom asked.

"You deserved that," Andy laughed.

"I saw him just sort of fake it to the left as though he was going out the door then, 'bam!' Flick pass! It was quite masterful," Tom said with some admiration.

"Why did I deserve that?" I bristled with the inference that I had done something wrong by speaking my mind.

"Because you buckled him," Andy said.

"Someone had to spell it out," I said.

"Quite cruel it was," Tom admonished.

"There's no need to hit a man when he's down, Nell," Andy said, looking quite disappointed by my apparent cruelty. "Look at him. He's being hammered."

We saw him through the window, pacing back and forth, holding the phone in front of his face, shouting into it.

*Bad lady!* He was shouting. *You very bad lady!*

"Karma," I retorted.

Tom and Andy snickered gleefully. Their loyalty was somewhat fluid. Encouraged, I went on.

"I just—I just can't bear the way you pussyfoot around him all the time," I said.

"There's a reason we pussyfoot around him," Andy said quietly.

"He turns," Tom confirmed. "It's ugly."

"You got off pretty lightly—if he just leaves it at that flick-pass." The 'if' was ominous. I leaned back against the sink and wiped my hands on a tea towel with some concentration.

"He doesn't scare me," I said with the bravado of someone who has had a stable, easy childhood. "Look at him, he's pathetic. Does he really think she's not in it for the money? Let her fleece him."

"If she takes all his money, he will have nowhere to go," Andy said. "And he will end up right back here. I don't want to get to the point . . . where I have to turn him out on the street."

"We're trying to gently maneuver him," Tom said, gesturing with his two hands, "in the right direction."

"Which is an eight-hour plane ride away from here," Andy agreed.

I saw Tom patting himself down for his smokes and lighter. They were both twitchy. About ten seconds away from retiring to the front porch for a smoke.

"Do what you have to," I said. "I'm going to bed."

"Say goodnight to Dad," Andy said.

"Give him a kiss," Tom added cheekily. "Might be the last time you ever see him."

"I can only hope."

# 16.

When the wedding invitation came, there was much debate about the merits of going. It became a common 'starter for ten' at dinner parties and other social gatherings.

"Andy's father is getting married in Thailand. Should he attend?"

The answer from those who did not know the full history was a resounding chorus of, "Yes, of course, it's family."

Andy delighted in a) asking people who didn't know the full history and b) keeping the details as sketchy as possible. So far we had canvassed the idea with my close friends who knew the full story, and a wide variety of different acquaintances from Andy's work (including the dopey nineteen-year-old receptionist and the barista with the mobile coffee cart in the foyer) who did not know the full story. The score, bearing in mind the branch-stacking tactics employed by Andy, was nine to four in favour of Andy going.

There was never any question or suggestion that I might go too. Firstly, I did not want to. Secondly, I did not want to. Thirdly, who would mind the children? Fourthly, before you suggest it, over my dead body would the children tag along to witness the unholy betrothal of a pervy old white geezer to a young Thai woman.

In my defence (if one is needed), we were strapped for cash, as we always were in those days. We were on one-and-a-half incomes and our saving-for-a-deposit plan was one step forward, two steps back. Meanwhile, average house prices were inching closer toward the million dollar mark every year. Who has that much money? Not us. In fact, we were beginning to resign ourselves to a lifetime of renting a large house with a strange granny flat goitre attached to its western wall.

I was picking up various bits of work here and there from specifically tolerant clients who would allow for the variations in commitment that children bring. It was mainly documentation work; a dull and technical process of detailing all the bits and pieces that make up large building projects. While the children were napping, I spent my time at a drawing board poring over window frames and guttering systems. It was non-glory grunt work that made me cross-eyed with boredom. Added to that, it was not an income that could be relied upon from month to month.

Andy had become, by default, the main breadwinner and in search of bigger money had moved into the private sector. It was not a role that sat well with him after years with the transparency and accountability of the City of Sydney (which he had loved). He was now working for a company whose boom trade was graffiti removal. He managed and coordinated a small team of workers who scrubbed other people's scribble (some claimed it to be 'art') off walls. It was well paid but entirely uninspiring (not to mention, absurdly profit-driven given they weren't actually selling anything). He struggled to find any sense in it and returned to me every night with that dead-eyed look of defeat that men have when they realise they have become but a cog in the larger machine of the economy; when the necessities of providing for the family have caused a downgrading of one's own dreams and desires.

It was a tense time of small children and violently see-sawing power between the main breadwinner and the main caretaker of the home and children. Our rapport was not at its best; our civility was stretched as taut as the strings of a violin and it depended on how well you played it as to how it sounded. Six years in, we had not yet reached the working equilibrium that comes if you can hang in there and make it to ten years; an equilibrium borne of a willingness to compromise without resentment.

We were both still clawing for supremacy. Andy longed to come home to a docile Stepford-style wife who would lay a blanket over his knees and set a drink in his hand while he stared numbly at the television and wiped the day's corporate horrors from his mind. I longed for a husband to come through the door and immediately run children's baths, heat up bottles, nurse the teething baby, read stories and wipe up spills while I shut myself in the bedroom and howled out the frustrations of domesticity and its dull, repetitive grind.

We both felt that we were disappearing into the quicksand of responsibility and we struggled violently to keep ourselves visible: to prove that our id still existed; vibrant and self-fulfilled, as it had been in the halcyon days of our twenties.

My issue (if I need to spell it out) with Andy going to Thailand to attend Hal's wedding was twofold. Firstly, he had admitted to me in a most candid moment that what he really wanted to do was go to the wedding then disappear to an island for a week to go scuba diving. This, to me, precluded the argument so often given that one must attend because one must support one's family. If Andy's main motivation was a little scuba holiday for himself, then the argument of 'it's family' did not apply. Secondly, I had an irrational fear (although perhaps not so irrational given his genealogy) that he would arrive in Thailand and, under the tutelage of his father, disappear down the rabbit hole of 'I love you long time'. (An offshoot nightmare scenario of *this* nightmare scenario was him coming home with the clap and giving it to me.)

Indeed, Hal had sent numerous emails pertaining to that sort of reunion for him and 'the lads'. At the eleventh hour, with Tom and Andy still resisting temptation, an offer came to cover the boys' airfares to get them there. An unusually generous offer by Hal.

And this was precisely the moment of Tom's defection.

The year prior he had been shunted out the other end of his drama degree, and found the world outside the university walls too big a dose of a struggling actor's reality. He did some 'suit' work (as in character suits like Yogo the Gorilla and Dorothy the Dinosaur), a bit part in a movie and some voiceovers. But ultimately, the cash flow was not viable. His only option now was to work to live while trying to keep the acting dream alive in the small spaces of life that remained.

He was currently weighing his options; the most realistic of which was teaching migrants to speak conversational English in some airless corporate classroom with fluorescent lighting and a mean false ceiling. After dedicating himself so fully to the craft of acting for three years, this ungratifying outcome pissed him off. He was at a loose end and ripe for corruption when Hal swooped.

Once Tom had defected, the pull to get Andy there increased to fever pitch, even including, for one brief moment, an offer to cover my airfare as well. The children then became the sticking point that allowed me to hold my ground. Andy presented various options to me. We talked about it in an abstract way but in essence, I knew he did not have a strong enough impulse to leave us. Perhaps he was afraid of the pull of his father and the amoral universe that had set him adrift in his childhood. For all his complaining over the years that I was 'too structured' and had 'too many rules', I was coming to realise that it was this sense of order that drew him to me. I kept him upright. I was a central fixed point around which he could orbit in safety. He liked the idea of going to Thailand but to his credit he did not like the idea of going alone. So Tom went alone.

We received a disc of photographs of Hal's wedding in the mail. In them, Tom appeared reborn, wearing the relaxed crumpled clothing of a holiday. Wild-haired and carelessly tanned, he faced the camera with the defiant air of a man who has found his freedom. He didn't look particularly happy, just thoughtful and somehow at peace. In the group shots he stood the way he had always wanted to live his life; slightly apart from the crowd. Hal was in amongst the locals, a tall, pink-faced, bug-eyed ogre towering over their petite brown bodies; his face split open in a grotesquely desperate show of happiness. Tom stood beside him, staring the camera down, as if to say, 'I've made my decision and there's nothing you can do about it'.

"Do you think he'll ever come back?" I said to Andy as we clicked through the photos on my computer.

"He can't. He's got no more money. He can barely afford the plane fare home now that he's given all his money to Phan."

He thought I was talking about Hal. "No, I mean, Tom," I said quietly.

Andy just sighed. We already knew the answer, even back then.

# 17.

Tom was an unreliable correspondent at the best of times. But Thailand seemed to swallow him whole, leaving no trace that he ever existed. He went AWOL and could not be roused via email, nor any one of the many mobile phone numbers we had collected in our contact book for him. Perversely, Hal kept in more reliable contact, emailing intermittently; spitting a hasty sequence of non sequiturs in his old-fashioned telegram-style communication across the screen, doling out valuable news of Tom in tantalisingly cryptic drips.

Hal's absorption of Tom into his white man's Thai paradise was all-encompassing. Ever the career shape-shifter, Hal had found work at a prestigious English elementary school in Bangkok, teaching local kids to speak English. The work was reasonably well paid when you factored in the relatively low cost of living in Thailand. It was the perfect crime for anyone who wanted to avoid the brutal capitalist grind of a Western city like Sydney. He presented it to Tom as such: easy work and reasonable pay in a city where white men can live well and be treated like kings. For Tom, already semi-trained to teach English to migrants, the final piece of the 'should I live in Thailand' puzzle fell into place.

Thus Tom's defection into Hal's world was complete. To my mind, Hal seemed to crow his victory at having snared Tom into his web. He gave the undeniable impression that the two of them were tom-catting their way across Thailand together in some sort of 'father-son-pleasures-of-the-flesh' bonding exercise.

It was from one of these emails that we first learnt of Sunisa. Hal focused mainly on her (apparent) wealth (detailing the condos and apartments she owned, how many cars and the sorts of designer clothes she wore), her youth (he incorrectly claimed she was twenty-two, she was actually twenty-seven) and the fact that Tom had been kind enough to 'fix' him up with Sunisa's sister on numerous occasions. This latter piece of information was given freely without any concession toward the fact that he was apparently now 'married' to Phan. It reminded me of the time he brought his mistress to the Tattersall's Club and we were all just expected to accept this as the order of things.

The obvious inference in this, as Hal hoped to convey, was that both Sunisa and her sister were, in essence, whores for the hiring. We both knew that any information given by Hal was to be taken with a heaped tablespoon of salt. But it was increasingly disorienting not to hear Tom's voice in all of this.

After a few hit-and-miss phone messages, a remote and disturbingly unfamiliar voice buried in the hiss of the vast distance between Sydney and Bangkok, Tom finally made contact via a temporary email address—the kind with an unmemorable sequence of numbers and letters in it—and sent through details of a Facebook page that we could all 'log onto' to keep up with his movements. At this point, Andy became quite despondent.

"He's gone," he said sadly one night, after trying to gain access to the page without actually joining Facebook himself. (Impossible, as we discovered. This was 2009 and just before Facebook became as de rigeur as an email address. There were still those of us who considered it some strange 'new thing' we didn't want to be part of.)

"He's my only brother and he's . . . just out of my life."

I didn't know what to say to that. I knew it was true. We had lost Tom to Thailand . . . and, more disturbingly, to Hal.

The fact that Hal was taking the trouble to keep in such regular contact was unusual and unsettling. Andy and I both sensed an ulterior motive. About a year prior to Tom's wedding, we received a typically truncated Hal missive in which the motive suddenly became clear.

> PLANNING VISIT FOR VARIOUS DENTAL AND MEDICALS. 3NIHGTS INCLUSIVE ARRIVe 21 AUG. GREG ANd JEAN NOT FORhtCOMING. HOPING TO IMPOSE ON YOUR HOSPITALity, MUCH OBLIGED. LOVE TO NELL, DANIEL, ELIZABETH AND BERTIE.

Hal had figured that he would still need to make regular trips back to Australia for medical and dental checks, as was the benefit of a free universal healthcare system like Medicare. Therefore, we were a place to land and a free bed. So it would pay to keep us on side.

"No way," I said, staring at the screen.

"It's just three nights."

"What's with the capitals?" I said distractedly.

"I think he has trouble with the caps lock or something," Andy laughed. "Seriously though, I may never see him again."

"I don't want him in my house," I said.

Andy swiveled the chair to look at me. "*Our* house," he corrected. "He's my father—besides, what excuse do we give other than *we don't like you.*"

I folded my arms. My mother would be aghast and I hadn't even told her any of the worst stuff. Even Maude had told me pointedly that I was to hold firm on never letting Hal stay at our house. *I don't want him near those children,* she told me. *Honestly Nell, they're such sweet children, I can't bear to think of him using foul language, or . . . having one of his turns in front of them.*

"Nell, don't put me in a bad position here," said Andy.

"You're putting us in a bad position," I returned, emboldened by the two mothers each sitting on either shoulder.

At that moment, Albert waddled up to the baby gate that was wedged across the study door and started shaking the bars like a monkey. It was feeding time.

"I'm asking you for three nights," Andy said, keeping his voice purposely calm. "That's all."

"Daniel!" I called out, still eyeing the offending and ridiculous telegram-style email. It was a wonder Hal hadn't put STOP between each sentence. Someone should tell him you can be as verbose as you like in an email, it wouldn't cost any extra and that capitals are akin to shouting.

"I'll never see Tom again," Andy said, with some added drama. "This is my family."

Daniel appeared at the gated doorway. "Yeah?"

"Can you take Albert and put him in his highchair?"

"I'll do it!" Elizabeth was there in a shot.

She picked Albert up virtually by his neck and tried to wrest him away from the bars. His little paws gripped with impressive strength.

"Not like that, you're strangling him," Daniel said. "Mum asked me to do it."

"I can do it," she said.

Albert let go and the two of them flew backwards, at which point Elizabeth, still hanging onto him and trying to right herself, fell over him and they landed in a clumsy tangle on the kitchen tiles. Albert's head made a sickening clunk. We all waited. There was a split second of terrible silence. Then he started screaming and we all breathed out.

"See what you did, stupid!" Daniel spat, outraged that his moment of authority as the eldest had been so clumsily turned to chaos.

"It was only an accident," Elizabeth wailed.

"You stupid idiot!" Daniel shouted in a voice so full of rage it frightened even me. He was clenching and unclenching his fists, his eyes were bulging out of his head.

"Daniel!" I said, horrified.

"Well, did you see what she did?" he shouted at me. His face was contorted.

"For god's sake, stop shouting at Daniel and get Bertie!" Andy shouted at me. There was heavy judgment in his voice and I didn't miss it. Bertie was lying on the floor on his back like an upturned beetle.

Andy pushed past me righteously, stepped over the gate and swept poor, wounded, howling Bertie into his arms, checking the back of his head carefully for blood and bumps.

"Lucky he's got a head like a rock," I said, trying to lighten the mood.

"I'm sorry Mummy," Elizabeth was sniffling and burying her face in my stomach.

"Just be careful," I said. "He's alright."

Daniel was feeding him marshmallows from a packet. Albert shovelled one in then put his paw out for another. *Quick thinking, Daniel,* I thought, but something else nagged at me; the force of his rage, the way he flicked so quickly these days from a compliant, helpful and reasonable child to a child who could not contain his violent emotions. His anger seemed quite literally to be something he struggled to keep within the boundaries of his own body. It burst through his skin, his eyes bulged, his teeth clenched together, his hands worked open and shut with the energy of it. Was this normal or was it some part of Hal's gene pool that we were experiencing, third-generation?

It could easily have come from my side of the family, of course. Both my father and I were known for our quick tempers, our explosive expressions of anger. My father's temper often got the better of him, manifesting in shouting or the futile kicking of inanimate objects. The crucial difference to my mind between his bad temper and Hal's violent one was that it was never directed *at* anyone and nor did anyone in our house ever fear for their safety. Indeed, my father often removed himself until he had cooled down sufficiently, at which point he would re-enter the family fold and apologise, offering an eloquent explanation for his sudden turn. And while I was never afraid of what my father might do to me, I did fear losing his approval. In Andy's case, he was afraid of what his father might do to him but he did not care one jot for his father's approval.

As to my inheritance of my own father's legacy, the latch on the laundry door was still bent back from when I'd recently shut myself in there and kicked repeatedly at the back of the door in a rage that I could neither contain nor display. Andy had no tolerance for extravagant displays of anger; raised voices, name-calling, hurling objects. And by that I mean he had no tolerance for it in other people. After the incident early in our marriage where he had barricaded himself in the spare room, I had quickly learned how not to set him off. If I look at it objectively, I could say that open displays of anger in other people brought back flashes of his life that he cared not to remember. His fight-or-flight response was, by virtue of his history, so close to the surface that he could not readily distinguish between a general venting of steam and a genuine violent episode. His response to an angry exchange of words was hair trigger and I had long ago developed a habit of pulling my punches, figuratively speaking.

As a result, it had been difficult to vent any kind of steam over the course of our marriage. I continually found myself pressing my anger downwards, pushing on it with force and the more I pushed down, the harder the upward force became. One night, after an argument, I had run deep into the backyard where the paspalum was hip-high to spend my unspent outrage. There in the cool darkness of suburbia, with a cathartic scream I had hurled my wine glass at the garage wall. It made a popping tinkling sound rather than the hard, satisfying smash I was hoping for. And as I looked up at the night sky, in search of cosmic wisdom, the only thing that became abundantly clear to me was that I would have to now find each piece of the broken glass and pick it up before morning, when the children would be roaming around with bare feet.

I watched Daniel now, back to his sweet angelic, helpful-beyond-his-years self, as he proffered the marshmallow packet towards Elizabeth in the ultimate peace offering. She quickly took four before I could apply any rules.

"I'm sorry Lizzie," Daniel said. "You just got me so angry because you shoved me out of the way."

I felt a wave of relief, seeing in him my own father's eloquence and willingness to express remorse.

"It was only an accident," she repeated through her mouthful of marshmallows, then gravely to me, "Do you think Bertie will be brain damaged?"

We all looked at Albert. His mouth was so firmly stuffed with pink and white marshmallows he couldn't even chew on them. He saw us all looking at him and tried to smile but could only let out an imbecilic gargling noise. Then he hit himself on the head with his own hand to celebrate his joy at being the centre of our attentions.

"*Will be* brain damaged?" Andy said.

It was amazing how ordinary life just kept rolling on over the cracks.

# 18.

One reason that the appearance of Hal's email (and his apparent impending arrival on our doorstep) so unnerved me was that Andy and I were in the midst of a marital Mexican stand off. It had begun when I started pulling my punches. There was only room in this partnership for one bad temper and Andy's temper, fuelled as it was by an inner child who sniffed danger in the flash of an eye, won out over mine. Andy's version of this would be that I do not communicate my emotions. For the record, I would agree wholeheartedly with that analysis. But I would add the qualifying fact that I do not communicate certain emotions for reasons of keeping the peace.

In any case, I had been not communicating my emotions for some time. Andy had been burying his in a binge-drinking session with work colleagues every Friday night, resulting in an unbearably pathetic and uselessly hungover husband emerging from the bedroom at around midday every Saturday. Our entire Saturday was wiped out by his hangover. He became particularly oafish, making morose requests for a cooked breakfast, taking a long bath when there was only one bathroom in the house, loafing around on the couch under a doona watching TV, all the while expecting me and the children to tiptoe around him. It got on my nerves but for months I held my tongue.

The week before Hal's email, Andy had really pushed it. He'd stumbled home at five in the morning. 5.09am to be precise. He thought he'd gotten away with it. I heard him trying clumsily to be quiet as he tip-toed into the room. I opened one eye and saw him lighting his way absurdly with the spark from a dead lighter. If I hadn't been so mad, I would have laughed. We both would have laughed. Then he dropped his clothes quickly onto the floor and climbed into bed with just his undies on. He didn't turn on the light, he just snuck in (or so he thought) and started snoring. When he was in a deep, thick, snorting sleep, I kicked him with my heel to make him stop. It was very satisfying.

The next day we were all in the car and I spoke my mind. Tired of constantly being the reasonable one while he behaved unreasonably, I lashed out and said something that reverberated into our marriage for the months to come.

The fact that I made this comment within earshot of his friend, Nick, only made things worse. What happened was this. We were driving along and Andy was practically incapable of speech. I had asked him three times what he wanted to do that day; picnic, take the kids to the park, work on the garden, and each time I was greeted with a vague grunting sound. I responded in my own passive aggressive way by plunging him into silence, hoping he'd hear the screaming subtext and ask me what was wrong, at which point I would finally voice my complaints with regard to Friday night binge-drinking; staying out until the wee hours of the morning when you've got a wife and three kids; and his general bad mood regarding having to work nine-to-five every day of the week (agreed, it's a hideous obligation, one I was secretly glad to be free of) while he imagined I swanned around having coffee with friends and tickling the children to make them laugh their sunny laughs. (True, I did have coffee with friends, but it was, as any mother knows, an exercise of deftly batting children away as you tried to finish each sentence and then eventually resigning yourself to the carpeting of your lounge room with popcorn if only to ensure you can finish one anecdote without interruption.)

His phone rang, he answered it on speaker phone. It was a friend from work, Nick. Andy announced the presence of his wife and children in the car, so as to preclude any bad language.

"Ah, Nell, how are you feeling this morning?" Nick had addressed me brightly after raking over the coals of his and Andy's 'big night'.

"Like a divorce," I said flatly.

It was a joke, sort of. I think I said it in order to get his attention. And I did get his attention, just not the sort of attention I had wanted. Instead of turning to me and saying: *Darling, I had no idea you were so unhappy, please tell me how I can fix things to make our life more closely resemble the ideal you have in your head,* Andy went into silent punishment mode. (My version. His version was that he was so upset and hurt he was unable to communicate with me.)

He did not speak to me, or look me in the eye for the whole day. Then the trump card; once the children were in bed, he stomped out of the house without explanation and returned half an hour later, making a beeline for the backyard. He pushed through the screen door, let it bang shut with a metallic slap and left the main door open despite the midwinter cold. I got up to shut it and that's when I smelled it, the sharp acrid smell of a cigarette just lit. My heart thumped to confrontation mode. Then I saw him out there at the picnic table, the red tip of his cigarette glowing at me. I went outside and stood there, waiting for him to look at me. He just looked straight ahead and ignored me.

"I thought you gave up," I said pointedly.

"I just started again," he said.

Six months before, he had undergone a course of hypnotherapy and finally given up smoking. It had cost $120 a pop: twelve weeks of regular weekly sessions. That's $1440 he was now sucking down and blowing out as smoke. I was furious. He was more furious. I could see that and I knew this mood. I stood behind him, wondering if it was worth wading into this now, knowing that mud would be slung. I wasn't up for it and I was still more annoyed that my justified anger earlier in the day had not received apologetic humble pie from him and instead had been seen and raised. I had a legitimate complaint. Why couldn't he just apologise for being a hungover bad husband bum? It wasn't fair. Smoke yourself to death, I thought. See if I care.

I decided to hold the moral high ground and wait for his apology. I turned my back to him, shut the door and went to bed. The stand off had begun.

One week later (when the email came from Hal), we still hadn't talked about it. We'd moved around it (and each other) carefully and while the moment had gone, the sour taste of it had not. We remained distant to each other. Andy slept on his side of the bed and kept his hands to himself. Normally we spent the night in a creep and crawl across the bed where he relentlessly sought me out, spooning me from behind in his sleep, as I tossed and turned and constantly changed position. He stopped trying to reach me.

Most unnervingly, Andy changed his behaviour. He smoked that packet of cigarettes over the course of the week then (to my knowledge) did not buy another. That Friday, he came straight home from work and helped with the children's bed and bath-time routine. He read stories, he helped Daniel with his spelling and reading, he changed Albert's nappies and fed him his night-time bottle. But there was something not right about it. He was polite to me, but his contempt was just below the surface. I could feel it.

He was making a point of making the marriage work in the face of what he saw as my willingness to just give up on it. He wasn't doing it to make things up to me, he was doing it to show me how it was done. We settled into this dynamic and the more it went on, the more we both forgot what had started it. Occasionally we would catch each other by surprise and share a joke, regaining our closeness for a split second. I started to gather my nerve, I began to think it might be safe to talk about it. Then three weeks later, Hal arrived and it became necessary once more, to paper hastily over the cracks; to polish up our veneer of the perfect family.

The first night of Hal's visit, Andy and I made an unspoken decision between us not to change our routine to suit him. In fact, we went so far as to aggravate him with our routine.

He had arrived in ill-fitting slacks and a skivvy bearing one small duffle bag with the only winter clothes he now possessed. His only other luggage was a large plastic shopping bag full of duty free stuff. I took it as the ultimate peace offering when Andy gently refused the large carton of cigarettes Hal proffered from within the goody bag.

"I've given up, Dad, remember, I told you that."

"You're sticking to it?" Hal said, surprised.

"He's been hypnotised," I said mischievously, but with a hint of pride that he had finally kicked the habit.

"Seriously?" Hal had said, still trying to put the carton of Dunhills into Andy's hands. "You're not going to lapse?"

"I'm done," Andy said. "Give them to Tom."

Hal looked around, from me to Andy, to the children, whom I was stultifying with television. Albert was strapped into his stroller, Daniel and Elizabeth were motionless on the couch, with their mouths hanging half-open like imbeciles, watching *The Incredibles*.

"Gee!" Hal crooned, "She's got you well trained, hasn't she? Giving up the evil weeds and everything. Never thought I'd see the day."

He chuckled to himself, as though enjoying a secret joke of his own along the lines of: *Poor bastard, he's well and truly under the thumb.*

Hal distributed his cheap gifts around and then Andy ushered him outside to the picnic table for a beer while I got the kids' dinner ready. At six o' clock, they came inside. Hal ensconced himself at the dining table with the newspaper spread out before him.

"Drink. Andy," he said. It was a demand, not a question. Andy ignored him. As did I.

The children were seated at the bench eating dinner. Albert was strapped into his high chair. His life at that point was an endless cycle of chairs with belts: high chair; stroller; car seat; high chair. Their collective whining was reaching fever pitch. Elizabeth did not like fish fingers and apparently had told me that last time I served them.

Daniel was trying to broker a deal. "If I eat all my fish fingers can I leave the carrots?"

Albert was making his feelings known in a more concrete way; by dropping his food straight onto the floor.

Elizabeth was whining and I mean *whining.* "I told you I *don't like fish fingers!"*

Andy was running Albert's bath with the bathroom door open, the roar of the water whooshing into the bath added to the general feeding-time-at-the-zoo ambience.

"Mum, *Mu-um!* Is that enough?" Daniel was asking, waiting for my approval so he could ensure a bowl of ice cream for afterwards. I had created this system where they showed me their plates and I cast my judgment. In hindsight, I should have made the system more absolute—no clean plate, no dessert—but it had somehow morphed into a game of difficult-to-define-degrees that required my visual confirmation. Sometimes they sought me out in the bathroom, proffering their half-eaten dinner plates for judgment at which point I usually screamed, "For god's sake, I'm on the toilet, get that food out of here!"

Albert, finally tired of seats with seatbelts started straining against his ever-present shackles and tried to wriggle himself free. The very annoying, straining sound he was making provided a discordant partner to Elizabeth's whining. Then the timer Andy had set so we wouldn't forget the bath (which we often did, not realising until the water had overflowed and began making a trickling noise onto the tiled floor) suddenly went off, a relentless, high-pitched rhythmic beeping noise.

Andy and I, both impervious by this stage of our lives to the cacophony of family, did not flinch at this sudden addition to all the other noise in the house. Neither of us moved to stop it. We just carried on what we were doing knowing it would see itself out in exactly sixty seconds. Hal looked up from his newspaper in panic.

"Smoke alarm! The smoke alarm!" he shouted into the cacophony of noise: the bath running, the kitchen exhaust roaring, Albert screaming, Elizabeth whining, the microwave whirring.

Andy simply wrested Albert free of his chair and carried him screaming to the bath.

"Andy!" Hal looked around helplessly. "The smoke alarm! Arrgh!" Hal's urgency for someone to notice the 'smoke alarm' was not so much a fear of some impending danger as annoyance that the ambient noise in the house was disturbing his newspaper reading time as he sat himself blithely in the centre of our busy family routine.

Needless to say, I did not give a stuff. I went into the study off the kitchen to calmly check my emails. I could still hear him from there.

"Nell! Andy! Something's ... the smoke alarm's going! It's ... Andy!"

Neither of us did anything to alleviate his discomfort. It was a little moment of collusion between Andy and me that warmed my heart.

Over dinner, Hal was up to his old tricks. We were left alone together for ten deeply uncomfortable minutes when Andy went out to the garage to retrieve another bottle of red.

"So, still drawing bus shelters, Nell?" Hal asked innocently. I laughed. I had long ago relinquished my ego to motherhood.

"No. I'm just doing bits and pieces here and there, nothing permanent."

"Too busy with the kids?"

"Yeah, it's pretty intense at the moment."

"Intense?" His ears pricked up. "You mean, with the baby and all?"

"Yeah, the first two years is always difficult," I admitted candidly.

"But you planned to have him, Albert?"

"Yes," I said, growing suspicious about where this was heading.

"You wanted the three."

"Yes," I said.

"Oh ... " he said with feigned surprise, "because Andy said you were iffy on the third, that he had to talk you into it."

It was true, there had been some discussion, which had been taken off the table when I had fallen pregnant unawares.

"I always wanted three," I said. "It was just the timing I wasn't sure of."

"But you love him now, dear little Albert," Hal said. "You don't regret it?"

"Of course not!" I said, horrified.

"And you're not one of these earth mothers, you know, breastfeeding until they're seven and that sort of thing. You like to have your career as well."

Hal had this very irritating habit: instead of asking questions *of* you so that you might tell him about yourself, he made statements *about* you. His statements were his own definition of you. They were, more often than not, insulting jabs that went right to the heart of whatever sore spots you possessed. Having a conversation with Hal wasn't so much an exchange as a constant test of your intellectual and emotional mettle. It was difficult to engage with him without appearing defensive and paranoid.

"Breastfeeding until they're seven?" I asked, not willing to let that one go through to the keeper. "What are you on about?"

He snickered, delighted that I'd kept the ball in play, which gave him the opportunity to explain it to me. He licked his lips in preparation.

"You know, these mothers who like to breastfeed their children until they're quite big. Apparently, they find it quite pleasurable, sexually."

"Right. I see." I stared straight at him, what was his point?

"It's well documented, they're quite inspired. They find the sucking on the nipple so sexually pleasurable that they can't stop."

Andy re-entered the room then, carrying a bottle of red. "Who finds what sexually pleasurable?" Andy asked, intrigued.

"I was just saying," Hal began as though he were expounding a fact that would be of use to everyone, "how it's quite well documented that some women find breastfeeding sexually pleasurable, you know, they have orgasms while they're breastfeeding."

I said nothing. What was there to say that wouldn't conjure up an image of me breastfeeding and having grateful orgasms for Hal to enjoy at his leisure?

"True?" Andy feigned some interest if only to keep things moving along.

"It's quite common," Hal assured him.

"Oh rubbish," I spat out. "That's a fantasy to soothe men who can't deal with the fact that sometimes breasts are just utilitarian objects."

"Not everyone," Hal demurred. "But there are some women who find it quite sexually stimulating."

"I have heard that," Andy said.

"Where have you heard that?" I said getting quite antsy. "Apart from here, right now."

"I've heard that before," Andy said. "Somewhere, I've read it somewhere."

"Where did you read that?" I insisted. I was aware that things were getting close to the antagonism that we had so effectively papered over since Hal had arrived. But I couldn't let it go. I knew my mother would not want me to let it go.

*Good for you, Nell.* I heard her voice encouraging me. *You speak up.*

"Settle down, Nell," Andy said, his face showing irritation with my self-righteous feminist stridency. "It's just a theory."

"I just heard it, that's all," Hal was coming on all sheepish and 'sorry to set you off crazy lady'. Then he muttered to no one in particular, "She's quite snaky."

"No need to turn," Andy said pointedly as he refilled everyone's glasses.

When he got to mine, I put my hand over the top. "Not for me," I said. "I'm going to bed."

I said my goodnights and went into the bathroom to brush my teeth. While I was in there I heard them muttering,"I just meant it as a general observation," Hal said, still feeling the humiliation of my tongue lashing. "You know, it's clinically proven."

"She's a bit stressed out at the moment, that's all," Andy said.

I left them there at the table talking. Andy didn't come to bed until after midnight. I feigned sleep. He climbed into his side of the bed and turned his back to me. I should have asked him there and then what they had been talking about. It may have opened up the channels between us; it might have fixed what needed fixing. But above all, I would have been ready a year later when it came back at me in another way.

It was my biggest mistake, turning my back to Andy when the only other person in the room *he* could turn to was Hal.

# 19.

Six months later, another Thai wedding invitation arrived.

*Together with their parents*
*Sunisa Samakthai*
*&*
*Thomas Straw*
*Request the pleasure of your company at their wedding ceremony.*
*Saturday the first of September, 2010*
*At the home of Rangsan and Aranya Samakthai*
*Nakhon Sawan Province, Thailand.*

By this time, Hal had gradually receded from our lives like a bad dream we'd once had. He had returned to Thailand and as long as he didn't need us, we did not hear from him. In fact, there was a fairly lengthy period of total radio silence during which Andy became more and more comfortable with the idea of just letting his father go and making no effort to stay connected. For a good while, we enjoyed the peace of a Hal-less existence.

But Tom's wedding brought the spectre of Hal right back into our present. Tom had already indicated to Andy that Hal was edging his way to the forefront of the proceedings and would need to be 'handled'. So not only would Andy have to spend time with his father, he would have to engage in direct hand-to-hand combat. Was it safe, or indeed kind, to let him go into that alone?

Andy would go, of course. The question became, would I? The children, again, became my sticking point but I was torn. Andy and I had only just come out of our bad marital patch. Without directly addressing it, we had just kept moving forward until gradually we didn't so much forget why we were mad at each other as conveniently allow ourselves some marital amnesia for the sake of just getting on with things.

The sour taste of our discord was still there, but we became better at living with it.

Albert moved from the just-walking baby phase into the more robust toddler phase and I began to see a light at the end of the child-rearing tunnel; the place where you get days back to yourself. I became less angry and Andy stopped doing Friday night drinks in such a hell-bent way. Things were gradually getting better.

But we weren't there yet. I thought we were one incident away from having the whole thing break wide open again. Which is why I moved heaven and earth to go to Thailand with him. The thought of delivering him, solo, to a place where Hal could get inside his head seemed like marital suicide. My parents tacitly agreed. They were surprisingly amenable to the idea of minding the children for ten days so that Andy and I could go on a holiday together.

The Hal-free period had galvanised Andy somewhat against his father. Andy made no contact with Hal prior to our arrival and our plan was to slip quietly into the country and only see Hal at the requisite wedding-related engagements. After all these years, Andy had finally figured out that the only way to deal with his father was to keep contact to a minimum.

At least, that was the plan.

II

# Land of a thousand smiles

**farang** – fa$^{L}$ rang$^{L}$ [noun]

1. non-Asian foreigner, [usually] Caucasian
2. guava, *psidium guyava*
3. foreign; non-Thai

## 20.

We flew into Bangkok on a Tuesday at 4pm. By the time we'd been ambushed by Hal in the arrivals hall and herded into Tom's convertible (intriguing), a dirty dusk was falling over Bangkok. As we came off the freeway and stalled in the traffic-choked streets of the city, I noticed the skeletons of buildings that dotted every other block; unfinished high rises like missing teeth in the otherwise lit city. Tarps, torn and flapping, exposed wiring just left hanging, a project abandoned mid-stream, the concrete frame now too far built to demolish.

"Ghost buildings," Tom said, noticing me staring at them. "They just run out of money and . . . "

The flow of traffic was organic, like the bunching flow of water through a narrow channel, carving out its own path. All around me there was a palpable disregard for the rules and regulations that ordinarily shaped my world. We were in Hal's jurisdiction now.

After we checked in at the hotel, we went across to Tom's condo and met Sunisa. The streets were half dug up, big potholes and piles of rubble pockmarked the narrow footpaths, tuk tuks and bikes and cars whizzed by. It was the sort of thing middle-class white people would be up in arms about; mothers with prams would be picketing councils with placards about the safety of their precious children being compromised. You've gotta love the Thais for their very high tolerance of life-endangering conditions. Entire families buzzed around the city piled four apiece onto dirt bikes, tuk tuks swayed on three wobbly wheels through heavy traffic with their lawnmower engines, no seat-belts, no speed limit, sewers running into water supplies, a guy doing calculus on the back of a bike as it whipped in and out of Bangkok peak hour. (Seriously, I saw that.)

A mangy old dog loped past us, it had a demonic look in its eye. I recoiled.

"Soy dog," Tom said.

"What's that?"

"Mangy old inbred street dogs. They're everywhere."

"Do they bite?"

"Not usually," Tom said. "But I wouldn't pat them."

At that time of night, the heat was balmy and gorgeous. We waded through it across the road to Tom's apartment. By now, I had that fantastic dislocated feeling you have when you first arrive in another country. In this night-lit setting everything was exotic. Even the poo-ey, ocean-outfall-like smell.

Sunisa was late back from work and slipped in quietly when I was out on the balcony, escaping the veil of cigarette smoke inside, trying to pretend I just wanted to admire the view. Of the freeway. And the building site next door. I was trying to get a handle on my panic that Andy would take up smoking again and die of lung cancer, leaving me a widow with three children to care for.

I heard Andy's voice change to a more-for-strangers tone and turned to see her there, a willowy slip of a woman in skinny jeans until she slipped off her six-inch heels whereupon, in bare feet, she became small and childlike. She padded across the room, soundlessly, (like she was gliding) towards Andy and Tom. She was so fragile and contained that even Andy, a failsafe social kisser for any occasion, kept his distance and shook her hand.

I re-entered the room, muttering, "Oh, I was just admiring the view," so it wouldn't seem I was huffing outside due to the fog of smoke inside—and approached her cautiously. I am an average-sized woman, I've had three kids and I'm no mere slip of a thing anymore, but by all objective accounts I'm not a heifer either. However, alongside Sunisa, I felt like the most enormous 'warning, wide-load!' pasty, inelegant cow. I took her cue and didn't go in for a big welcome-to-the-family embrace, more for the fact that I imagined me coming towards her with my big tuck shop lady arms outstretched and my ruddy fat face howling a big white lady sound might cause her to run and hide in the bedroom and perhaps not even come out for the wedding.

I took her hand in mine. It was slim and brown and warm. I was already pink-faced and sweating profusely from the heat. She was latte-skinned and immaculately unsweaty. Not even the smallest bead on her top lip.

"I'm very pleased to meet you," she said, meeting my eyes briefly. Then she sat by Tom tucking her legs neatly beneath her, seemingly not bothered by the smoke that wafted around her face, her hands clasped neatly in her lap (as opposed to batting belligerently at the smoke).

Tom was talking about the time Hal peed on them from the upstairs balcony of Sunisa's parents' house. Yes, you read that sentence right. He weed on them. Not intentionally in a 'I piss on you!' sort of way, but in a careless, bit drunk, not really caring about the sorts of social mores most people do, way.

"We were sitting outside and felt this . . . " Tom mimed feeling the first sprinkles of rain.

"We think it's raining," Sunisa giggled.

"He's up on the balcony taking a leak." Tom's face was screwed up, incredulous.

Andy snickered.

"Is there no toilet?" I said, an ulterior motive of trying to gauge the conditions we would be living under for the coming weekend.

"Yes, there's a toilet. But it's downstairs."

"He pissed on you?" I asked Sunisa, watching for signs of life.

"We think it must be raining," she giggled.

I made a mental note to get her alone later to see what she really thought of Hal. Maybe she just thought that's what old *farang* men were like. In fairness, he pretty much fitted the profile in Bangkok.

"One thing I will ask you to watch out for," Tom said, addressing Andy and me more seriously, "is Phan."

He ground his cigarette out into the overflowing ashtray on the coffee table.

"She'll white-ant me," he said. "She'll sidle up to the locals at the wedding and tell them I'm a bad man."

"She's not a nice person," Sunisa said with some authority. "She try to sell me Hal's house."

"That house is his retirement plan," Tom said. "He used the last money he had to build it out in the country so he'd have somewhere to run to when he retires."

"She ask if I want to buy it," Sunisa confirmed. "In Thai, so Hal don't know."

"Did you tell Dad?" Andy asked Tom.

"Yeah," Tom shrugged, then affected his Hal impression. "Nah, she loves me mate. She loves me."

"I don't like her," Sunisa said. "She try to involve me because we both Thai, she try to make me . . . " Sunisa struggled for the word.

"Complicit," I said.

"Yes." Sunisa gave me a grave look.

She wanted me to know very definitely that she was not complicit in this treachery against Hal. I wanted to assure her that it would not compromise my impression of her at all in any case. But it was a difficult thing to explain in simplified English words with no tenses.

"Phan's brother and his mates moved into the house while Hal was in Bangkok," Tom went on. "They moved all his stuff out and all theirs in. When Hal went back, Phan's brother came out with the electricity bill. 'You pay bill,' he told him, because the electricity was about to be cut off. Hal was all, 'nah, fuck off, aaggh not paying'. The guy left. His mate told Hal, 'he's gone to get his gun, I'd pay if I were you.'"

"Did he pay?" Andy said.

"He paid." Tom lit up another cigarette and blew out smoke, sat back. "I tell you, it's the fuckin' wild west out there."

Andy shot me a glance. He chuckled and took my hand. He knew my mind was wheeling out of control, thinking about going out there on the weekend. To the wild west. I was no seasoned traveller. I'd never done the backpacking thing, never driven a fetid old-sock-smelling Kombi around Australia, never trudged through Europe on a wing and a prayer, or trekked the Himalayas with a pack the size of a small mattress strapped to my back, whistling *I Still Haven't Found What I'm Looking For* when I squatted behind a bush to empty my watery bowels.

I'd been to France and America but on a strictly three-star, all accommodation booked and confirmed-to-have-sit-down-potties-before-lift-off rating.

"You okay there, my sweet?" Andy asked, knowingly.

"Good-good," I said tensely.

Then Sunisa got up and said ever so politely, "Excuse me, I need to take a shit," and went into the bathroom.

Andy and I looked at Tom for explanation, not knowing whether to react or let it go. Tom wheezed with laughter, his eyes screwed up.

"I've been meaning to tell her," he said between wheezes, "that it's not a polite way to say I need to go to the toilet."

"Good sport," Andy cackled and bent over double like one of those bobbing birds as though bowing to the joke. I thought I might wet myself, seriously, I couldn't breathe.

Tom snickered and shook and lit up another fag. I pretended my mirth was driving me outside for fresh air and retired once more to the balcony.

# 21.

The next day we awoke to a steamy Bangkok morning. I'd turned off the airconditioning the night before, set as it was to 'frigid Antarctic'. By the morning, the windows were fogged with steam and the air was cloying. I got up and opened the balcony doors expecting a fresh gust of outside air. But if possible, it was hotter outside than in. A thick smell of raw sewerage wafted in.

I stood out on the balcony looking down at the swimming pool; all tropical landscaping and bridges. A mirage of cool for the *farangs*.

Then I went back inside, shut the doors and turned the airconditioning back up to full Antarctic frigid.

We had a full day to ourselves before Maude and Stan arrived. So we went shopping. We hopped in a cab, sat in bumper-to-bumper traffic for about half an hour, talking in broken English to our friendly cab driver, Mr. Boonya, then arrived at a big old bargain Mecca in the city called MBK. It was a rabbit warren of stalls and shops and escalators and retail cubby holes, row upon row of sparkly shoes that caused me to hyperventilate (I needed to brace myself against a wall and clutch my excited heart), bags, sundresses, sunglasses, silk scarves, pashminas, frilly bras for tiny breasts (I was continually ushered to the special sizes, big white lady norks section, which secretly thrilled me), more sparkly shoes and tiny, tiny, *tiny* pants that looked perfect on hangers but would fit no white woman.

Seriously: *tiny* pants. I kept calling for larger sizes, even the XXXL would not go past my upper thighs. Did these people not have bottoms? I started scrutinising locals' bottoms as I boom-bahed my fat white lady arse through the shopping complex. What's with the pants in this town?

After about half an hour of forced togetherness, Andy was edgy. Admittedly I am annoying to shop with. I go into a trance at the best of times and with all those sparkly shoes I was unreachable; on another planet called Cheap Shoe Heaven.

"Let's meet back here at 1pm," Andy said as I stood clutching four pairs of spangly flats, my eyes spinning like pinwheels.

I was mindful of the fact that Andy did not have a watch. "Maybe you should buy a cheap watch," I said, knowing that him not having a watch would be the ultimate excuse to be late.

"Yeah, maybe," he said non-commitally before wandering off to the electronics and illegally-copied DVDs floor.

I spent the morning wafting, drifting, trying not to make my run too early. I bought two pairs of sparkly shoes, three scarves, a skirt with floaty aqua layers and gladly paid two baht to use the sit-down toilets on the third floor. I arrived back at the allotted meeting place at five minutes to one, knowing that my being late would put Andy in a bad mood.

At ten past one, I realised there was no such worry in *his* mind and told myself to remain calm and not make such a big deal out of little things. We were on holiday after all. At twenty past one, I was running through all the times I'd left Andy waiting in the past and arrived to find him incandescent with rage. At 1.25pm, and excruciatingly conscious of having no mobile phone, I was pissed off.

He appeared on the escalators, side-stepping people to get around them, pulling one iPod earphone out of his ear, his T-shirt slightly damp with sweat. He smiled, waved, made a show of looking like he'd run all the way from Phuket to get here twenty-five minutes late. *Selfish.* I thought to myself righteously. *Just like his father.* He saw my tantrum erupting and took my hand.

"I'm starved, let's get something to eat," he said evasively.

"I've been standing here for twenty-five minutes," I said tersely.

"Sorry darling, I didn't have a watch."

He looked at me. I was trying to convey my raging fury with an evil dagger stare. He took in all my shopping bags. "Looks like you got some good stuff," he beamed. "Let's go and sit down and compare purchases."

He held up his own bag full of illegal DVDs, electronic gadgets for the kids and a pair of cheap shoes. As he herded me towards the food hall, thin-lipped and trying to remain terse, he said brightly, "How'd you go with your money? Do you need some more?"

Andy was well-practised in dealing with temper tantrums. His method was evasion at all costs, which spoke volumes about his childhood. He had a maddening way of just riding over the top of it and pretending it wasn't happening. It was the way you handle a toddler. Oh look, what's this? Car keys, see? See how they jangle and make a loud noise?

There were times I found this diminishing. Sometimes I needed to have my anger moment. But then I had to remind myself that he grew up with a father who was not only like a toddler, but had been known to throw heavy objects indiscriminately when in a rage.

"What's with Tom's car?" I said over lunch. "Did you find out?"

"It's Sunisa's," he said. "She bought it last week."

"What does she do again?" I said pointedly, meaning, *surely not enough to buy a Mercedes convertible outright.*

"She owns a couple of shops."

"A couple of shops that sell gold?" I asked.

"Shoes, dresses." He raised his eyebrows at me again, meaning, *I know, it's a bit fishy.*

"What's that worth then, a Mercedes?" I was still trying to make my point and engage him in my line of thinking.

"One point three million baht apparently," he said. "Second-hand." As though that made it less fishy.

"So, 43,000 dollars," I said. "And she just bought it outright, no loan or anything."

"Supposedly," Andy said, trying to appear nonchalant, just to annoy me.

I put down my chopsticks with some emphasis. "What do you reckon is going on there?" I asked.

"I don't know. But isn't it interesting," he said, adopting his gossipy old woman tone, "how Tom always ends up with women who are independently wealthy?"

We both snickered into our stir-fries, bonded by our treachery, two like-minded little gossips picking over the rubble of other people's lives with glee.

Later on, in the swanky air-conditioned comfort of the hotel bar, we discovered that Maude had her own theories on all of this. You could always count on Maude to have her own theories on everything, disseminated in hushed, scandalised whispers and preceded meaningfully with the word, '*Apparently . . .*'

Maude is the sort of person who always creates a bigger story than is necessary and, if nothing else, you have to appreciate the effort she goes to. I'm the sort of person who is willing to believe *anything* as long as it makes for a good story and some excellent hissing-behind-hands-in-the-corner gossip.

To my delight, Maude's theories on Sunisa were typically colourful and fully fleshed out with scandalous augmentations. I was as eager to believe them as Andy was eager to dismiss them (verbally, and in the company of fellow men, at least) as unfounded gossip. We were settled on a couch in the corner, talking in code (as we frequently did), knowing that the menfolk would disapprove of our gossiping. I had raised the issue of the convertible Mercedes. Where did the money come from?

"I think the *other* is still around," Maude said with a meaningful look.

She was ensconced on the beige couch, resplendent in a plum coloured silk blouse, a glass of chilled wine in her manicured hand.

"Hang on, what *other*?" I said, not getting it. Obviously I'd missed some details somewhere along the way. I shifted closer.

"The *American,*" Maude said.

"The American?"

Stan looked over at us suspiciously. Maude was doing that really obvious thing she does when she talks about things she shouldn't be talking about; she puts her hand up over her mouth and then talks without moving her lips. Presumably so no one can read her lips. As a teacher of the deaf, she's a lip-reader from way back. She claims to be able to read entire conversations from the far side of a room and assumes everyone else is doing the same. As a teacher of the deaf, she doesn't consider however, the volume at which she speaks, which for the most part gives her away more readily than the movement of her lips ever would.

"You ladies okay over there?" Stan asked.

"Oh yes," Maude raised her glass to him then muttered out the side of her mouth, "Stan thinks I should stop gossiping about it."

"Your drinks okay?" he continued. Stan's life mission was to ensure that everybody had a fully charged glass.

"Very happy, darling, thank you," Maude smiled again.

That was enough; ladies happy, drinks okay. Stan was a wonderfully uncomplex sort of a man with very little subtext. He went back to his conversation with Andy.

Andy looked longingly at me and Maude gossiping. Even though he tried to disapprove, I knew he longed to be in our conversation. He could tell there was something good going on in the corner he wanted to be privy to. I would have to give him a very detailed post-gossip briefing later on.

"The American boyfriend," Maude continued. "Or whatever you call it, I don't know if boyfriend is exactly accurate." There was an upwards inflection and a light scoff on this last bit, a very meaningful upwards inflection.

"Right," I said, taking that in. "So is he still giving her money, do you think?"

"Well," she cocked her head, "I don't think a couple of dress and shoe shops would cover the cost of a Mercedes convertible, do you?"

"One point three million baht," I confirmed incredulously. "Outright."

"And that's their third car," she continued then counted them off on her peach-coloured fingernails. "There's a Peugeot, some sort of hatchback thing and now this convertible."

"How does Tom feel about the whole thing with the American?"

"Oh, he's quite worried about it. They've had to hide the fact they're getting married. I mean," Maude let out a sigh of exasperation. "Honestly the whole thing is . . . " She took a deep breath. "I'm finding it all very worrisome," she said, her face naked suddenly with the vulnerabilities of a mother.

"She seems very nice, very . . . genuine," I said to reassure Maude.

"Do you think?"

"Yeah, I had a pretty good chat to her last night." Sunisa had struck me as a perfectly genuine woman. I was impressed by her.

"She's terrified about meeting you," I said. "Apparently, the mother-in-law's approval is a very big thing in Thai culture."

"Well," Maude raised her eyebrows, not willing to give Sunisa any leeway at this point.

"She's got herself into a bit of a state about it," I confided. Tom had told us how she'd been a wreck for the past few days, worrying about what sort of impression she would make on Maude.

"Well, if you say she's genuine," Maude conceded.

We sat in silence for a while, sipping our drinks, listening idly while Andy and Stan compared travel stories. Andy was telling the one about his backpacking days in Thailand, when he'd sprained his ankle riding a motorbike and had been laid up in a hammock on the beachfront for three days, drinking rice whisky to dull the pain. He was up to the bit where a violent storm rolled in. I could tell because he was enthusiastically miming being flung about by gale-force tropical winds as he lay in a hammock.

Maude said, "God, Nell, I'm absolutely terrified about seeing Hal again." She put her hand up to her chest. "Just *terrified*."

## 22.

Thursday was as sticky and stinky as the day before. We braved the breakfast buffet at the hotel, bypassing a 'muesli' of stale cornflakes and rice bubbles, casting a cautious eye over ectopic eggs and cardboard-like bacon before opting for some sweet fluffy pancakes with syrup. Coffee was weird, juice was cordial and the plate of spam and processed cheese cut into triangles and fanned meticulously, with a pickled onion jauntily aloft each corner, defied logic.

Tom and Sunisa suggested we hire a long boat and go up the river to see the snake farm, the giant gold Buddha and some famous temple. Just between you and me, tourist attractions bore me numb. All that waiting in queues, standing in crowds reading plaques, shuffling from one attraction to the next, trying to make some sort of connection with the local culture . . . I'd sooner do another 100 laps of the MBK.

But Andy loved it. Plaques? Couldn't get enough of them. Temples? Bring 'em on. Giant gold Buddha lying down sideways? You've gotta see it while you're here.

I agreed to go on the long boat expedition as long as I didn't have to get out of the boat and go into the snake farm or the temple or to walk around the giant gold Buddha. My idea of tourist activity is to sit on my arse while the city goes by. I thought a boat ride would be nice. Who doesn't like boat rides? Maude confided quietly that having seen the gold Buddha and the temple before, she and Stan would be spending their day looking for a third-world tailor to exploit in classic

Anglo-empirical style: *Tailor! Sew us your finest linen garments and make it snappy*. So it was just the four of us, plus an unexpected fifth.

When we met Tom and Sunisa at the front of the hotel, there was a small brown-skinned boy in a striped T-shirt and shorts standing between them, gripping both their hands. I guessed he was about four.

"This is Sunisa's nephew, Bon," Tom said.

The little boy smiled shyly at us. Andy did a bit of, 'Hey there little tiger! Look at you!' work that only made the child scootch further behind Tom's legs.

"He very shy," Sunisa said, looking at Bon with what one could only call motherly eyes.

"You ready to go on a boat?" Andy said to Bon with his face frozen into a Mr Number One Fun grin. To Andy's credit, Bon peeped out from behind Tom's legs and smiled a little. "You want to see some snakes?" Andy then augmented that with some me-no-speak-Thai-but-me-can-mime work. "SSsssssss!"

He affected a snake with his arm. Bon giggled.

"He is like my own son," Sunisa said proudly.

"Sunisa pays for all his schooling and clothes and food and stuff," Tom added.

"He live with my parents," Sunisa said. "My brother he . . . "

She shook her head.

Andy and I waited to arrange our faces appropriately for the rest of that sentence: condolences, judgment, horror. He what? He dead? He incapacitated in some way? He ran off?

"He don't work."

Oh. That'd be judgment then. I did some frowning and nodding that I hoped looked sympathetic towards both Sunisa and her brother and whatever it was that prevented him from working. Sheer laziness as it turned out. I'm not being all white and judgmental here, Sunisa told us that herself. "Thai men very lazy. Women expected to support whole family."

"We're very close," Sunisa said, indicating the boy. "Sometime, he call me Mum."

Later on, when it all came out, I thought back to this conversation. She needn't have provided that alibi for herself. I didn't know the Thai word for mum anyway. So if he was calling her Mum, I wouldn't even have noticed.

"Oh, that's . . . nice," I said at the time, unsure what the proper reaction should be. Was it sad that he didn't have a mum? Or was it nice that they had such a close connection? Or both?

At the riverfront Sunisa did some impressively gentle bartering on price with the local boatmen. She stood with her Ralph Lauren tote hooked over her arm talking softly. Then listened. Then talked softly again. Then walked over to Tom and shook her head. The boatman called her back. She went. She talked softly again. Never once raising her voice or gesticulating wildly with her arms (or heaven forbid pointing) the way a white woman would. The final clincher was when she stood in silence looking at the ground for what seemed like ages while the boatman talked intermittently, in short stabs.

She proceeded to plunge him into a very long, awkward silence that made me wonder if they had actually been talking about hiring a boat at all. It seemed far more protracted and serious. Then finally, just when I was about to say, 'Oh for god's sake, how much?' she looked up at him and agreed.

Tom saw me fidgeting impatiently and said, "Relax, Nell, you're on Thai time now."

"It's like Fiji time," Andy concurred. "Juuuust relax."

"When we get to the village on Saturday," Tom said, "everything will be on Thai time. I have no idea what's going to happen or when. You'll have to be prepared to go with it."

The phrase, 'when we get to the village on Saturday' was becoming a guaranteed precursor to something that would make me tense.

"Great!" I pasted a fake smile to my face and followed them past children jumping into the light brown river, past roadside food stalls with what looked like fried dog's balls on them and past a lot of people shouting what sounded like, 'buy my duck!' to where the long boat was docked. It was rocking and creaking and looked like it had been banged together with random planks of timber. I looked out at the beige river, where boats whizzed past at speed obeying the same right of way rules as the Thai roads: whoever gets there first has right of way.

The driver was perched on the pointy tip of the boat and had no teeth (not his fault, I know, but still, did he have no teeth because he was generally careless in his approach to life and if so, how would that affect his boat-driving skills?). I plonked myself down in the centre of the boat where I reckoned there was the best chance of flotation if the boat spontaneously disintegrated while we were buzzing past the giant sideways gold Buddha.

We buzzed out to the centre channel at a nice, leisurely putt-putt rate. I enjoyed the view of the city from here: impossibly tall buildings built right on the shoreline against a blank overcast sky, the soft diffused light, the bridge that looked exactly like the Anzac Bridge and made me feel suddenly homesick for bright blue cloudless sky, clean air and blindingly cancerous sunlight. Big bunches of banana leaves floated in the river along with chunks of timber and oh, what's that? Some sort of reptile the size of a komodo dragon, belly up, limbs in rigor mortis and body bloated to bursting. How quaint. It bobbed and swayed like an inflatable pool toy.

Then the driver cranked it up to 'so fast only one end of the boat stays in the water' and we were off, zipping through the busy main channel of the river with water spraying back over us.

Then we turned into a side canal and slowed to a crawl. As we putt-putted along the rank canal, Tom pointed out the falling down houses with rotting decks right on the waterline, the obligatory washing lines strung across windows, miniature temples out the front of every home, the crumbling cancerous concrete, the giant sideways Buddha that mercifully we didn't stop at. Pretty soon, talk, as it would continue to do, turned to Hal.

"Do you know if he's coming to the engagement dinner?" Andy asked.

"He called yesterday, said he and his mates are a scratching."

"He'll turn up," Andy said. "He won't want to miss the chance to be in the same room as Mum."

"I know. He'll either turn up unannounced or he'll call at the last minute to say he's coming after all," Tom said. "Whatever fucks things up."

Tom lit up a fag.

"Will he cause trouble?" I said.

"Most definitely," Andy said calmly.

"You have to keep him away from Mum," Tom said to Andy.

"Maybe he won't come," I said hopefully.

"Maybe."

"He's sulking," Tom said.

"Because we tried to sneak in without seeing him?" Andy asked.

"Yeah. He's hurting," Tom said with the slightest edge of sympathy.

"Tough shit," I said aloud, involuntarily. I'd meant only to think it.

Tom looked at me sideways. I was never sure where he stood on the whole Hal thing. He had followed him here to Thailand, after all. They worked at the same English school and it appeared they spent considerable father-son time together.

"How do you feel about him using your wedding as some sort of pimping exercise?" I said, referring to the set up between Jeng and Ivan.

"Yeah," Tom said carefully, he always approached criticism of Hal to me with some discretion. "Bit unseemly."

Then he sniffed out a giggle at the sheer unseemliness of it.

"It's just so wrong," Andy said, laughing helplessly.

"He's demanding two separate bungalows at the wedding," Tom said, staring out at the riverbank, a small, perplexed smile on his face, "One for him and Phan and one for Jeng and Ivan."

"What did you say to that?" Andy said.

"I said balls. They'll have to take shifts."

"Humping shifts," I confirmed.

We all guffawed and snickered. Sunisa looked at us blankly then shifted her gaze back to the middle distance as Bon cuddled in close to her.

"Does he embarrass you at work?" I asked Tom.

"He can't embarrass me any more," Tom shrugged then flicked his butt into the river. There was a sense of resignation about it; fait accompli.

I looked at Tom as he squinted at the riverbanks running alongside us. He was the spitting image of Hal. How deep did his loyalty to his father really go?

"Do I have to talk to him?" I said to Andy.

"To who?"

"To Hal?" I said. "If he comes to the dinner, do I have to talk to him?"

"Be pleasant," he warned.

"It's difficult."

"I know." Andy put his arm around me. "But for your own sake, just be pleasant. Don't take him on. It'll just get ugly."

"Yeah," Tom said. "Nell, I don't want to be one of those 'it's my day' people, but if we could all just work toward containing him rather than smacking his chops."

I laughed. I did enjoy their familial turns of phrase: *smack his chops* was one of my favourites, *just calling to touch your base* was another. All Hal's legacy, ironically enough.

"I know it's hard," Tom said. "But just for me and Sunisa. Could you just do that for us?" He put his arm around Sunisa, kissed her and spoke in his pointedly delicate turn of phrase. "I don't want my lovely lady here to witness such things." Sunisa looked at him trustingly. Put her head on his shoulder. Having found a loving, hard-working *farang* to share her life with, she considered her destiny fulfilled.

She obviously had no idea what she was marrying into.

## 23.

As it turned out, Sunisa did have concerns, but they were more of the traditional kind. She had worked herself into a state about meeting Maude. As we wandered around the temple on the river that day, where monks in orange robes wafted by in the background, she was very quiet. I assumed it to be shyness. So I started peppering her with 'tell me about your culture' questions to fill the silence. She answered politely for a while and then after, 'Why is the Buddha sideways?' I simply ran out of questions. We fell back into silence, still walking aimlessly, side-by-side and I was about to suggest we rejoin Tom and Andy.

"I very scared to meet Maude," she said suddenly in a quivering voice. She was near tears. I assured her that she had nothing to worry about, even though I knew better. She had everything to worry about. Maude was formidable, she would eat this demure girl alive. She would not for one minute take her at face value and would sniff out all that was phony and unacceptable about her in an instant. She would cast one practised eye over her and make a judgment on the spot: a judgment that would be difficult to shift for years to come. She was a mother and she was protecting her youngest cub.

"You'll be fine," I lied. "Maude is very nice. Very warm."

"Yes, but in Thai culture, mother-in-law's approval is very important," Sunisa said gravely.

I tried to think of a culture in which the approval of the mother-in-law was not that important only to decide that it was pretty much a universal conundrum; the competing roles of wife and mother, the tug of war for control, the lifetime of care given over with misgivings to another woman who may or may not have his best interests at heart, the severing of apron strings and all that. It's a minefield of emotions whatever latitude on earth, whatever tribe, whatever city you find yourself in.

Women have layers and layers of subtext that need to be negotiated with assiduous cunning; to disregard that is to do so at your own peril and have the relationship blow up in your face. Added to that, women hold grudges like sponges hold water. There was no easy way around this emotional obstacle course she was about to embark upon. The only way was through it.

I looked at her. She was a picture of apprehension and, to a Westerner's eyes, submission or weakness.

She was standing now with her head bowed to the ground, where usually she stood perfectly upright with her head balanced beautifully on a proudly elongated neck. One arm was crossed defensively over her body, gripping at her elbow so tightly I could see the whites of her knuckles. She was folded in on herself, giving in, admitting—to a white person's eye—ineptitude and unworthiness with her body language.

"Just be honest," I said carefully. "And be . . . " I grasped for a word, a simple word to encapsulate the meaning of forthright or assertive, which I knew at heart, this young woman was. I also knew that Sunisa sitting in the background silently and meekly with her head bowed would only reinforce the cultural stereotype that raised a kind of obstinate competitiveness and suspicion in Western women. It was Maude's feeling that Sunisa would not be an equal partner to Tom. I thought about how I could help Sunisa overcome this preconception. "Make sure you look her in the eye."

She nodded unsurely. I knew this was anathema to her culture. But hell, I'd been bowing and using praying hands all over Bangkok as a sign of respect, why shouldn't I tell her a thing or two about how our world works?

"In Australia, not meeting someone's eyes can seem shifty, like you're guilty of something."

She nodded again, slowly.

"When you are introduced to Maude, just make sure you meet her eyes like this . . . " I held her gaze steadily, in a friendly way, not in a creepy 'I'm looking right into your soul' way. There was an important and subtle distinction. If she got it wrong she could end up eyeballing Maude like a Scientologist conducting an audit.

"It's considered polite and respectful," I said.

"Thank you," she said, smiling. "I will."

Later on, Andy told me that this was categorically the wrong thing to say. That I should have just told her to be herself. Which was indicative of nothing more than the fact that Andy was a man and found the ways of Thai women pleasingly affirming to his masculinity.

I saw Tom and Andy coming across the lawn. There was a monk wafting around behind them, resplendent in orange robes, looking at the sky. I got out my camera to take an opportunistic photo.

"Nell," Tom said, putting his hand up to stop me.

"Oh sorry!" I put the camera back into my bag, thinking it was some quaint local belief that their soul would be stolen by the camera.

"You mustn't go near the monks," he said.

"They will bone up," Andy snickered.

"They will what?" I said.

"Bone up," Tom said, sniffing with laughter at the look on my face. "It's true, they're quite notorious for it. They don't get to see women much, so they get a bit . . . excited."

Even the monks in this country were obsessed with sex.

Meanwhile, the same afternoon, by the hotel pool, after counselling Sunisa like a trusted friend, I am ashamed to say I behaved treacherously and inflamed the situation against her.

Maude had confided in me that, as directed by Tom, she had bought gifts for Sunisa and her parents. For the parents, again as directed by Tom, she had bought cheap Australiana stuff: an Akubra, a purse made out of a kangaroo pouch (which, for some reason, I kept imagining as a kangaroo scrotum). But for Sunisa, she had oscillated wildly. Tom had hinted heavily that Maude should give Sunisa her grandmother's wedding ring. Maude had thought about it and was considering having it re-set into a pendant as the setting was very old fashioned and more than likely too large for Sunisa's dainty fingers.

"Then I thought, oh blow that, and I found another ring in my jewellery box that didn't have so much, you know, emotional meaning for me," she said looking around furtively for Andy and Stan, who had gone to the business centre to check emails. I calculated that Maude and I had about ten minutes to gossip freely.

"I know that sounds terrible, but I just don't know about all this, Nell. It's very worrying."

"What's worrying you?" I asked, still trying to remain impartial, but desperate to get to the nitty gritty of it while we still had eight minutes left.

"Oh, that there's 'the other' still in the wings somewhere and all this money, where does it come from . . . ? You know, something just doesn't feel right to me."

Her eyes darted from side to side. "They've had to hide the fact that they're getting married from the other one," she said. "I mean, what am I supposed to think?"

"Give her your grandmother's ring," I said sliding gleefully down the slippery slope from impartial to treacherous betrayal, "on their tenth wedding anniversary."

God I'm duplicitous. Despite my sway in empathy towards Sunisa that afternoon, my loyalty was ultimately tribal. Maude got my implication of 'as if that's ever going to happen' and guffawed.

"Yes, that's right," she hooted. "She can have it if they make it to ten years."

We both chortled into our beers. All we needed was a cauldron bubbling away between us to complete the picture.

At this point I should clarify that my objection was more to do with Tom's insistence that his mother take so immediately and without question to this young woman she had never met; and that she should relinquish to Sunisa a much loved keepsake from her own mother. It was typical of Tom and it's fair to say we all had become somewhat gun-shy of his historically fickle proclamations of undying love. Over the years, we had been subjected to a great number of women with whom we were expected to bond immediately.

Every summer holiday, there was a different one, each one as impressively ambitious and accomplished as the last: an elegantly upright stage actress; a sweet but steely-eyed cadet journalist; a single-minded graphic artist with her own studio. And just as we got the hang of the last and whatever quirks she possessed, she was gone and a new one presented. At which point, with no allowance for mourning the last one, we'd have to start all over again with an unknown quantity. We could no longer conduct familiar gossipy conversations but would have to allow for the newcomer and be on our best behaviour all the time; ask about her family, did she prefer red or white? What were her hopes for the future (Maude's question, not mine), where did her family hail from? Did she have brothers and sisters? Politely enquire as to how she slept the night before (again, one of Maude's standards). We also had to make sure we didn't get too plastered and frighten her off.

This might go some way to explaining our reticence toward Sunisa. That and the massive cultural chasm that yawned wider with every day we spent in her homeland. We'd grown attached to so many of Tom's girlfriends before, only to see them blithely replaced.

Yet there was another element: racism, pure and simple. Considering the impressive parade of strong-minded Australian women Tom had attracted over the years, there was an unspoken feeling that with Sunisa, he was settling for an easier, more submissive option. In hindsight, this was an entirely ill-founded assumption. But you can't blame Western women for the rising of their hackles on this issue. We are encouraged to be outspoken, forthright and to put ourselves first, then ultimately we are punished for it when men grow tired of us and fall back on a more submissive option.

"So anyway, it's a sapphire, and I had it reset," Maude went on when we'd recovered our composure. "It looks lovely. Do you think it'll be okay?

"That sounds fine," I said.

"Well, we'll see." Maude shifted in her seat. "I just couldn't bear to part with Granny's ring."

## 24.

That night, I tried to redirect the pre-dinner meeting of Sunisa and Maude to the hotel bar, where it was airconditioned and no one would smoke. But Tom said it was essential that we all convene at his apartment. He had a special surprise for all of us that couldn't be given in the hotel bar.

As we sat in Tom and Sunisa's stuffy apartment politely anticipating Sunisa's arrival, with the celebratory champagne chilling seductively in an ice bucket and the minutes stretched to fraying with the unbearable elasticity of Thai time, I began to consider that there was one more crucial thing I should have told Sunisa regarding our culture; that we tend to adhere to the time structure set by clocks and watches.

"Where's she gone, Tom?" Maude said. It was the third time she'd asked the question. I think I'd asked it twice. The first time it was a perfunctory, 'Where's Sunisa?' question that seemed socially polite and indicated that she figured highly in our thoughts. The second time, we were simply trying to ascertain how much longer she might be. And this third time, Maude was actually saying: *What could be so important that she would keep us all waiting like this?*

"She's having her skin bleached, for the wedding," Tom said.

That was bad. Maude cast a look in my direction, eyebrows raised with obvious disapproval.

"How extraordinary."

"I guess it's like white girls having spray tans," I said, wanting to put Sunisa back on even ground now that she'd set herself so far back with the tardiness thing.

"Spray tans?" Maude was aghast. "You're joking?" Maude's hand was splayed upon her chest in horror and I hadn't helped the situation. Now she just thought all young women, white or Thai, were weird.

"They don't really get spray tanned do they?" Maude looked like she might be about to vomit. Although that could've been because of the stifling heat and the vague smell of wet shit coming in from outside.

"Oh yes," I said. "It's very common. They all wear strapless gowns, a tiara with a veil sprouting out the back and have a spray tan. It's the trend."

"My god."

She looked at me as if I might be one of them. "Did you get a spray tan?"

"No," I scoffed. "And I didn't wear a tiara either." I said this with some disdain for the trend. "Although I do regret not wearing my hair up." I'd thought about that a lot.

"Oh, your hair looked lovely!" Maude enthused. "Just gorgeous. I remember thinking that as you came down the aisle."

Maude and I talked about my hair for a good ten minutes while the men all stood around us like sentinels with beers, trying to decide whether to hive off to another conversation or to endure the inane chit-chat about hair to its conclusion. Andy and Tom retired to the balcony for a cigarette (Andy's third that evening, I was counting), which left poor old Stan sitting with the ladies talking about hair. He took it well, settled back into his seat and only harumphed twice before excusing himself to the bathroom.

As soon as he was gone, it was on. Maude dropped her voice and said incredulously, “Getting her skin bleached?”

“She’s got the most beautiful smooth brown skin, I can’t believe it.”

“Do you think she’ll get here soon? I’m *desperate* for a glass of that champagne.”

“Thai time,” I said knowingly.

Maude groaned, then waved her hand across her face. “It’s so hot in here!”

“I told you, didn’t I?”

Maude rearranged her face into a grin, which meant Tom and Andy were returning from the balcony.

“Tom, it’s a bit hot, could we switch the airconditioning on?” Maude said.

“Of course, Mama Bear,” he said. “I’m just so anti the airconditioning, I forget that other people like it.”

He moved to the wall to crank up the AC.

“I don’t want to be a big sweaty pig the first time Sunisa sees me,” Maude said.

The key scrabbled in the lock. We all sat to attention as the door opened and Sunisa entered. I scrutinised her skin. She didn’t look any paler. She slipped off her shoes and turned to face us all; slowly and with great trepidation, as though we were a firing squad. Her shoulders were bowed over, she was clutching at her elbow, her head stooped forward. I willed her to stand up straight. Maude rose and I followed suit, realising too late that now we were all standing around her awkwardly like a forest of big sweaty *farangs*. She was wearing skinny jeans and a tight striped tank top, while we flopped about like fat camp inmates in big loose cotton clothing. She was an immaculate package of smooth skin, glossy dark hair, almond shaped eyes and impossible cheekbones.

Tom went over to Sunisa and kissed her, arranged her hair back from her shoulders, spoke Thai in a low soothing voice. Sunisa smiled at him shyly and nodded. Her teeth were straight, perfect and white.

"Mum, this is my lovely lady, Sunisa," Tom presented her to Maude.

"It's so lovely to meet you," Maude said with her best for strangers smile on.

It was uncharacteristic and not an entirely good sign that Maude stayed where she stood. She did not immediately swoop Sunisa into a welcoming embrace the way she had with me all those years before. The cultural divide was thorny and Maude stood stubbornly on her side of it. Sunisa bowed deeply with her palms flat together, the greatest of Thai respect, and then offered Maude her tiny brown hand which Maude clasped between both of her own to offset the formality of a handshake. I thought that was a good move. Then I watched closely and with an enormous surge of Henry Higgins-esque self-satisfaction as Sunisa's eyes dipped up from the ground, met Maude's and stayed. Then she smiled her gorgeous wide Cheshire smile and said, "I am very pleased to meet you, Maude."

Then I nearly cried out with joy when she stepped forward and kissed Maude gently on the cheek. I wanted to applaud her. I knew how hard that was for her to initiate contact like that, to meet Maude's gaze and not fold into a gesture of respectful submission.

After everyone had become acquainted and the champagne opened, Tom directed Sunisa to sit on the couch between Maude and me. For a split second the revelry of initial introductions died into an awkward lull as we were sucked into a black hole of intense social discomfort. I spied a booklet of photos on the coffee table and keen for a conversation starter, I picked them up and asked Sunisa if I could look at them. She nodded enthusiastically. It worked a treat, with Sunisa able to point out various members of her family to Maude and tell her a bit about them. It was all going really well until I flipped over and there was Hal's leery face grinning out at us.

"Oh!" Maude recoiled visibly. "There's Hal."

He was standing in between Sunisa and her sister, his arms around both of them so that each hand hovered menacingly just over one of their breasts. The girls were none the wiser to this hilarious prank as they smiled genuinely for the photo.

"Nice," I said flatly.

Sunisa giggled politely. "We didn't realise what he is doing."

"Yes," Maude said. "I can see that." She flipped the photo over and still looking at the booklet said, "He used to take photos at the beach, with topless women in the background. So I'd be there smiling away and then he'd just shift the frame to the left to take in a topless woman."

Andy and Tom were listening in now. They snickered like naughty school boys.

"Come on, Mum, that was good sport," Tom teased.

I looked at Stan, who shook his head at me and rolled his eyes.

"Oh yes, good sport," Maude said disapprovingly, playing her part to perfection.

Sunisa clapped her hand over her mouth horrified. Maude, sensing her confusion as to whether this was funny or horrible let out a big hoot of laughter.

"Isn't that terrible!" She smacked Sunisa lightly with the back of her hand for effect. "I shouldn't laugh. But isn't it terrible? I'd get the photos back and there I'd be smiling away, with some woman in the background."

Maude then mimed a woman with big boobs, looking sort of pleased with herself, flopping her boobs around for the camera.

"Those were nice photos, Mum," Andy said facetiously. "We've got one in a frame on our mantelpiece."

"Oh, you don't!" Maude said, taking the bait for effect. "Do you?"

She looked at me for confirmation. Playing the patsy for everyone else's amusement.

"Yes," I confirmed. "We've just framed you out, I hope you don't mind."

Stan, thrilled that the talk had moved off Hal and what a larrikin he was, exploded with relieved laughter and then went into a coughing fit of mirth. Tom snickered like a jackhammer. Andy looked at me appreciatively. Sunisa had the vague smile of someone who got the general gist but had missed the subtle details.

"My sister is afraid of Hal," Sunisa said, obviously emboldened by the free talk about bosoms.

"Really?" I said, eyeing Maude with meaning. "Why's that?"

"My sister have very big . . . " she gestured 'bosoms' as she grasped for the word and then unfortunately came up with ". . . very big tits."

"Bosoms!"

"Breasts."

Maude and I corrected quickly.

"Bosoms," Sunisa said. "And when Hal meet her the first time he is just looking at her . . . her tits . . . "

"Bosoms."

"Breasts."

Again, in unison.

". . . her . . . bosoms saying, 'yes, very nice, verrrry nice.'" Sunisa was giggling at this memory. Maude and I exchanged a glance, not sure whether to keep things neutral or not. Then Maude broke ranks.

"How revolting!" she said with equal emphasis on both words.

"How terrible for your sister."

"Yes," Sunisa sobered up a bit; she'd sussed out whose side we were on. "If she's coming over, she ask 'Is Hal there?' and if we don't want to see her, we just tell her, 'yes, yes, Hal is here'. So that she don't come."

"Do you see them often?" Maude probed. "Hal and Phan?"

"Yes, sometimes," Sunisa said non-committally.

"And is she a nice lady?" Maude asked, all innocence, knowing full well that she most definitely was not.

This was one of Maude's sly tests and Sunisa hesitated, torn between discretion and truth. Maude cocked her head to the side, as though eager to know. Sunisa looked at me, I widened my eyes as though to say, 'Go on'. She looked back at Maude then screwed up her nose and shook her head slowly.

"She is not a nice person."

"Oh. What a shame," Maude said, as though she gave two hoots.

But the answer had been noted. Sunisa had scored massive points for straight-talk over inscrutability.

Talk ground to a halt again and before Maude could interrogate Sunisa about having her skin bleached, as she was itching to do (her gaze kept shifting curiously to her arms and décolletage), I gestured to Andy to give Tom our wedding gift. It was wrapped in Alfoil as I hadn't been able to communicate the words, 'wrapping paper' effectively enough to any of the local Seven Eleven staff and had been directed towards the kitchen wraps instead. Tom unwrapped it and I suddenly felt bad that I hadn't figured Sunisa in the gift. I'd been so blasé about it when Andy had mentioned that we should perhaps buy something that would suit both of them.

"I don't know her from a bar of soap," I'd said with characteristic short-sightedness toward this scene we were currently in. "What am I supposed to buy her?"

So we'd gone with an espresso coffee maker, which was very much for Tom. Now, sitting beside Sunisa and having seen how she took such care to greet Maude in a culturally appropriate way, I felt like a bit of a cow. Then Maude gave Sunisa a small square package beautifully wrapped with gold ribbon.

"This is for you, Sunisa," she said. "Just something little."

Sunisa unwrapped the gift carefully. We all watched as she peeled away the wrapping and found the blue velvet box. She gently prised the small box open to reveal the sweetest ring I'd ever seen in my life. It was an oval shaped sapphire in a delicate gold setting with two small diamonds either side. It sparkled cleanly in the bright artificial light of the apartment. Sunisa drew a sharp breath. She said nothing and kept her head down, looking at the ring. We all waited, suddenly wondering whether it was some kind of faux pas or bad luck to give the bride a ring before her wedding day. Maude caught my eye, worried; *was it inappropriate*?

"It's an Australian sapphire," Maude said to fill the gaping silence. Sunisa nodded, still looking down at it. Then she sniffed and lifted her hands to wipe surreptitiously at her eyes. She was crying.

"It's very beautiful," she said, tears dropping into her lap.

"Do you like it?" Maude said hopefully.

Sunisa couldn't speak. She was weeping. She nodded her head furiously then carefully slid the ring onto her finger. She looked at it incredulously. She was completely overwhelmed.

"Wow, that really suits you," I said. It was hard to believe that Maude could have come up with the most perfect ring for someone she'd never met.

"It is so beautiful," Sunisa managed to say between the tears that were now rolling freely down her cheeks. "I am very grateful. Thank you so much."

I felt my own eyes welling up with tears. This was completely unexpected. Here Maude and I were talking about this gift as though it were some kind of consolation prize, some afterthought and here was Sunisa, genuinely moved by the gesture. Maude caught my eye and put her hand on her heart. Then, in the most telling gesture of the night, she put her arm around Sunisa and kissed her firmly on the side of the head like one of her own children.

"Welcome to the family, my love," she said.

# 25.

Later that night, as promised, Tom presented his 'special gift for everyone'. He shuffled us all into the spare bedroom where the computer was and instructed us to take a seat. We stared at the screen and waited while Tom mucked about with buttons and settings.

Then a slide show began with musical accompaniment. The song was, *Everyone I Love is Here,* by the Finn Brothers and the slide show was made up of all the Straw's old family photo albums. I secretly hoped that with the song title so blatantly laying down the boundaries of Tom's affections, Stan's mug would turn up somewhere, no matter how briefly or perfunctorily, or that it would stay strictly a 'before Stan's time' affair so as to offset any perceived snub.

"I found all our old photo albums at Dad's," Tom said. "I scanned all the photos and I've put them together in a bit of a slide show for everyone to keep."

Everyone made 'aww, isn't that nice' noises and we settled in for the show. There's something slightly unnatural about six people sitting in a room staring at a computer screen. Beyond that general awkwardness, it must be discomfiting to watch a slide show of one's past family life and ex-husband, when one's current husband is in the room.

Maude must have felt Stan's discomfort as she offset the sweaty silence in the room by providing a bubbling-oh-isn't-this-fun-and-not-at-all-awkward-for-Stan running commentary to all the photos.

The first section was devoted to Maude. "Oh I was so young, look at those hot pants. I used to wear these hot pants and drive around in my convertible MG, all the teachers at the school thought I was completely incompetent as a parent ... That's a nice one of us, Tom, you've got your Batman suit on again ... there's my car, I used to whizz around Glebe in it ... and there's my dancing class, you boys were so embarrassed by me, there's me and Mum, that's a nice one and Dad ..."

Then Andy got a look in. "Oh there's Andy on a horse, he was so good with horses, he used to go in all these gymkhanas and win ribbons, oh and there's the house in Drummoyne, remember that house? It was two semis and we knocked down two walls to make one big house ... oh there's Hal. I remember that holiday, Andy you were always so brown like a little native and when you were young you had this long blonde hair ..."

Then Tom ... "Oh you two were so sweet together, that's your cousin Sam, she used to live next door do you remember? She's into all sorts of occult things now, she's a pagan or something, very strange ... oh there's Hal again ..."

Then Sunisa got her own section. Which put paid to the 'before Stan's time' disclaimer I was hoping for.

"Oh lovely ... that's a nice photo of you Sunisa ... don't you photograph well? Lovely ... gorgeous ... don't you look lovely?"

Then I got a look in with one photo taken in our backyard three years before. "Sorry Nell, that was the only photo of you I had," Tom said.

Then the finale. And what a finale it was. Photo after photo after photo after photo featuring Hal, an endless homage that began with his past glories as an actor. An old black and white press shot of Hal and his young co-star as Conrad Cobden, the responsible older brother in *The Adventures of Charlie Cobden,* then another as Constable Kirkpatrick from *Magpie Creek.* An old black and white newspaper clipping of Hal and Maude looking glamorous at a black tie event, Hal and Maude getting married, Hal and the boys, Hal's mug on the famous real estate posters, Hal, Hal and Maude, Hal and the boys, Hal, Hal, Hal, Hal . . .

Suddenly Maude stopped talking. The absence of her until-then constant chatter was felt immediately. An intense silence fell over the room. I felt the sweat beading on my forehead in the stuffy air. I did that thing where you try not to move or breathe too deeply as though that will stop you from being present in a moment that is deeply uncomfortable.

I felt Maude's uneasiness as though it were my own: it was so pronounced it leached out of her body and into mine. Photo after photo of her past life, including the ex-husband she had left flashed up on the screen. I willed it to end. But it didn't, it kept going and going and going. I knew then there would be no nod, no matter how perfunctory or basic, to Stan, who was sitting quietly but surely behind me in the dark. Stan, who had provided them all with a bedrock of paternity for the past fifteen years.

Then it ended. The screen went dark. We all sat absorbing the awkwardness of the last five minutes of slideshow devoted entirely to Hal and his apparently happy memory.

Then, as though we had conjured him, Tom's phone erupted; a paradoxically jaunty tune that blooped and bleeped at nerve-jangling pitch. He checked the caller ID then answered curtly.

"Mate," he said. "Good sport."

Locked into the role of audience, and because he was standing in front of the screen we'd just been watching, we all transferred our attentions en masse to Tom on his phone, as though he were now the show. He plugged one ear with his finger. Nodded at us. Rolled his eyes.

"Alright then, see you there, mate, you know the restaurant? Over."

He hung up. We all waited.

"That was Hal. He's decided to come to dinner after all."

"Oh well, that's good," Maude said in a tone of voice that implied the exact opposite. "A bit last minute, will the booking be okay, Tom?"

"Yeah, yeah, should be fine."

Sunisa was already on her phone changing the booking for four more.

As we all filed out of the room, Tom took me aside. "We need to keep Dad away from Mum."

"I know," I said.

"We'll have to make sure they're at opposite ends of the table," Andy said. "He'll try and sit next to her."

"Nell, you may have to form a sort of a buffer zone," Tom said snickering nervously, knowing this was a recipe for disaster. "You might have to sit with Hal on one side and Mum on the other."

"Great," I said. "Bring it on."

Andy eyed me. He gave me a warning look.

"I know. I know," I said. "Don't worry, I'll be nice as pie."

I sat next to Maude in the cab on the way to the restaurant. We couldn't talk freely about the slide show—the Hal homage—because Stan was in the front seat, strong and silent as the Rock of Gibraltar. He was feeling it. We both knew it. Stan was an old-school gentleman; he held doors open, got the ladies drinks and always carried the bags. It must have been difficult to continually hear those legendary 'Hal the milk-bottle-chucker' stories and then watch as Hal is celebrated as the great patriarch. Maude rummaged in her handbag and found her lipstick. It seemed to focus her, looking into a small sliver of mirror and applying orange across her lips. She fluffed her hair and muttered simply, "I'm really not looking forward to this."

Then she laughed nervously as she clutched my forearm.

The cab stopped. We got out to the familiar wet shit stench of Bangkok. Without warning, the heavens opened like a giant bucket of water emptied unceremoniously onto the earth. Even Stan had to laugh as we ran for cover inside the very restaurant where Hal was waiting.

1 Thai baht = AU$0.0357846119

1600 Thai baht = AU$48.00

160 Thai baht = AU$4.80

# 26.

While everyone else was dreading the engagement dinner, fearing a scene or incident, I was harbouring a secret and perverse fantasy that something terrible would happen. I was hoping that Hal would so openly show his true colours and publicly disgrace the family that it would excommunicate him from proper society for the term of his natural life. Then we would no longer have to qualify our reasons for cutting him off; to ourselves or anyone else. I was hoping for that definitive moment, the proof, the mitigating circumstances.

My mother had some years before had a definitive moment with her own sister in law. My aunt Marjorie had what would now be diagnosed as borderline personality disorder. She was mentally unstable and not in any charming or amusingly eccentric way. For years, my mother felt obligated by marital affinity to accommodate her erratic and manipulative behaviour. Then one day, during a protracted and increasingly accusatory phone conversation about whether or not my father was available to speak to her, Marjorie became completely unstuck from her fragile social moorings. She hissed the word 'Bitch!' down the phone at my mother.

My mother said, "Goodbye Marjorie," and by goodbye, she meant forever. She replaced the phone in its cradle with a satisfied finality; her obligation to accommodate Marjorie within my father's life had just come to an end.

I had been hoping for some time for a similar sort of event with

Hal. But he was as yet too controlled, too sly to turn in company and show the scaly underbelly of his personality. While the majority of his friends had fallen away over the years, having sighted in some unguarded moment his scales, there was still a small posse of people around him who thought he was just a fun guy who sometimes took things too far; a loveable larrikin.

Part of this posse accompanied him to the engagement dinner. Jean was among them. I think she had a sort of tolerant view of him borne of Christian charity towards the less fortunate. She also did not listen to what he said. She just tuned him out, assuming he had some sort of tourettes. She wasn't really paying attention. Why would she? He was an old friend of her husband's who came around occasionally for dinner and sometimes stayed in their spare room. A bit player with no power, or so she thought.

On one occasion, Hal had been staying at Jean and Greg's house in their absence and came around to ours for dinner. It was autumn, not bitterly cold but a bit of a cold snap. Amid various conversational comments about the weather, Hal boasted without shame that he'd left the heater on at Greg and Jean's. Andy and I had waited for an explanation of this, given it wasn't even cold enough for us to have dragged our heater out of the attic yet. Hal explained to us that the morning before Jean and Greg had left, he'd dragged a heater out of the cupboard because he was cold. Jean had told him curtly to put it back and suggested he perhaps put some socks on instead. Hal's revenge, in their absence, while he was enjoying the comfort of their home free of charge when even his own son would no longer take him in, was to crank the heater up to maximum every time he left the house. Simply to get his own back. My point is, if Jean had been paying better attention, she may have also paid less in heating bills that quarter.

At the engagement dinner on Thursday night, we had taken our seats at a long table in a private upstairs room of the restaurant. When Maude, Stan and I arrived, Tom directed us to the far end of the table, with him and Sunisa placed strategically at the midpoints. I was on Sunisa's left side, followed by Maude, then Stan. On Sunisa's right hand side remained an empty chair, to be filled eventually by Hal. At the far end of the table was a guy named Joe, an old childhood friend of Tom's with some family connections to the Straws. We all chatted politely and waited; the spectre of the empty chair and who it would hold grew more ominous with every minute that ticked past.

Then, in a burst of noise and movement, he arrived, heralding himself with slow applause above his head. He was flanked by Jean, Greg and Ivan. Phan was a notable no-show, which Andy told me later was a massive slap in the 'small face' to Sunisa. Indeed, at the sight of him arriving without Phan, Sunisa looked down at her lap and went very quiet.

People stood to make their greetings. Maude turned in her chair and fixed a pleasant smile to her face; a smile I knew to be entirely false. No doubt, Hal knew it too. His eyes scanned the room like a searchlight and landed upon her immediately. He swooped towards her. She stood up in her place and braced with one hand upon the tabletop

"Hello, darling!" He lunged forward and there was a moment of awkwardness. He tried to land one on her mouth and she moved left, he swung left with her, she swung back right and he landed one on her cheek.

"Hello, Hal, good to see you." Maude's smile was utterly too wide, her eyes too sharply pinned. Then he stood in front of her and took her in from head to toe.

"Yes, hello," he repeated.

Stan stepped forward then, all stocky build and rugby neck, and thrust forward his hand.

"Hal," he said in a genial manner.

"Hello, Stan. Good," Hal said.

Then Stan did something that completely unnerved Hal. He produced a camera from his pocket and said brightly, "Photo?"

He pointed the lens at Hal and Maude. I stood behind them with a horrified look on my face. Stan caught my eye and winked cheekily. He made sure I was framed into the photo.

"Say cheese."

Hal gripped Maude around the shoulders and drew her in. Maude tried not to recoil. The flash went off. The spell was broken. Everyone moved to their seats and resumed the business of dinner and chit chat. That moment we had all been dreading, the moment we had all focused our terror upon for the past forty-eight hours had been and was gone, captured by Stan in a blinding flash of light that lasted barely a millisecond: frozen in time, and already relegated to the past. We moved on.

The night then passed relatively uneventfully, save for when Hal called the waiter a dunce, ordered three bottles of overpriced wine (even though Tom had begun the evening by requesting that we all stick to beer as the price of wine in Thailand was exorbitant) and tried to snaffle Sunisa's entrée for himself when his steak (the most expensive item on the menu, his favourite trick when part of a group booking) was taking too long to arrive. All this seemed relatively minor given the circumstances.

I did notice, however, Tom and Andy taking it in turns to retire to a separate table with Hal, where they would light up and smoke furiously at him as they talked, shrouding themselves and their conversation mysteriously in a veil of cigarette smoke. I wondered at the time what they were talking about and why they had to keep themselves separate from the rest of us like that. Sometimes it was all three of them, other times just Hal and Andy, or Hal and Tom, occasionally Tom and Andy.

Stan continued to court mischief by taking photos of Hal, calling out to him at intervals and demanding that he smile. It surprised me that Hal could not see through this ruse of Stan's. He had so little regard for Stan that it did not occur to him that he was being gotten the better of. He assumed, vainly, that Stan simply wanted photos of him. He smiled his best headshot, Hal's-your-real-estate-pal smile for Stan's camera, posed himself accordingly with one elbow bent outward, larrikin-style, and waited for the flash to capture his image.

When not capturing his very soul with the camera, Stan sat at the far end of the table watching Hal's antics; a look of wry amusement on his face.

"Stop staring," I said at one point, alarmed by his outright willingness to engage Hal in some sort of showdown.

"He's ordering another bottle of wine," Stan chuckled. "I best make sure I get me a glass. "Look at him. Silly old bugger. He's like a toddler."

"Stan!" Maude warned. "Do not make a scene."

"What?" Stan widened his eyes innocently. "I'm just enjoying the show."

At that point, Hal began shouting out for the waiter, "Slaves! Slaves!"

Stan made an audible sound of disgust, being the sort of man who was unerringly respectful to waitstaff and left a healthy tip.

When it came to pay, a minor fracas broke out. As Andy began to work his way around the table collecting money, methodically noting who had paid, Tom's friend Joe, drunk to the point of stumbling and incoherent, decided to do the same. He collected random notes from people and couldn't remember who they'd come from, eventually thrusting an unkempt wodge of notes into Andy's hands for counting. The collective bundle came up noticeably short and everyone looked around pointedly . . . who hadn't paid? An uncomfortable tension settled across the table as most of us were thinking the same thing: Hal.

"Balls son!" Hal shouted boldly. "Has it come up short?"

Instead of pointing the finger, Andy counted out the notes again on the table in front of everyone to prove there was money missing. I looked at Maude. She raised her eyebrows at me knowingly. Stan reached into his back pocket for his wallet. Maude put a hand on his arm to stop him making up the shortfall. Andy reiterated the amount that needed to be put in by each person (not counting Sunisa and Tom as it was their dinner). Joe, the guy who had collected random money in a drunken guerilla rampage, piped up with, "I can't remember who I took money from." He giggled and added, "Or how much."

"Did everyone put in 1600 baht?" Andy said tersely. He looked uncharacteristically dark and angry.

Everyone concurred. Except Hal, who wasn't listening, he was shouting things at the waitress, who had tried to enter the room quietly to clear the tables and get rid of this ugly, loud bunch of *farangs*.

"Waitress, I need service!" He shouted in a booming tourettes-like monotone. "I need to be serviced by the waitress!"

Ivan snickered, appreciating the bawdy wit. Greg smirked, not quite wanting to condone it openly. Encouraged, Hal kept going in a loud, expressionless monotone, so that if you weren't tuned in, you would just assume he was shouting inoffensive rubbish.

"Big white cock needs servicing."

"Dad!" Andy said.

Sunisa indicated to the waitress, who was now pale with fright, that no more wine was to be ordered.

The waitress backed away uncertainly. Hal was now shouting, "Vino! Vino! Vino!" And added, *"Jing-joh! Jing-joh!"* with his hands, making jumping kangaroo paws. This, apparently, was his best Thai party trick. *Jing-joh* being Thai for 'kangaroo'. Him being Australian. Oh hilarious. Especially after you've seen it once every fifteen minutes for the last three hours.

"Oh dear," Maude murmured under her breath.

"Hal!" Stan barked in an authoritarian warning tone.

"Shh!" Maude warned Stan in return.

"Dad!" Andy said again. "Did you put in 1600?"

"Yes, yes." Hal flung his hands towards Andy dismissively. "I gave my money to Joe. *Jing-joh, jing-joh*!"

Ivan laughed, throwing his head back like it was the best larrikin joke he'd ever heard. Greg grinned indulgently, the goody two shoes vicariously living it up via the class clown. Jean just had a benign smile set on her face that I couldn't read. Joe collapsed back into his chair. His work here was done.

I looked at Stan. His mouth was open, appalled. Maude just muttered, "Oh he's gone mad."

She looked the other way as though averting her eyes to a terrible accident.

Hal was becoming agitated. He got out his wallet and leafed through the notes in there, as though to prove it was now missing 1600 baht. Then he reached across the table and grabbed a wine glass that was still half full of wine, threw it down his gullet greedily as though to ensure he got the maximum value.

"No more wine, Tom?" he asked, looking around again for a waiter.

"Has everyone given either me or Joe 1600 baht, per person, not per couple?" Andy said again, trying to stay calm.

Another thick silence settled across the table. Tom began to grind his teeth nervously. He looked into the middle distance to avoid his gaze settling accusingly on Hal. Sunisa looked increasingly distressed and then started shuffling in her handbag for money.

"No, not you." I said, stopping her. "It's your dinner."

"Alright," Andy said, rubbing his hands across his face in big circular movements. "I'm going to come around the table and get 160 baht more from everyone."

"Balls!" Hal shouted. "I'm not paying more because some dunce hasn't paid his share!"

"Here, Andy." Stan waved 500 baht at Andy. "For me, Maude and Hal."

Andy took three and gave back two pointedly.

"It's the principle," he said quietly.

Stan took it back reluctantly and folded it into his wallet. Andy moved around the table until eventually he was standing over Hal.

Hal looked up innocently. "What?"

"Come on, cough up. 160." Andy wiggled an open palm expectantly.

Hal dipped into his wallet with some pain. He pulled out some coins.

"More," Andy said.

Hal giggled and put some notes down.

"You're nearly there, three more of those," Andy laughed amiably, if only to keep the tone light.

"He's fleecing me just like his mother did," Hal shouted to the table.

"Shh!" I hissed, the noise escaped from me involuntarily, as a reflex. Hal looked at me, his glazed eyes were sharp all of a sudden, dangerously so. I turned my other cheek and gazed off intensely at a speck on the back wall.

"What did he say?" Maude said loudly, herself full of drink.

"Shh!" I shooshed her, too.

Stan said intrigued, "What's that thing he keeps doing, jing jong?"

"It's Thai for kangaroo," I said flatly, even though that still didn't explain it.

Maude said, "Oh dear." And again. "He's gone mad."

She rummaged in her handbag for the situation cure-all: lipstick. We both sniggered nervously, floppy with drink. We had been over it an hour ago, which was the point where we had run out of polite inclusive conversation with Jean who was sitting opposite us. We had surrendered long ago to a mutual tired, drunk silence as we waited for things to wind up.

"Am I offensive?" Hal said looking up innocently at Andy for reassurance. Then he turned and jing-joh-ed Sunisa a few times because she seemed to find it funny (or alarming, her reaction for both was much the same—polite giggling.)

"Just settle," Andy said sternly.

"160 baht for a steak and three bottles of overpriced wine, he's not done too badly for himself," Stan muttered to Maude and I.

Hal was counting out coins, giggling sheepishly as he laid each one into Andy's palm. Andy waited until the debt was fully paid. Under the watchful gaze of the entire table, Hal counted out coins thriftily like he had scorpions in his wallet and confirmed in most people's minds that he was the short-changing culprit who had started it all.

Perhaps it was from here that the communal sense of loathing began to spread. But still it was not enough yet for me, figuratively speaking, to hang up the phone for good.

## 27.

After the dinner Maude, Stan and I went back to the hotel and had a brief, candid post-mortem over a nightcap by the hotel pool. Andy had gone on to Tom's apartment for more drinks and some brotherly bonding; their own post-mortem most probably augmented by about one million cigarettes each. I assumed he'd be late, they'd probably get into a game of cards or something, whatever it was they did when they were together, beer, red wine and talking rubbish, the latter fuelled by the former. To be honest, I was glad Andy had someone he could be close to. I didn't know that Hal would be part of the team.

It was past eleven and the air was still thick and balmy. We sat outside in the hotel pool bar, our skins lightly coated by that ever-present layer of sticky perspiration. There was no breeze and the smell had sort of settled around us. We must have been well on our way to being acclimatised, because there were no comments about the smell, no sniffing at the air with distracted distaste, nor any wafting of hands across our faces in idle salute.

Maude's conclusion on the evening was that Hal had gone quite mad. Stan concurred. "No, he's not right in the head. But I got some great piccies of him."

He fished his camera out of Maude's handbag and showed us The Hal Series, as he had decided to call it. "It's not finished yet," he said. "I've got to get some of his wife for Bev."

"Bev's desperate to see what Phan looks like," Maude said. "She said, 'make sure you get some photos of Hal's Thai wife.'"

Stan scrolled through his Hal series for us. In each one, Hal affected the same headshot photo face: teeth-baring grin, dead watery eyes beneath his fop of carefully maintained, boyishly bowl-cut white hair, elbow cocked outward larrikin-style.

"He's like a cardboard cut-out, just inserted into each photo," I laughed. Stan roared with laughter too. Maude hooted and wheezed and ended up having to wipe her eyes with a tissue. It wasn't that funny, but we were all releasing the tension of an evening where we had sat upright at a table and made polite conversation to drown out the screaming subtext of family dysfunction.

"He's really lost his looks," Maude said sadly. "He was handsome, like a classic matinee idol." She looked to both of us, trying to convince us. We stayed bonded in silence.

"You saw the photos in the slide show?" She said to me. "Didn't you think he was handsome?"

"Not my type," I said.

Stan snorted, but I could sense him retreating behind his eyes, the way he always did when talk turned to the unsung virtues of Hal Straw.

"He was a good father," Maude seemed to be convincing herself. "Very good with the children, not responsible, but fun, you know? They adored him."

There was another silence. Stan folded his hands in his lap and looked down at them. I decided to bail her out.

"Yeah, he's good with Daniel," I conceded, sensing her desperation to make peace with herself. "He always brings fantastic presents. He has a good instinct for kids."

"It was only when they got older and started to answer back . . . " She looked at Stan, who had checked out of the conversation and was occupying himself sipping his beer and setting it carefully back onto its coaster. She put a hand on his forearm and said, "Well, anyway . . . "

Then she gave me a conspiratorial 'he's grumpy' look and excused herself to the bathroom.

When she was gone, Stan and I regarded each other across the table, both knowing we were and always would be outside witnesses to this fractured family history. Then Stan spoke. "When we were first married," he began quietly, "if I came into the bedroom at night after she'd gone to sleep, she'd sit bolt upright and make this terrible noise . . . " He imitated Maude's dramatic gasp, a primal expulsion of air, underpinned by dread and terror. He did it well enough to pull me back from thinking this was a funny, madcap family history to be gossiped about around a wooden poolside table. It presented it to me in the cold light of what it really was, the two words no one had ever mentioned—domestic violence.

It shocked me, this revelation. Despite being in this family for ten years and hearing all the stories, this small, idiosyncratic detail from Stan coldly exposed the very bones of it. It put paid to any suggestions that Maude may have exaggerated one word of it.

"What was that about ?" I said, without thinking.

Stan looked at me, gravely, knowingly. Then he shook his head. We knew exactly what that was about but came to a mutual decision not to define it aloud.

## 28.

When Andy came in, it was past three and he was drunk. I could tell by the way he crawled across the bed on all fours and crouched over me saying, "Nell are you awake?"

I snapped awake in an instant. I'd waited for his return, reading until the early hours then dozed off when it was past one.

"What's going on?" I said. "Why are you so late?"

"I needed a debrief with Tom." He was thick-tongued with hours of drinking. "We had to wait for Hal to leave."

"To leave where?"

"To leave Tom's apartment," Andy said. "He came back for a drink with the lads after the dinner."

"How annoying."

Andy shrugged. "I figure it's probably the last time I'll see him, so . . ."

"So, did he leave?"

Andy's eyes glittered with mischief. "Well, then Phan turned up."

He went into the bathroom and peed long and loud with a great drunken sigh. I waited. He came back out and stood by the bed. "And then what happened?" I asked.

"She started going through those photos of Sunisa's, remember the one with him and Sunisa and her sister, where he's got his hands over their boobs?"

"Yes," I rolled my eyes. "So hilarious."

"And she started screaming at him, 'You want to fuck her! Why don't you fuck her! Go on! Go and fuck her!'" Andy giggled. "And Hal's going, 'No, no lovely lady, I love you my lovely lady.' Trying to kiss her. But she just kept screaming at him. And then . . . "

He paused tantalisingly.

"Go on then, what?"

"And then Phan starts ripping up the photo and throwing the pieces at him."

"Nice work." While I didn't trust Phan's motives one jot, you had to admire her chutzpah: she didn't stand for any of it.

"She ripped up Sunisa's photos," Andy repeated, a bit flummoxed as to why I wasn't on Sunisa's side on this. "Those weren't her photos to rip."

"What was that photo doing in there, anyway?" I said by way of reply. "A photo of her father-in-law with his hand over her boob. What's with that?"

"Anyway, then . . . " He paused again to refocus my attention on the story at hand. "Sunisa told Phan to get out of her apartment. And Phan just started going *off* in Thai. And then they're both shouting in Thai."

"Oh my god."

"Apparently . . . " he said, as he pulled off his clothes and got into bed, "apparently, there's some issue with Phan and Sunisa. Phan keeps telling Hal that Sunisa is a fraud."

"Why because she's willingly marrying a *farang* who has no money?" I scoffed.

"I don't know. But Sunisa was pretty freaked out. She just disappeared into the bedroom and wouldn't come out until Phan was gone."

He burrowed under the covers against the arctic blow of the airconditioning.

"It's something to do with the dowry money."

"Do you reckon Sunisa's parents just randomly made up that 'traditional sum of 300,000 baht'?" I said.

"Probably. You can bet that there's one price for a Thai man and another for *farang*," Andy said.

"Where did Tom get 300,000 baht?" I said, wondering suddenly if he had hit Maude up for it.

"Sunisa's paying it," Andy said.

"Is that why she's a fraud?" I shrugged. "So what? Who cares. Let Phan call her a fraud."

His pores oozed the sweet rotten rummy smell of alcohol and he reeked of cigarette smoke, but I decided to let that go. I sat up and turned on the light, wide awake now. He was just beginning to snore lightly.

"No way," I said, nudging him awake. "You've woken me up, what happened next?"

"Hal and Phan left," he said. "She's probably beating him with a stick as we speak."

We both sniggered, it was a pleasing visual.

"There's more," he said.

"What else?"

"You don't want to know, do you?"

"Yes," I said, then "no," then finally, "maybe not."

I was cautious all of a sudden, thinking some things were best left in their dark family corners.

"I think I need to tell you," he said. His voice was muffled under the covers. "I need to talk about it to someone." For a moment, I thought he'd fallen asleep. Then he said, "The dinner was *appalling*."

"I thought he was pretty well behaved," I said, "apart from not contributing to the bill and a bit of alarming 'service-my-cock-waitress" work at the end *and* ordering the most expensive thing on the menu plus three bottles of overpriced wine that we all ended up paying for. We got off pretty lightly, I thought."

"*You* got off lightly," Andy agreed. "Because Tom and I spent the entire night shielding you all from it."

"From what?"

"From his . . . " he grasped for the word to define it, ". . . his Hal-ness."

"What did he do?"

"He was evil."

"What did he say?"

Andy rolled onto his back. "Are you sure you want to hear this?"

"Yes." I didn't want to know, but at the same time I couldn't stop myself from finding out. "Go on," I nudged him again as he momentarily thought better of it. "Tell me."

"Well he started off just the usual," he affected his best impression. *"Why would you run off and fuck that old cunt."*

"Meaning, your mum and Stan."

"Correct." He smiled as though I were prize pupil in the school of Straw. *"Disgraceful old cunt."*

"Charming, but enough. I get the picture. Anything else?"

"Well, he was trying to tell me how good his life was."

"Right."

"How happy he was with his young Thai wife." Then he did Hal again, *"Look at that old bitch, so glad I don't have to have a go at that every night any more."*

"What? Was he talking about Maude?"

"Yes."

"Vile. What did you say?"

"I just humoured him," Andy said. "I was trying to keep him under control, he was talking really loudly."

"So, what did you say?"

"I said, 'That's great Dad, I'm glad you're happy'."

"Well done."

"Thank you," he said. "But then it went on."

"Go on."

"He started going on about Mum taking all his money and giving it to *that fat cunt*."

"Aaarrghh! Change the record pal!" I said. It was like tourettes, Hal said the same things every time.

"I know, but then—and this was really good—I said, come on Dad, we all know who took your money.'"

"Bam! Take that!" I mimed some punching.

Andy laughed. "I know, I thought that was quite brilliant of me. And I sort of patted his hand, very gently."

"Good one."

"See, it's important to not get riled up and just keep calmly batting back."

He mimed the calm batting back of Hal's poisonous comments. I thought about that for a minute. It was so sad that Andy had to approach his own father with such a sharp presence of mind, that he could never just relax and be around him. He had to be on his guard the whole time, waiting for barbs, trying to keep his mind in the game. That wasn't a relationship. That was emotional combat.

"But that's what happens, no one reacts and so he just keeps doing it. Everyone acts like it's normal and so he's allowed to continue to behave that way," I said. "I can't stand the way you all tiptoe around him."

Andy propped himself up on his elbow and looked at me. "We don't tiptoe around him because we're too weak to stand up to him," Andy said, offended. "I've done that. I've had a stand-up fight with my father. I've landed a punch. I can handle him. We do it to spare everyone else around us from incidents."

"Why?"

"Nell, you've never seen the worst of it, you've seen a few little things here and there. You haven't seen what we've seen."

"I've heard about it," I said.

"Well, I've lived it."

"You shouldn't have to do that," I said quietly. "It's unfair that you have to be so guarded all the time."

"It's the only way to handle Hal," Andy said proudly, as if he'd finally figured it out.

"Right," I said. "What else?"

"Then he turned on us."

"What do you mean, he turned on us?"

I was getting a screaming sensation that I should stop now and bail out of this conversation. But I also had an overwhelming urge to keep going.

"He started telling me our marriage was in trouble."

"Right," I said, my heart racing. "And that was based on what evidence, given he's been in Thailand for the past two years and you don't even speak to him . . . do you?"

"He was going, you're not happy are you? Tom tells me you still hump around. You're still a humper aren't you, son?"

"What?"

My blood ran cold. I thought back suddenly to all those Friday nights he had been out drinking, in particular, the morning he had rolled in at five. What else would you be doing until five in the morning, I thought to myself, with a woman's logic that drinking is not an activity unto itself. I had always pushed away the possibility of infidelity. But it had been at the back of my mind since our 'I want a divorce' argument. What if I had missed the bigger picture? What if the reason he'd pulled himself up and started behaving like the perfect husband these past twelve months was because he was facilitating some extra-curricular love life behind my back. My mind was spinning with conspiracy theories.

"Why would he say that?" I said.

"I don't know, just to get it out of me." His face shut down a little. I sensed something more that he wasn't telling me.

"To get what out of you?"

"That I'm unhappy," he said. "That we're unhappy."

I went silent. It was three thirty in the morning. We had to be up early to get on the minibuses that would take us to the village for the wedding. Did I want to open up this can of worms now? Did I have the energy to rake over it one year later?

"Why does he want you to be unhappy?" I said.

"Because he's desperately unhappy."

"That's his own fault, he did that to himself. No one created that situation but him." I was sitting up in bed waving my arms around, making big karate chop motions with my hands to emphasise my point.

"I know that," Andy said. "Why are you so angry with me?"

"It's sick," I said. "It's sick that a father would try to create so much unhappiness in his children. What is wrong with him?"

"I know. He's twisted," Andy agreed. "But you should've heard me, Nell, I was brilliant, I just batted it back calmly."

"Don't you see, though?" I said. "You shouldn't have to do that. You shouldn't have to go in expecting ugliness. Can't you see how ripped off you've been all your life to have a father like that? He's not a father. He doesn't deserve your loyalty or your love. He's such an . . . an . . . an animal!" I heard myself sounding a bit ridiculous and hoped Andy wouldn't pick me up on it. But it was almost worse when he didn't laugh it off. He went quiet and sad instead.

"I can see that," Andy said. "But it doesn't help to sit around feeling sorry for myself."

We sat in silence for a while.

"Do you want to hear what I said in return?"

"Yes. Go on."

"I said, you're wrong. I'm very happy with my life. I love my wife and my children."

It sounded like a line to me, not the truth. It sounded like the lines he had to say to keep his father at bay. I made a mental note to get back to that later.

"What did he say?"

"He said, 'Nah, balls, really? You're happy? You don't regret that mistake child that you had?'"

"Was he talking about Albert?" I asked, my heart leaping into my throat with outrage.

"Yeah," Andy sad sadly. "Isn't that awful, his own grandchild."

"Oh my god!" I was alive with adrenaline now. My children! My beautiful baby Albert, how dare he call him a mistake.

"I want to punch him!" I said.

"You can't," Andy laughed. "You'll ruin Tom's wedding."

"It's not funny. It's hideous."

"There's more. Do you want to hear it?"

"No," I said resolutely. "Please don't tell me any more."

"I need to tell someone. I need to tell you," Andy pleaded.

"Go on."

"Then he says, you told me, Nell wants a divorce because you've been humping around."

That chilled me. It was close enough to some sort of truth, a twisted, uglier version. Or was it the truth?

"Why would he say that?" I said evenly.

"Because he's a mad old fool," Andy said, trying to laugh it off now.

I didn't laugh. I stayed stonily silent. He looked at me. I was sitting up staring straight ahead with my arms folded. I was trying to figure out where to start. I was rolling back in my mind to the source, trying to remember who had said what and why; why I'd blurted out that I'd wanted a divorce twelve months ago. I couldn't get the facts straight. Why hadn't we laughed about it and moved on? Why had I been so wary of Andy's moods for the past year? Why had I moved heaven and earth at the last minute to get the children sorted so I could come to Thailand with Andy? Things can get so lost in the everyday if you let them. Life just rolls on over things and you forget why you were mad, why you were hurt, why you had inched away from each other. But it chipped away at your closeness and created a distance, which was how people ended up losing each other.

"Nell? Are you okay?" Andy said, his voice bristling with a real warmth.

I felt like I knew him again. I felt safe enough to ask. "Why would he say that thing about divorce?"

Andy lay down, then rolled over, away from me and said, "Because I might have said something to him about it."

"You *might* have?"

He rolled over, put his arm across my lap and nestled his head into my side. "I let my guard down," he said, his voice muffled. "See what happens? You let your guard down and he stores it up."

"When did you let your guard down?"

"The last time he stayed with us. I just needed to talk to someone. I was so hurt. It knocked me for six when you said you wanted a divorce."

"It was just meant to get your attention," I said. "I didn't really mean it."

The truth was, at the time, in that moment, I absolutely meant it. It wasn't something I felt from day to day, but in the heat of that particular moment the feeling was quite real. That's why it was so unnerving that Andy had told Hal about it.

"I just . . . it would never occur to me, to leave you. No matter how bad things got. I love you so much," he said. "It made me realise I had to protect myself, to keep my distance a bit from you."

"Well that's not going to work," I said. "What kind of marriage is that?"

"Well what kind of marriage is it if you just shoot off that you want a divorce when things get hard?"

"I didn't feel like I could talk to you about it."

"Well talk to me now," he said.

"I didn't like it when you drank yourself into oblivion every Friday night, stayed out until three in the morning and then had a hangover every Saturday."

"I know," he said. "But I've stopped that, did you notice?"

"I did," I conceded, then emboldened I went on. "And sometimes I don't feel like I can express my feelings without you getting angry. It's like you're angry that I'm unhappy. So I push it down and cover it up, then it comes out in a burst of 'I want a divorce', when you least expect it."

"We took a vow," he said, trying to wear me down with black and white righteousness. Bringing me back to the vows we took on our wedding day was one of his favourite moves. Personally, I didn't see that moment as the ultimate promise of trust and devotion. I saw things more as an ongoing quid pro quo: a commitment that was subject to the changing conditions. But commitment nonetheless.

"But that doesn't mean you can behave how you want and I just have to wear it," I said.

"Is that what you're doing, just wearing it? Is this marriage so unbearable that you just have to endure it?"

His voice had a hard edge to it, he was pulling away from me.

"No. But I should be able to express . . . dissatisfaction . . . without copping months of silent treatment as punishment."

"Dissatisfaction? You said you wanted a divorce."

"I was trying to get your attention!" I shouted.

"Hey!" he hissed. "Keep your voice down!" That was that. I was silenced. Shamed by my apparent loss of control. I felt gagged, muted and stymied and my unspent rage over the whole thing was still simmering. The unfairness of not being able to have my say.

"I've just spent two hours with my father," he pointed wildly in the direction of Tom's apartment, "with him crowing at me that my wife wants to divorce me."

"Well, you're the one who told him about it," I said.

"Oh, so I'm not supposed to talk to my father, is that it?"

"Um . . . that would seem a sensible option."

"I can't just cut him out of my life, Nell, I've told you that."

"Yeah but you don't have to tell him about our marital problems."

I felt Andy take a suck of breath. He prided himself on having a shiny exterior for everyone (including his father) to admire. It was anathema to him that we should admit to having problems. Because then Hal would be right; about him, about us.

"Do we *have* marital problems?" he asked, slyly.

It was a dare, an invitation to step on either side of the line. My answer would define me as either with him or against him. I realised then, I was too tired to take on the challenge. And this was no place for spilling everything onto the floor. What if we couldn't gather it up again in time?

"No," I said in a small voice. But there was something more I had to know. "That thing your dad said about you humping around . . . "

"Nell, come on," Andy dismissed it outright. "Think about it, if it were true would I have brought it up?"

It was good logic, but I started thinking it might be some sort of double fake. A seed of mistrust had been planted.

"Nell?" Andy said plaintively. "We're okay, aren't we?"

I wasn't able to answer that honestly. I couldn't say yes, but if I said no, we would be obliged to spend the night raking over months of problems, here, in Thailand, where we couldn't afford to fall apart.

In the face of my defiant silence, he tried another more definitive tack.

"Do you love me?" I heard in his voice the damaged child asking for reassurance.

I realised then, that this was exactly what Hal wanted to do; to pull us apart with doubt. So, I pushed the doubt aside and decided to be blank and pure and trusting. How else did you get close to someone? "Yes," I said, "But your father's a fuckwit."

We both chuckled, a small shimmer of understanding sparked

between us. Just enough to get us through. We slept on separate sides of the bed that night and we didn't touch. Hal had come between us.

# 29.

The next morning, in the parking undercroft of Tom's building, I had a panic attack. We had come for the requisite post-dinner breakfast that Tom had organised for everyone. Included in the wedding guests were about six of Tom's work colleagues, fellow teachers of varying nationality from the school where Tom taught.

I had coffee first at the hotel and then made my way separately to Andy. In the foyer of Tom's building, I ran into Jean and we went up to the apartment in the lift together, making polite chit-chat about what the village wedding might be like.

Jean was one of these people who regarded Thailand with a liberal and non-judgmental eye as the land of 1000 smiles. She found the people just lovely and had already indulged in two Thai massages (not the dirty nudge nudge, wink wink kind, but the kind where they bend your body around like a pretzel) and a pedicure. She showed me her painted toenails with the novelty of a person who didn't normally have painted toenails. She was an earthy woman with a natural pretty face. She was fiftyish and looked, I reckoned, exactly her age. She wore not a scrap of makeup and had gone 'a bit native' you might say, dressed in a matching sarong and top ensemble that she had bought at the night markets. Her long hair was still slightly damp and tangled from a swim in the pool that morning. Maude and I were still clinging to the dignity of tailored linen and capped sleeves. We had not gone in the pool for fear of a) giardia and b) exposing our fat whiteness to the slim brown

Thai people who were folding towels beside the pool. I asked Jean about Pattaya, given Hal's intention to do some sex touristing with his mate Ivan. From what I knew Jean and Greg were devout Christians and their tagging along on a Hal-led sexpo did not fit.

"Oh, it was lovely, I just lay by the pool and read a book," she said.

"And Greg?" I said, digging for something more truthful. "How did he go?"

"Oh, they just went off and did their own thing," she said. A flash of something crossed her face. "Greg didn't stay out late, he's come straight from a conference in China so he's pretty tired."

"And Jeng and Phan?" I dug a little deeper. Jeng was Ivan's blind date. Remember how Phan had demanded some white cock for her sister and Ivan had selflessly offered himself up?

"Oh, they just did their own thing. How are your children? You've got three now?"

She seemed genuinely interested in my kids. By the time we got to the twenty-fifth floor we were talking about my famous bus shelter. Apparently, Hal had bragged to Jean and Greg that I had designed it single-handedly. Strange, given he always found a way to put a patronising, negative spin on it whenever he brought it up with me.

I had to fess up and explain that I was working for a firm at the time and it was a team effort, accredited to the firm's collective name. It intrigued me that Hal would brag about me like that to Jean and Greg. I wondered what else he had told them about me. The only things he told us about Greg and Jean were unflattering comments about Jean's lack of culinary and housekeeping skills. 'The house is filthy, she's one of these slothful academic types' or Greg was a 'scroogey old tight-arse'. I'd imagined him doing the same hatchet job on us at the other end. Apparently, he'd instead been cleverly painting a pathetic picture of himself as the outcast father who just adored his children.

On the twenty-fifth floor, Jean and I stepped out into the hall and both looked one way, then the other. There were about ten apartments per floor. I couldn't remember which apartment it was. Jean hadn't been here at all and was expecting me to lead the way. We heard the sound of a party coming from one direction and both followed it to a door. I knocked timidly.

"I think it's this one," I said.

The door opened. A cloud of stale cigarette smoke held aloft on beer breath wafted out. An unfamiliar face stood there, holding the door open looking at us quizzically. He was a gnarly guy with a Mohawk, one forearm was entirely covered by tattoos exposed by a barely-covering-his-nipples singlet top. He was holding a can of beer in one hand. I looked inside for a familiar face—Andy, Tom or Sunisa—and saw only strangers. A carton of beer had been ripped opened and already plundered in the middle of the bare floor. Call me uptight, but nothing about this scene fitted, to my mind, the idea of 'breakfast'. When Tom had said 'we'll be hosting a breakfast tomorrow morning before the trip' I had naively envisaged a Merchant Ivory-style spread of pastries, fruit and silver coffee pots down a long trestle table about which we would all waft and pick. It was only nine o'clock in the morning. I'm not judging, but it was all a bit undergraduate for mine.

I was considering how long would be polite to stay before I could leave when I saw Andy on the far side of the room. He put up a hand to wave us in. The guy holding open the door had lost interest and wandered off into the haze. I was about to step inside, planning to head straight for the balcony, say hi to Tom and get the hell out of there when no one was looking, when Jean said, "Nup," and turned on her heel saying, "I'm not going in there. I've got allergies." She was already back at the lift lobby pressing the down button. I grabbed the opportunity with both hands.

"Me too," I said following her.

"Let's wait downstairs," Jean said, smiling at me without a hint of guilt that she might have to explain to anyone why we hadn't joined. "I can't go in there, my eyes will swell up."

"Yeah, I've got asthma," I lied.

"Oh well," Jean concluded. "No way."

I was beginning to like Jean. Which was lucky because when the lift doors opened to the foyer and we saw Hal coming towards us, hers was the arm that guided me straight past him as I had a bizarre and completely unexpected panic attack.

Here's what happened. The lift doors slid open. At the same time as we stepped out into the foyer, Hal appeared through the front doors like an apparition from a nightmare. He was flanked by Ivan, whose short-man legs pumped him along in shiny polyester pants, and Greg who was tall and lanky and drooping from either the heat or the burden of Hal's constant company. But it was Hal who loomed towards me in slow motion with his pale wet eyes, his idiotic grin, his stupid foppy hair, his hateful soul.

There was no avoiding some sort of greeting and I wasn't sure I could pretend any more that this was normal. Hal's eye caught mine and he smiled at me, as if we liked each other! Then he put his hand up to wave at me gaily. As if he hadn't said all those hideous things about me and Andy and my beautiful baby Albert, our family. As if he hadn't tried to wedge open the fissures in our relationship just for sport.

I was focused on all the hateful things he'd said. I called them up, one by one, like incantations, as though to remind me to keep on track with my outrage. *That mistake baby . . . you're still a humper, aren't you son . . . divorce . . . fat cunt . . . so glad I don't have to have a go at that any more . . . your marriage is in trouble . . .*

In reality, you can easily let most things go if you choose not to hold onto them. Hate is a choice. And I chose at that moment to hang onto it with a white-knuckled vice-like grip. A deep, violent well of utter loathing turned inside me like a viper uncurling, about to strike. I struggled to push it down in case I took a swing at him, or worse, suddenly shouted out something random like, 'You cocksucker!', which was more likely. That's when it happened, my hatred morphed into pure panic.

I have never had a panic attack before; it was anxiety gone feral. The palpitations of my heart became so violent that I could feel it pulsating in my throat. It was the most violent, juddering sensation. My entire body shook with it. I felt as though I could suck in air but not expel it. I became hysterical with oxygen. I broke out into a sweat, my hands shook. I was the epicentre of an emotional earthquake radiating outward through my body from the central point of my hammering heart.

By then the minibus was waiting in the undercroft to take us to the village. The engines were idling, sending a putrid burning plastic, carbon smell into the thick hot air beneath the building. As Hal loomed closer I thought I might be sick. Then Jean deftly stepped around me so that she was on the side that would pass by Hal. She greeted him with a friendly no fuss, nothing-to-see-here 'hello' at the same time as she took me by the arm and guided me right away from him.

She walked me out to the front of the building and sat me down on a step. I took a few deep breaths and tried to get a grip on myself. She didn't ask what it was about but she did ask me if I wanted a drink.

I nodded. She went into the convenience store and bought me something sweet and fizzy. She handed it to me and then said simply, "I think there's something wrong with him."

I could only stare at her.

"Seriously, I think he has some kind of mental problem." She said this thoughtfully as if it were a revelation she had just recently arrived at. (In Pattaya, as it turned out.)

There was too much to add to that. So, I just laughed in a slightly unhinged way. She looked at me with some concern and said, "Are you going to be alright to travel eight hours in the bus with him?"

# 30.

Something about that moment, seeing me react to Hal and realising I was not allied to him in any way, seemed to turn a key in Jean. Until then, she'd stayed distant and impartial, unsure about where the loyalties fell in this complex family web. But seeing me react to Hal so violently, she suddenly understood a little bit more about where I sat. After I'd gulped down the cold, sweet fizz of a Fanta outside the convenience store, Jean suggested we go and sit in the bus, where the aircon was already cranking.

We took two rows of seats at the front and sat with our backs against the windows, our legs stretched out, not facing each other. There was a tentative newfound intimacy to it and without prompting, Jean told me about her time in Pattaya with Ivan, Greg, Hal and Phan.

This time her version was more truthful. She had lain by the pool with her sudoku book in order to block out what was going on around her. Ivan, having rejected the sacrificial offering of Jeng had gone whoring every night with Hal, leaving Jeng to return alone to the hotel room. Some nights, Jean said, she could hear Jeng knocking hopefully at Ivan's hotel room door.

"It was just awful," she said, covering her face. "Just before we left Sydney, I accidentally opened an email from Hal to Greg about the trip to Pattaya." She shook her head. "I was almost sick. I was literally packing my bags to go and when I read that I started unpacking them."

She took a sip of water. She was still trying to choose her words carefully. There was still some part of her that was keeping me at a distance.

"Greg talked me into coming. He convinced me we could just have a nice time by the pool. Which we did. We just had dinner and then let them do their own thing."

"What does Greg see in him?" I said.

"They're old friends," Jean said. "Greg feels some sort of responsibility towards Hal, I think."

"Why?"

"He's got no one else," Jean said this with compassion for Hal and his current situation.

This told me she did not know the full family history. I was itching to tell her but I felt it wasn't my story to tell. It was Andy's history. Self-preservation had kicked in, too. If I told Greg and Jean the full story, would they take Hal in the next time he landed in Sydney? In the end, it was a tactical decision, not an ethical one, of family privacy that made me keep my mouth shut.

I also made a decision regarding the two days of wedding celebrations in a small village in close quarters with Hal Straw. I decided that the only way to handle Hal in such claustrophobic and trapping conditions was to simply pretend he didn't exist. I decided to send him to Coventry.

Gradually everyone wandered down from the apartment and started climbing into the buses. Andy was one of the first and Jean took the opportunity to move further to the back of the bus and get busy with her sudoku, leaving us to our conversation. She said nothing to Andy about what had happened with Hal, but as she moved away she laid her hand on my shoulder, firmly, just long enough to let me know that we were now allies in some small way.

As people clambered into the bus, I told Andy about my Coventry plan. He was dubious.

"You can't just ignore him for two days," he said, no doubt worried my behaviour would set off a turn in Hal.

"Why not?"

By now everyone else had filed in except for Hal. He was still outside stuffing around with his bags in the luggage compartment, taking plastic shopping bags in and out, unable to decide what he could do without for eight hours and what he couldn't. We were all waiting. Maude and Stan had been spirited away to the safety of Sunisa and Tom's car, which had scooted off with a jaunty 'toot-toot!'.

The bus was idling while we all waited for Hal and Phan who, aware of the captive audience inside the bus, were now making a bit of a 'daffy couple' show of it, giggling and fussing with their things outside the luggage compartment. Someone sighed loudly; I think it was Joe. Then Ivan got up and went out there to see what the problem was.

"I'll just avoid him," I said to Andy.

"You'll only make it worse. He'll seek you out," Andy predicted.

"I'm sending him to Coventry," I said proudly.

"Nell . . . " Andy pleaded. "Remember, this is Tom's wedding. Don't make a scene."

At that moment, Hal and Phan boarded and I demonstrated my method to Andy; I simply turned my cheek and looked the other way.

"G'day mate," he said to Andy then, "Nell."

I ignored him. Andy nudged me. I turned my face toward him and gave him a tight, closed-mouth smile with glazed, far away eyes.

"Hello darling," he leered at me, smiling sort of sheepishly as though he was slightly afraid of me.

*Hello fuckface,* I thought to myself.

Then he moved on as Phan pushed him to the back of the bus playfully like they were the cutest married couple in all of Thailand. Andy snickered, he couldn't help himself. "He's terrified. Did you see that?"

"He should be," I said, satisfied.

Then a slight ruckus broke out at the back. "I'd like to sit with my lady," Hal was saying.

There were no more seats left together, just a single row down the side. Everyone looked at him. No one was prepared to budge. Joe was sitting with a work colleague of Tom's, a young guy about the same age.

"You two! Move!" Hal demanded. "You don't need to sit together. I need to sit with my lady."

Joe just eyeballed him. And I mean *eyeballed* him. It was impressive. Hal's back was to me so I couldn't see his reaction. Phan stood behind Hal, still waiting to be allotted a seat alongside her most prestigious accessory: her *farang*.

Jean, I noticed, just buried her nose further into her sudoku puzzle book and pretended it wasn't happening.

"We're not moving, mate. Sit over there."

"Dad," Andy called out warningly. "Just sit down, we've all been waiting for you."

"They must be homosexuals. Have to sit together. Are you poofters in love, are you?" Hal said in a nasty, twisted tone of voice.

I have to admit, for all my bravado, even I was frightened. It was the way things just turned so suddenly on a dime without any normal build-up to it. It had an unpredictable psychopathic vibe about it that turned my stomach.

"Hey Hal!" Andy called out. "Settle down!"

He must have taken his seat, a single one, with his 'lady' in front of him. Andy twisted back around and put his hand on my knee soothingly. "It's going to be a long day."

An hour later we pulled out onto the open freeway and left Bangkok behind. I felt a strange pang of familiarity for the place. I turned and watched it retreating, a smoggy brown smear of high rise, as all around us the road stretched through the heat with the scrubby province unfolding either side. There was the occasional ostentatious hut built right on the freeway, but mainly just bushland and fields. At one point, I saw a family of five piled up one behind the other on a dirt bike, trying to make a U-turn in the middle of the busy freeway. My heart leapt into my throat as they wobbled out, regained their balance and spun off in the opposite direction, the small children clutching their mother from behind, her face furrowed with the worry of a risk that had to be taken.

Inside the bus, the airconditioning roared. Hal was quiet for a time and the driver put the radio on in order to assault us with some very bad nasally Thai pop music. Andy sacrificed his iPod to me for an hour while he read his book. I listened to Sheryl Crow and watched the scrub and dust and windblown palm trees go by, wondering when and if I would develop some kind of fondness for this place. It certainly wasn't now. There was nothing exotic about the landscape; it looked hot and uncared for, blasted into submission by the heat.

About two hours in, the bus pulled off the freeway into a truck stop. The driver got out and slid the door open with a roar. The heat came in like a hot gust from an opened oven. Everyone piled out. The driver held up both hands indicating ten minutes. I waited until Hal passed and I got out to go to the loo. Andy went to the shop to get some snacks. I went to the toilet, where I planned to stay until it was time to get back into the bus, and so avoid any unnecessary collisions with Hal.

In the bathroom, as I accidentally pissed on my hem, I made a mental note to not wear a long skirt again. There was a plastic bucket of dirty water by the side of the ceramic pit with a scoop in it: the flusher. You swished your effluent away with a scoop of water and then (in lieu of toilet paper) you splashed your undercarriage. It was a good system, quite refreshing really. As long as you could ignore the fact that the cleanliness of the water could not be counted on. In pissing on my hem, I balked and stepped into the sluicing bucket by mistake. My precious flush and sluice went all over the floor. I had no paper. Bodily functions are hideous when not surrounded by Western commodities.

When I came out, I stood at the sink with my antibacterial liquid and surreptitiously squirted some onto my palm. Jean emerged from a stall and I felt suddenly self-conscious about my over the top antibacterial approach, given she was more of the gone native type. She had accessorised her matching sarong and shirt ensemble with a printed Thai string bag slung across her body. She probably didn't judge the levels of sanitation like I did. "Ooh, can I've some of that?" she asked.

I squirted some into her hand. We rubbed our hands together in a companionable routine of two *farangs* obsessive-compulsively eradicating the under developed world from their skins.

"How you going?" Jean said.

"I'm good."

I was about to elaborate and thank her for looking after me that morning when Phan and Jeng emerged from their stalls. Phan preened her loose poncho-style polyester top into place as she strutted to the sinks. She was wearing black leggings over her stout legs and clicky high heels. Jeng followed in her shadow, looking decidedly less optimistic in a collared T-shirt and plain knee-length shorts, a pair of rubber flip flops on her feet. Stocky and boyish, she'd given up the façade of 'pretty lady'.

"Hello girls," Jean said brightly.

"Hello," Phan said sing-songingly in the way that Thai people spoke English. Jeng just nodded silently and didn't meet our eyes.

Phan stood at the mirror and fluffed her short hair into place, got out some lipstick and instructed Jeng to stand still while she put some on her. Jeng stood obediently while Phan fussed over her. Then they left, chattering quietly in the modulated tones of Thai.

"Poor Jeng," Jean said, shaking her head sadly. "I feel so sorry for her. Ivan took one look at her at the airport and wouldn't even speak to her."

"Why'd she come?" I said.

"She's still hoping, I suppose," Jean sighed.

I followed Jean outside into the suffocating heat. Phan and Jeng were standing with Hal, Greg and Ivan like two high school girls hanging with the cool group and wanting everyone to notice them. Jeng stood back on the edges of it while Phan was right in there chatting away to everyone; the social butterfly and her homely sister.

"I'm going back to the bus," I said, making a beeline for it while Hal was otherwise occupied.

"I think it's locked," I heard her call after me.

It was. I looked around and saw Andy sitting on the seat outside the shop, tucking into a bag of lollies. He waved me over. I went and sat down next to him. "Sweetie for my sweetie?" he asked, proffering the bag. I took a red jelly snake. Then Hal came and sat down right next to me and I nearly choked on my snake. I turned my head away from him and gazed into the middle distance at the cars passing on the heat-blurred freeway. Andy leaned across me.

"Hi mate," Andy said.

"Gee it's hot isn't it?" Hal said, blotting his forehead with a hankie. He looked particularly old and shabby in this heat, his pasty skin appeared to be melting like wax.

Then he addressed me directly. "You hot, Nell?"

He leaned right into my eyeline with his big leery face, his watery lizard's eyes. Mercifully, at that moment, the bus driver appeared and unlocked the bus. I just got up and walked to the open door as though it had called to me personally and I had no choice but to move towards the light. Andy was right, this Coventry thing was going to be much harder than I thought.

# 31.

The bus trip seemed to last for days. We made two more stops at similarly soulless truck stops (but really who am I to judge, it's not like we have culturally vibrant truck stops where I come from) where I again weed on my hem and knocked over the sluicing bucket. This time I spent the time out of the bus moving around constantly so as to avoid becoming a sitting duck for Hal's unwanted advances. He was determined to get to me. I'd see him coming towards me and I'd duck into a shop and hide behind the shelves. When he came in looking for me I kept moving, moving, too busy to stop, got to go over here, over there, busy, busy, busy. At one point, I was actually at the cash register about to buy something when he spotted me and came and stood next to me. I dropped my purchase on the counter and wafted out of the shop in my 'oh I've just got to go over here suddenly' way, while the girl at the checkout yelled out to me in Thai: Hey crazy white lady, you forgot your giant bag of chicken chips. Each time, I managed to avoid him with my busy moving tactic.

Just when I thought we'd never get there, the bus turned off the main freeway onto a smaller road. We'd been travelling for about seven hours by that stage and the mood in the bus had settled into a silent weariness. Even Hal had been quiet for hours. Then the bus driver did something inexplicable. He flipped down a video screen at the front of the bus and started playing a DVD of (scantily clad but clothed nonetheless) dancing girls. Hal applauded loudly and shouted something witty like, "Thanks for the mammaries!"

I braced myself for their clothes to come off, or for some vague pornographic thing to happen, but no, it was just dull and inexplicable footage of bored-looking girls dancing in an ever so slightly suggestive way. Occasionally they bent over and pushed their breasts together, which sent Hal into a frenzy: "Jugs, jugs, we want jugs!" Or they danced close to the camera so the view was virtually up their skirts: "Pussy cam, Pussy cam, Hello Kitty! Show us your opening!"

One scene of dancing girls cut out and another started up. They were all filmed at big outdoor occasions, on stages with crowds dancing around below them. The dancing girls seemed practically comatose and were gyrating half-heartedly. They weren't even dancing in synch. The music accompanying it was a migraine-inducing Casio keyboard generated Thai version of an industrial dance beat.

"What the fuck?" I said to Andy.

"Just don't look," he said, nose in his book.

"I don't understand," I said unable to move my eyes away from the screen. "What is this in aid of? Are we supposed to enjoy it?"

Andy looked up thoughtfully and said, "It'd be so much more interesting if they just took their tops off."

"I actually agree with you."

We snickered. I looked around at Jean. She was gazing intently out the window. Hal caught my eye. "These are the dancers they'll have at Tom's wedding," Hal boomed out to me from the back of the bus as he pointed joyfully at the screen with a big thick stabbing forefinger. "These dancing girls. They'll be at the wedding." I risked another look. Phan was nodding her head furiously, as though she were the proud tour operator.

"*Farang*/Thai wedding is very big deal. Sunisa's family will put on big event," she said.

I smiled my close-mouthed, valium smile at them and turned back around. Apart from everything else, I didn't understand what Phan was doing joyfully joining the wedding bus tour when eight hours before she'd been ejected from Sunisa's apartment for tearing photographs into tiny pieces and shouting slanderous Thai insults at the bride. What was her story?

"You've got to admire his tenacity," Andy said with regard to Hal's determination to engage me. "He's not giving up."

After another five minutes of the industrial beat music and the bored girls in short skirts doing the occasional pelvic thrust to the camera, I looked back to see if anyone was interested. Only Hal was looking. Even Ivan had lost interest and was nodding off with his head lolling back and his mouth half-open (he still had his polyester pants on by the way, just in case you were wondering). Everyone was either reading a book, sleeping or listening to music on headphones. I leaned forward and said to the driver, "Excuse me, could you turn that off please?"

He turned his head to look at me and I realised that he was no longer watching the very narrow road, which butted straight up against the corn fields. "Huh?" he said, veering into the middle of the road.

In the interests of road safety, I turned instead to his co-pilot in the passenger seat. "Um, I was just wondering if you could turn the DVD off, I've got . . . " I was about to give an elaborately verbose explanation of my headache then decided to go a bit pidgin English, Hal-style, "Me got headache," I shouted grasping my head. Then I pointed at the screen. "Too noisy."

The guy frowned at me, not comprehending the idea that I would want him to turn the in-flight entertainment off.

"Off?" he said.

“Yes please,” I said, then added, “*kop koon caaaah*” (thank you) to show that I was culturally sensitive. He gave me a look like I was a nut-case and leaned forward to switch it off. The screen went blank.

“Balls!” shouted Hal from the back. “Turn it back on!”

“Now you’ve done it,” Andy said without looking up from his book.

“Me want the pretty ladies!” Hal called out. “Clam cam, Clam cam!” he started chanting.

Phan giggled and slapped him playfully. “You stop that. Nell no like it,” she said, as though I was some sort of prude who was offended by girls in short skirts.

“Too much for you, Nell?” Hal shouted at my back. Then to Phan, in a loud voice he said, “She’s a devout Catholic, you know. Very proper. She doesn’t like the rumpy pumpy.”

The driver looked at me questioningly. I shrugged, defeated. He turned the video back on. Hal cheered.

“Serves you right Miss Prudey Pants,” Andy said.

About an hour later, the bus turned off the road again onto a smaller dirt road and it became apparent by the growing frequency of huts along the road that we were travelling through the centre of a small village. Large fields of corn stretched out on either side of us and I could see the jagged shapes of mountains in the distance.

As we bumped along the dirt road, locals came out of their houses and watched the bus go by, their hands shielding their eyes from the glare of the afternoon sun. Some wandered out in a daze, barefoot, and stared slack-jawed as though aliens had landed. Others smiled toothy smiles and waved happily (as though the prophecy had come true).

They were petite brown people with well-honed wiry limbs. Their faces were flat with wide prominent cheekbones and small, neat noses. The men were as delicate and defined as the women. The young women were pretty and open-faced, the older women sort of gnarled and worn-in by a life of hard physicality. The older men were like tough old bags of leather with no teeth and no stuffing.

I felt big and round and pointy-nosed. Above all I felt fleshy: fleshy with the excesses of the West. I felt all the food I had unnecessarily eaten over the course of my life, food I hadn't *needed* to eat, but which I had gorged myself on for the pure sensual pleasure of it sitting in evidence all over my body. Even my full set of teeth seemed ostentatious.

A small contingent of villagers began running behind the bus. The bus turned again into what looked like a back laneway, then pulled up at the back of . . . a house? The house had been added to at the rear with smaller and more rickety lean-tos made of rusty tin and rotting timber that finished at a cartoonishly small, comically crooked outhouse. A washing line was strung between the house and a tree. The ground was light brown mud with big puddles of water set into it. There were various buckets and containers piled up, some bags of rubbish, a haphazard explosion of pot plants.

"Is this it?" I said doubtfully to Andy.

We had been told we would be taken straight to the accommodation. All I could think about was getting out of the fricken bus, straightening my legs and going to my 'room' (assuming it was a room and not some kind of open air longhouse) with my book. I was already thinking about lying on the bed and reading the afternoon away beneath a slow-turning fan.

We all got out. That was when the noise first hit us: an ear-piercing blast of Thai pop music was being broadcast across the village to herald our arrival. Everyone winced and looked around for the offending source. Eight hours in that bus, we all had headaches. I looked up and saw a speaker stack, at least two stories high, sitting in the middle of the laneway. It was on a trailer, trucked in just for us, emitting speaker-crackling shards of bass and drums, guitar and nasal whiny singing out into the hot afternoon.

No one said anything. A few locals stood around looking at us but no one came near. We all stood in the mud and the suffocating heat being assaulted by Thai pop music. Then I spotted Maude coming from the front yard of the house across the lane. It was a large, ostentatious house made of concrete. It was painted white with a pitched roof at the centre of things and ornate decorative eaves in lurid blue. In the front yard, there were chairs and tables set up beneath a mish mash of makeshift marquees of blue tarpaulin stretched over sticks staked into the ground.

Maude virtually ran towards me. She gave me a 'look'. "We have been here for an hour and a half," she muttered behind her hand, obviously at the end of her tether, "just *sitting* here."

"Where are we?" I said.

"This is . . . " Maude began and then, as a local man came towards us, she pasted a big fake smile onto her face and started speaking loudly as if there was nothing weird going on, ". . . this is Sunisa's parents' house," she said grinning at me through clenched teeth. "Isn't it lovely of them to welcome us to the village?"

"Where's the accommodation?" I said, bewildered and feeling like I was about to cry from exhaustion.

"Oh, it's miles away from here," Maude said with an extravagant 'god help us' inflection.

"What's going on Mamaa?" Andy said, sensing that Maude and I were working each other up into an outraged, spoilt white woman frenzy.

"I was just telling Nell that we have been here for an hour and a half. Just sitting here. No one has said anything to us. They've all just peered at us from a distance."

"Well it's pretty remote, Mamaa," Andy said, laughing lightly at her. "They've probably never seen a white person before. They're probably afraid you're going to eat them."

I snorted through my nose. I *did* feel like a big fat eating machine waddling into their village looking to consume anything that didn't move.

"Oh! Very funny!" Maude was in no mood for fat jokes. She'd already told me earlier that she was worried they would run out of Thai silk to wrap her in during the ceremony. Apparently, part of the tradition was for the groom's mother to be wrapped up in Thai silk. "I tried to go for a walk down the lane," she said, "and they all told Tom to tell me not to go because it's not safe. Because of the dogs."

I looked around and saw mangy dogs lying flyblown in the heat. One of them blinked at me. They looked too tired to do anything but lie there. Still, there was something deeply disturbing about the possibility of a wild dog. Which made me think of Hal. Where was he? Then I saw him still sitting in the bus, staging a sit-in, no doubt.

A neat wiry Thai man approached us. He was, it has to be said, dapper. He had a triangular head and his face was almost entirely covered by a pair of mirrored aviator sunglasses. He was tiny and perfectly formed, his pants were pulled up jauntily around his armpits and belted at his miniscule waist. His collared shirt was nattily tucked into them. He walked with a bow-legged duck swagger, with his hips forward like he owned the place. (Which apparently he did.) As he got closer Maude started speaking in her loud 'for strangers who don't speak English' voice.

"Oh, here's Sunisa's father. Hello Rungsung!" she shouted, even though he was now standing right in front of her. (For the record, his name was actually 'Rangsan'.)

Then she nodded when he nodded, which set off a frenzy of nodding all around. We all nodded at each other.

"Rungsung . . . " Maude began, shouting as though he were miles away, "this is Tom's brother, Andy, and his wife Nell!"

He made praying hands and bowed to us. We bowed back. Andy overdid it, he put his praying hands together and bent himself right over from the waist.

I saw then that Rangsan had a spectacular mole on his pointy chin, with an unapologetic spurt of black hair sprouting out of it. No kidding, the hair was about three inches long. He grinned at us, his teeth were impressively white and straight and all intact, which gave away his relative affluence. He gestured towards the marquees, where there were chairs and tables set up. A group of locals had already taken roost at one of the far tables and they all lifted their hands and waved as we looked across at them. They 'cheersed' us with their glasses of beer.

"All drinking Tom's beer," Maude muttered to me disapprovingly. "Tom's beside himself."

Sunisa's father continued to herd us over to the chairs with big magnanimous arm gestures. *Come-come, sit-sit, be my guests.*

We followed and sat uncomfortably in the shade of the tarpaulins. Sunisa's father then distributed Tom's beer with a generous flourish. We all took a glass and nodded, more nodding. (I don't want to sound spoilt, but the beer was warm.)

"There's Mum," Maude said to me. Her voice held a slight edge, as if she was expecting something from me. I looked over and saw a brown potato of a woman standing with her hands behind her back, overseeing the proceedings sternly. She was a stout, frowning potato with a potato head that grew straight out of her body. Her neck and head were just one entity. Her snub nose was slightly pig-like.

"Isn't that surprising?" Maude said meaningfully. I got the meaning; Sunisa obviously hadn't gotten her looks from her mum. Just as importantly, we were no longer the fattest women in the village.

"Not what I was expecting, at all," I agreed slyly.

Maude waved. The woman's face crinkled into a smile and she waved back.

"Just enjoying a drink!" Maude shouted and enunciated lavishly. "Thank you!" Then she turned back to me. "Tom's beer for the wedding," she muttered. "He bought it for the party, now they're just serving it up and drinking it all. He's beside himself."

Stan wandered over. "Hello Miss!" he said, giving me a big kiss on the cheek. "How was your trip with my best buddy Hal?"

"Excruciating."

Stan roared laughing. "Well, we were very comfortable in Sunisa's car, very comfortable indeed."

"Oh, stop it, Stan, no one's in the mood for those sorts of jokes," Maude said.

"Not enjoying the ambience, my dear?" he teased.

"Oh go fuck yourself," said Maude.

Stan's eyes went wide with shock. Maude was wearily unapologetic. Thailand—its heat, its squat-hole toilets, its murky morality—had finally worn her down. In that way, she was like a canary in a coalmine, signalling to the rest of us that things were now officially untenable.

# 32.

Two hours later, when all the beer for the wedding was gone, they packed us back up into our bus and trucked us out. At Joe and Andy's instruction, we took a brief detour via the bottle shop to pick up some beer to take to the accommodation. Everyone gladly proffered forth the required notes to contribute. Everyone except for Hal.

"We're only light drinkers," he protested when Joe fronted up to collect his contribution.

"Yeah, well everyone's putting in so . . . " Joe said gruffly.

"Come on Dad," Andy bantered. "Cough up, mate."

"No, we're light drinkers, we won't be putting in." Hal's voice went up a notch in intensity. I didn't look. There was a thick silence all around me.

"Come on Dad, you'll have a beer. It's only 10 baht."

"Well we're just light drinkers," Hal repeated again, his tone full of fight.

"Dad, give us 10 baht, you cheap prick," Andy laughed, still trying to keep it light.

"Forget it." Joe dismissed it angrily. "Let's go."

As they exited the bus, Hal bleated after them one last time.

"We're just light drinkers."

They returned with two cases of beer carried aloft on their shoulders triumphantly. Everyone cheered. The bus coughed to life and we were off again, bumping along the dirt road to our accommodation. I was bone weary and dying to be alone. We'd been in company for the whole day and the time at Sunisa's parents had been extremely trying; sitting at a table while more and more villagers rocked up to partake of the free beer and get a good eyeful of the *farangs*. We were being 'displayed' for status. It was a very big deal for Sunisa's family to be hosting a group of *farangs*. Hence the unscheduled entrapment.

About fifteen minutes out of the village we turned off onto a small track that ran through a large cornfield. The corn was as high as the bus and the track was so narrow the leaves brushed against the windows. The sun was just setting, casting a lovely soft gold light across the corn. I felt pleasantly travel-weary, knowing that some respite was ahead of me; a bed and a fan and some quiet reading time.

We bumped along through the corn track and finally came to a clearing. A sign in Thai heralded the name of the resort. We looked out the window at what greeted us.

A terrible unspoken disappointment settled across the bus. I don't know what I had expected, but it wasn't this. Actually, I did know but it was embarrassing to admit. The word resort, which had been bandied around for the past week had conjured up visions of a sparkling kidney-shaped pool, quaint thatched roofed huts with Vogue-style interiors and perhaps a bar in the centre of the pool where a man would be serving large pink cocktails liberally adorned with tropical fruit. A hammock, a banana chair, a gazebo, a buffet breakfast with bacon and pancakes.

There were four single huts on a rise to our right. These were apparently the luxury huts. (They had sit-down toilets and airconditioning.) They were little concrete bunkers all dolled up to look like mini Swiss chalets, with tall-pitched, rusted tin roofs and curly woodwork. There was something terribly tragic about them, like a toothless smile: they were trying but still they were shabby and unloved. At the centre of the clearing was a large open air longhouse type structure: the kitchen and dining hall, where we would have all our meals. Beyond that were the cheap rooms. A row of motel-like doors on a low rectangular-shaped building cum long-shack made of what looked like fibro, its walls a dirty pink colour.

Tom, Sunisa, Maude and Stan were waiting for us in the long-house. They waved the bus in and we parked. Everyone got out and Tom herded us into the open air dining room to allocate our rooms. I sat at a table with Joe, thinking he was the safest bet to keep Hal away from me. Andy was talking to Tom, looking at the piece of paper with everyone's room allocations on them. As Joe and I sat in companionable silence, Hal approached and threw a scrunched up 10 baht note across the table at Joe.

"There, that's for the beer," he said ungraciously.

"Forget it," Joe said in a low dangerous voice. "I don't want it." He tossed it back.

Hal picked it up and threw it back again. Joe was a tall, well-built guy. He had an easy smile but his eyes were now hard.

"For the beer, we're just light drinkers." Hal flicked his hand dismissively at Joe, as though *he* was the tight-wad in all this. Joe picked up the money and threw it back.

"Mate, stop throwing your fucken money at me." He said this in a low angry voice that made my stomach curl. Then he eyeballed Hal again. He held his gaze and just glared at him: cold and mean.

Hal glared back, his eyes watery and watchful, getting Joe's measure. He lifted his chin just ever so slightly, as though to say, 'right, I've got you now', then let it go. Hal put his hands in his pockets and rose up onto his toes ever so slightly; defensive or offensive, it was hard to tell.

Then Tom called us all to attention and the moment passed into something else.

Tom addressed us all with the aplomb of a host. He apologised for the basic conditions and urged us all to enjoy the experience. He thanked us all profusely for coming all this way for his wedding. We were all touched and suddenly the eight-hour journey did not seem such an imposition.

Andy and I were allotted one of the motel rooms. The luxury suite was reserved, fittingly, for Stan and Maude. Hal, Ivan, Jeng and Phan were bunking in one of the bigger huts on the rise. Hal had demanded that he get a hut to himself and one for his whoring mate. But Tom had disregarded this request and put them all in the same hut.

Over the next few days I would see Jeng sitting alone in the dining area after dinner looking a bit out of sorts, as though filling in time until she could go back to the hut. Ivan would be pacing the perimeter.

Thankfully, we were at opposite ends of the compound. We took our bags down to the motel rooms. Jean was already down there. She came straight back out of her room with a look on her face.

"I ain't showering in that bathroom," she said. "Is there a hose somewhere?" She then went hunting for a hose.

I went inside and put my bag down on the tiled floor. It was a small room with a low, straw-stuffed ceiling. The double bed with a mattress in the corner had no bedding. There was a so-low-it-might-take-your-head-off ceiling fan and a small low table. The window had bars on it, a torn fly screen and a view of the old broken farm machinery behind us. A stench of wet wee was coming from the bathroom. When I opened the door I saw a concrete room with the requisite porcelain squatter, a piece of hose coming out of the wall and a water bucket with a plastic scoop. I backed out.

"Is it okay?" Andy said.

"Oh dear."

"Quite reeking," was Andy's summation.

I went to the bed and sat down. The mattress was like a Ryvita biscuit. I tried to convince myself that I could sit here and read and got out my book. It was dark, just coming on dusk and I turned on the light. It buzzed to life and continued to hum, a hideous bright fluoro. I turned it off again.

"I'm going for a walk," Andy said. "Care to join me?"

"No." I lay back on the bed. "I think I need to lie down for a while."

"There's a computer up in the kitchen apparently, internet access, 10 baht for ten minutes. Why don't you go and check in with your parents, see how the kids are doing?"

"In a minute," I said.

"If you do," he said with the seriousness of a man about to impart some rules, "Make sure you lock this door. And take your passport and any money with you."

I closed my eyes and tried to be completely still. The heat was thick and impossible: the air seemed to sit *on* my skin and cling to it. The fan turned but made no breeze. At the moment, I just wanted to be wherever Hal was not.

About an hour later I heard voices coming from the dining room: laughing and shouting, general social hubbub. I wandered up and saw that dinner was on. A wizened old Thai lady whose broad flat face was a map of lines was shuffling out of the kitchen, weighed down by two plates piled with food. She put them down in front of Joe and another guy, then turned around to make another slow shuffling trip to and from the kitchen. Her back was bowed over with age and I wondered if she'd still be alive by the time I got to place my order.

Tom's friends from the college were sitting together, knocking about with the ease of travelling buddies; drinking beer and chatting idly about nothing in particular, their legs up on chairs, leaning back with cigarettes held out and away from their bodies luxuriously. There was one girl amongst them—holding her own—blonde and subtly voluptuous, pretty in a wholesome, natural way. She sat on the plastic chair with her legs crossed underneath her, yogic style.

Andy was in the thick of them, in his element. He already knew all their names. As I came over, he introduced me. I won't bore you with their names, suffice to say there was about six of them and they were all under thirty and all from different (Western) countries. They all spoke fluent Thai (as far as I could tell, by the way they ordered food from Grandma) and their easy, bright rapport reminded me of the sorts of friends you make when you're at uni or travelling. Transient friends, in the moment friends. Their conversation was peppered with jokes and smart comments that made them seem familiar with each other, but I sensed too that they didn't really know each other beyond the country they were in.

I sat down and struck up a conversation with the cross-legged girl. She had the fluid social skills of someone who has been travelling for years. She was Canadian and her name was Brittany. I asked her if she'd order me some chicken and rice and she said, "Oh I don't speak Thai. I'll ask Ben."

"You don't speak Thai?" I said, confused. Didn't she work at the international school? Didn't she live in Bangkok?

She rolled her eyes. She was used to this reaction. "I've been in so many places where I've made an effort to learn these obscure languages, then I just move on and never use them again. I just can't be bothered anymore."

She rattled off the languages she could speak. They were obscure and there were about four or five of them. Two different African dialects, some version of Portuguese she'd picked up in South America . . . she also spoke French and Spanish. I was impressed by her nonchalance.

"Don't you get frustrated?" I said. "I get so frustrated when I can't communicate."

"I just get one of the guys to speak for me," she said unashamedly. "It's easier."

She got Ben to order me a chicken and rice. There were a lot of words involved in the ordering of the chicken and rice, more to-ing and fro-ing than you would think. Granny seemed to be shouting, something like, '*No more food! I have no more food! Kitchen closed*!' And Ben just gave it back to her in the same stabs of abrupt Thai words and grunts. Finally, she sighed and shuffled her old bones back to the kitchen.

"Is everything alright?" I asked Ben.

"Christ, she's grumpy," he laughed in his cockney lilt.

"Is she going to spit in my food?" I said, worried.

"Oh . . . did you want that?" He motioned to call her back to add it to the order.

Andy told them I wanted to check on our kids back home and so Ben leaned back and shouted some Thai words at the man behind the 'bar' (a large chest fridge that had all our beer stashed in it). He gestured behind him to an old steam-driven computer with a big fat IBM head. It was sitting on a table with a chain around it that secured it to the wall as if it were some sort of unruly prisoner that had tried to escape before.

I went over and sat down, gave him my money. The party continued around me as I logged into my emails. I was just starting to enjoy the ambience in the longhouse, the easy company of young people, the floaty travelling feeling. Then I saw my father's email address pop into my inbox and I nearly cried with joy. A hollow-boned feeling of homesickness nearly knocked me off my chair. Then I opened the email.

Hi Nell,

Here is the daily report. The kids are being excellent. Elizabeth and Daniel went to the Halloween party at the local community hall and returned triumphant. Elizabeth won the best dressed prize for her cross-dressing Luke Skywalker costume and Daniel won best dancer for his Moonwalking. Albert stayed home and watched The Incredibles for the 50th time, while wearing his Mr Incredible outfit for the fourth day running. (Tomorrow your mother has vowed to peel it off him to wash it.) We offered to get him something different from the video shop as a treat but he (not so) politely declined. Initially we thought he would have to be heavily placated with the others allowed to go to a party, but in truth, I think he enjoyed the peace and quiet.

I made them pancakes for breakfast and it was nice to have such enthusiastic customers. I wasn't so enthusiastic when Elizabeth wanted to borrow my tape measure (to measure her pancake) and put her maple syrupy fingers all over it. This afternoon, to keep the peace, your mother went down to the local hardware store and bought Elizabeth a tape measure of her own. She has been measuring things all afternoon. Incidentally, the vase in the living room is 235mm high. The dog is slightly bigger.

Speaking of the dog, Albert has developed a certain fondness for her kennel. We can't keep him out of it. The other day we were beside ourselves when we couldn't find him. Elizabeth finally hunted him down, curled up in Peggy's kennel, fast asleep. Peggy is happy for the company. In the ensuing search, Elizabeth also turned up a pair of Grandma's reading glasses and a long lost shoe of mine. We will be forever in her debt.

On Friday, I took Daniel with me to my lecture at the institute. I was worried he'd be bored and start heckling me, but he got to sit in the AV booth with the tech and work the slides for me. He did a sterling job except when he got curious about the workings of the slides and put his hand in front of the projector casting a big fuzzy hand shadow over the screen. Then emboldened, he did a quick rabbit shadow puppet just for good measure. It really brought the house down and was so much more interesting than anything I was saying. But his favourite task was during question time when he got to ferry the cordless microphone to each person asking a question. We worked like a finely tuned machine. I'd point out the 'lady in the green coat up the back' and he'd race towards her with the microphone like a pro. It was the most entertaining lecture I've ever given and in the end, I think people were only asking questions so they could watch Daniel dart up the aisle towards them with the microphone.

He was very helpful and even carried my notes for me without dropping them all over the floor. He told me he might like to be an architect when he grows up and enquired as to the lucrativeness of the profession. He has since changed his mind and this morning was back to wanting to be a famous saxophonist.

We will take Daniel and Elizabeth to school tomorrow and Bertie to preschool. Bertie insists that he usually has sprinkle sandwiches for his lunch. Elizabeth has concurred and added that she only likes biscuits that are pink. Is this right? Your sister has taken them all to the movies to see Monsters vs Aliens in 3D. We hope Bertie can sit still for the duration, otherwise they might be back here sooner rather than later.

Gotta go, my oven timer has just gone off, I'm making slow-cooked lamb.

Love Dad

I began to sob involuntarily, stupidly, at the basic decency of my own father. In light of what I had witnessed over the past few days, I felt suddenly that I hadn't been grateful enough for his measured reliability; his good humour, his willingness to see the best in all of us, his simple goodness, his exemplary parenting. It's a funny thing, you only really notice parenting when it is spectacularly bad. When it is as it should be, you take it for granted.

I missed my kids and my family. I felt like a child again wanting my mum and dad. I wanted the safety of their morality, the steadfast caring that they had given me over the course of my life. I felt as though I had gone out into the big bad world and consorted with the wolves. I tried to contain my emotions but it all just got on top of me. I was sobbing. I had opened the floodgates and now I couldn't stop. I thought I would quietly remove myself from company and go to my room to sob it out. Then I heard Hal's voice behind me.

"Bad news from home?"

I stayed staring at the screen. I didn't turn around.

"It's fine," I wiped at my eyes.

But then Hal started shouting and drawing everyone's attention to me. "What's wrong, darling? Something gone wrong? The children!" he said in a panicky voice. "Are the children okay? There's been an accident."

He was trying to guess why I was crying. It wouldn't occur to him that someone might simply miss their family so much it moved them to tears.

"I'm fine." I stood up to make my exit.

"Andy! Andy! Your wife! Your wife!" Hal was calling out across the room and now everyone was looking at me. "Nell's upset, something terrible's happened at home. The children!"

Andy's face went pale. He stood up so suddenly that he knocked his chair over. Now we really were making a scene. "Nell!"

I was running now, running through the darkness with my husband yelling out at me from behind. The entire dining room had stopped to watch. "Nell, what the hell's going on?"

So much for fitting in with the young people.

## 33.

A rooster woke me up. Its crowing reminded me of Hal. The day was only just showing the first rays of light but the heat was already audible, the sound of bugs was rising in crescendo with the sun. And Hal the rooster was prowling around outside. It was like a bad joke.

I lay in bed until sunlight began to creep across the windows. The heat was stifling. Andy was snoring and showed no sign of stirring. I got up, went to the bathroom and tried not to breathe in. I sloshed cold water over myself and squatted to pee.

I heard the hiss of breakfast frying up in the kitchen, the hot greasy smell of oil in a wok, as I ventured to the dining room alone. Luckily Ben was already there, tucking into his breakfast. He greeted me, asked me how I slept, and ordered me the same again. He was reading a book so I sat at a separate table and proceeded to read mine, happy for the open agreement that breakfast was a sacred time of silence. There was some sort of coffee and tea making facility along the wall, but I didn't trust it. I longed for a newspaper, but made do with my book and the view of distant mountains, which was quite contemplative in the mist of a hot morning.

I was deep into chapter sixteen when I felt Hal's presence. He went over to the coffee and tea wall and busied himself there for a while. I buried my nose further into my book even though I had not read one word since I'd noticed him. Even so, I turned the page, just to make things seem authentic. I was acutely aware of his every movement. He came towards me and I thought, *surely not!* He was carrying two cups of coffee. He set one down in front of me.

"Coffee, darling?" he asked and then answered in one swift movement.

"Thanks," I said, my heart already racing with fight or flight.

He had me cornered. He stepped over the bench seat and sat down next to me.

"There's sugar over there," he said, "if you want it."

"Right. Good." I took a sip of my coffee for good measure, so as not to appear too churlish. It was cloyingly sweet and dusty-tasting; it bore no resemblance to coffee. Not his fault, but my initial reluctance to partake in the coffee was vindicated.

"There's sugar there if you need it," Hal repeated again.

"Good."

"If you need it," he said.

To say we sat in uncomfortable silence would be a massive understatement. I plunged him actively into a deep void of wordless air and continued to (pretend to) read my book. I had no idle chit-chat for this man. I kept my mouth shut. He shifted uncomfortably and said again, "There's sugar over there if you need it."

It was farcical. Then it got even worse. Maude appeared, coming up the steps from her bungalow with the misty mountains as her dramatic backdrop. Hal's back was to her, but she saw us sitting there and her eyes widened. I tried to widen my eyes back at her to convey the thought, *don't come over here.* But I must have accidentally conveyed the thought *please help me* instead and so she came and sat down at the table with us. To save me. It was magnanimous.

"Morning!" she said brightly. "How did you sleep, Nell? You sleep okay? I was sooooo comfortable. Tom's given us the room with the aircon so we just cranked it up, so comfortable. And I took the Stillnox, I was out like a light."

She was babbling. I knew she was nervous as hell because her mouth just kept moving.

"Good sleep Hal?" she said.

"Yes, thanks darling. Although we don't have aircon, so a bit rustic. And, of course, sharing with Ivan and Jeng, that's a bit awkward. Not getting the royal treatment by any means. But that's alright," he sighed. "Just glad to be here, to support Tom on his big day."

Maude, to her credit, took none of his bait. She rode over it with more bright small talk about nothing.

"Oh, is there breakfast?" She looked around. "What are you having, Nell?"

At that point, Granny shuffled over and plonked my rice and chicken in front of me. "Er, this." I said pointing at the plate.

"What's that called?" Maude said peering at it. "Is it fried rice or something? Is there toast?"

She looked around hopefully, presumably for the crisp white-shirted butler who would bring her a plate of toast and marmalade covered by a silver cloche. But there was only Granny with her broad wrinkly face and her oil spattered apron.

"No toast," I said to Maude.

"Oh, alright then. I guess I'll just have one of those." She looked up at Granny and smiled her brightest smile.

"Hellooooo!" she shouted. "Can I have one of those?"

Granny said something in Thai back. Maude put one finger up and then pointed at my food, to indicate, *one more please.* Granny frowned and looked around for someone to translate what the crazy white lady was saying.

"She wants some food!" Hal shouted. Then, just to compound the racist sense of entitlement, he spat out random scraps of Chinese. "*Sheh sheh—nee how gob gai*!"

Granny shouted back in Thai and waved her arms around.

"She's quite waxy," Hal said recoiling, then he spied Ben hunched over his breakfast. "Hello! *Nee how,* hi there, need help!"

It was telling that Ben, at the sound of Hal's toddler-like cries for help, did not move a muscle.

"Hey Ben?" I said.

Ben turned around, his face amiable.

"So sorry," Maude apologised for interrupting him, then she opened her mouth to continue in that vein but Hal interjected, "Need some food here." He patted the table in front of him to reiterate where the food was needed.

"Are you able to help us?" Maude said smoothing over Hal's rudeness, "We seem to have a bit of a communication breakdown."

"No problem," said Ben.

He spoke to Granny in Thai. Apparently, he ordered two more. Granny shuffled off. Hal shouted after her.

"Not too hot! Not too hot for me please! *Sheh sheh*! Tell her not too hot."

Both Ben and Granny ignored him.

"Oh dear," Maude said, adjusting her shirt along her shoulder line.

"She's probably going to spit in it now," I said.

"Oh, I think you're right," Maude tutted as though it were inevitable.

"Would you like a coffee, darling?" Hal asked, getting up. "I got Nell a coffee, she hasn't had any of it, but would you like one?"

"Oh lovely," Maude said. "Thank you, Hal."

He got up. Maude and I looked at each other. My instinct was to run while his back was turned. But Maude sat tight. She straightened up as though to say, "I can handle this, just watch me." I think she thought they were making progress. It was unlike her to underestimate Hal like that. When he came back he put the coffee in front of her, the devil's downpayment on her soul.

Then he said, "Gee Andy's getting fat, isn't he? I got quite a shock at the airport when I saw how fat he was. He's quite bloated in the face."

Maude looked at me, lost for words (completely out of character). It was the last thing she had been expecting. Her mouth was open, but she was not saying anything.

"I think he looks very happy and healthy," she said finally.

"Must be all the grog, is it Nell? He still drinks a bit, does he?"

"He's given up smoking," I said. "Everyone puts on a few kilos when they give up smoking."

"Yes, right. Is that it? Because he's quite bloated, in the face. He doesn't look well at all." He made a gesture towards his face to illustrate how hideous he obviously thought Andy was.

"I don't agree. I think he looks fine," Maude said curtly.

"He was always very unhappy having to change jobs to bring in more money for you and the kids," Hal continued. "He loved his garbo job, didn't he?"

"Senior contracts manager," I corrected. "At the City of Sydney. Yes, he loved that job."

"Such a shame he had to give it away; the pressures of family, you know. Is he still going out on those all-night benders?"

"No," I said.

"Because last time I visited, you were having some problems, weren't you?" He sighed. "He was always a pants man, wasn't he Maude?"

He leered at Maude, conspiratorially as though this were a secret family pride she was in on. Maude looked at him and simply blinked with distaste. She turned her body ever so slightly away and spoke only to me.

"So, you spoke to your parents?" Maude said.

"I got an email," I said.

"How are the children?" Maude said pointedly.

"Yes, the children, how are they going? Your parents looking after them?" Hal said, trying to access the conversation.

I gave Maude a recount of my father's email and as I was talking, I noticed her eyes glassing over. She was smiling at me, but her mind was elsewhere. When she began to blink furiously I knew she was on the verge of tears. She clutched my arm and said, "Darling, could you show me where the bathrooms are please?"

We stood up. I took her toward the 'toilet facilities'; two little pee-holes with curtains for privacy tucked behind a partition wall at the back of the room.

"Excuse us, Hal," Maude said, still smiling.

As we walked across the room away from him, she began to shudder and sort of crumple up into herself. We slipped behind the partition wall and she collapsed into me. She sobbed, she was inconsolable for about two full minutes. She tried to apologise, but was unable to speak.

"I had my meltdown last night," I said, unfazed.

"I just . . . I just . . . " she began then she busied herself with finding a tissue in her bag to dab at her eyes. "I just always hoped that one day we could put our differences aside and be proud of our children."

She dissolved again. "I thought no matter what, we've got these two gorgeous boys we can be proud of. And all he does is just find the negative in everything. He just spreads unhappiness wherever he goes."

And then as though trying to make sense of her own history she added, bewildered, ". . . he wasn't always like that."

"I'm sending him to Coventry," I said. "I suggest you do the same, otherwise he'll keep upsetting you."

"No," she said, pulling herself together. "I'll be fine. I just have to be ready. I just wasn't ready that time."

"That's what I mean, though. It's exhausting having to be on your guard all the time. Just ignore him. Pretend he isn't there. If he comes up to talk to you, just look the other way," I demonstrated my Queen of Sheba turn the other cheek look.

Maude clutched my arm and did a big breathe-out whisky laugh. But she was crying too, a mass of hysteria going both ways at once.

"It makes him really nervous," I said. "I was doing really well until he sidled up and trapped me with a cup of coffee."

"Oh, the coffee!" Maude agreed. "Wasn't that sly?"

We heard voices gathering outside in the dining hall. "We should go back out there," Maude said. Ever the country-bred girl, she was always keen to do the right thing and keep up appearances.

"Yeah, your chicken and spit is probably ready."

"Will you just stay here while I go to the loo?" Maude said. "I'm afraid I might fall in."

She disappeared behind the curtain. I heard her muttering to herself, "Oh dear."

And then the inevitable spill of the sluice bucket.

III

# Tom's Wedding

**Thai** > English

**Sin sot** > dowry

In Thailand, bride price (locally known as sin sot and often erroneously referred to by the English term "dowry") is common in both Thai-Thai and Thai-foreign marriages. The bride price may range from nothing, if the woman is divorced, has a child fathered by another man, or is widely known to have had premarital relations with many men; to 10 million Thai baht (US$330,000) or more for a woman of high social standing, a beauty queen, or a highly-educated woman.

# 34.

By eight o'clock, the heat of the day was already in full skin-searing swing. The sun bore down and the thick humidity closed in on our pasty white skins, forming a film of sticky sweat.

After breakfast, I had changed into my wedding outfit: a blue and green cotton sundress. I also added a small short-sleeved cotton cardigan to cover my fleshy upper arms and keep small Thai children from grabbing hold and swinging from my fleshy First World bingo wings. I had a pair of blue sparkly flip flops that had cost me the princely sum of 300 baht at the MBK and I put them on in honour of the special day.

We all waited in the dining hall while the bus idled some more carbon monoxide into the humid air. Then Tom appeared in all his wedding glory. He was wearing a cream coloured Nehru-style suit with gold brocade around its mandarin collar and a matching gold brocaded sash across his body. He moved stiffly in it like a child, not entirely comfortable but secretly pleased with its tailored formality.

Everyone applauded when he appeared.

Hal shouted something inappropriate like, "He's ready to consummate!" Tom flicked Hal a small, irritated look and responded to the applause graciously with a subtle bow.

Everyone took various photographs of Tom with their groups of people. At one point Maude and Hal were required to stand either side of Tom and I noted Maude's faraway look when Hal leant forward across Tom to say something to her.

Tom gave a small preamble, outlining what the wedding ceremony would entail; apparently, a lot of traditional stuff involving clumps of rice stuffed into vases, dancing for one kilometre down the street while stabbing giant palm fronds in the air and finally tying money to the bride and groom's wrists for luck. We all boarded the bus. I sat with Maude in the front seat, Andy sat up the back to contain Hal, as requested by Tom.

It was only eight-thirty by this stage, but already I felt the tiredness of having woken at five am creeping in behind my eyes. Tom had flagged that it would be a long day of 'Thai time' where we were to expect the unexpected and try to go with the flow. This was not my forte. With Hal also prowling around trying to be my best bud, it promised to be a long and difficult day of culture shock and in-law related tension.

The bus bumped along the dirt road to the village and we all sank into an anticipatory silence. As we neared Sunisa's parents' house we heard the obligatory Thai pop music blaring from the three-storey speaker stack, no doubt heralding the arrival of a busload of *farangs* that had come to eat them out of house and home. (Lock up your pets and children.)

The bus pulled up and we saw a great bustle of colour and people in the front yard. As Tom had predicted, the whole village had turned out (mainly for some free booze and food but also to celebrate the betrothal of one of their most treasured daughters). Everyone seemed to be busy, apart from the men who were mostly kicking back around the tables hooking idly into the beer (occasionally they raised their hands in salute to us). I was grateful for the hubbub of activity to smokescreen our arrival.

But as we got out of the bus, they all stopped what they were doing and turned to stare. We were like zoo exhibits being unpacked out of our crate. An audible rumbling of awe moved across the front yard like a Mexican wave; an eruption of Thai chatter commenting openly on the strangeness of the sight of us. Some squinted disbelieving, others smiled big, toothless smiles and laughed amiably, others pointed and guffawed. I have never felt so ridiculous in my life.

Maude, to her credit, assumed they were admiring us. She waved a jaunty royal wave at everyone and said, "Helloooo!" loudly at whoever was looking at her.

It worked; women nodded and prayed toward her. She nodded back and did some half-hearted praying hands after finding no takers for her initial forthright offers of a handshake. Tom had schooled her in the cultural inappropriateness of handshaking, to which she had replied, "Oh, blow it, Tom, I just don't give a stuff!"

She was wearing a hand-painted silk number she had bought from a boutique back home. It was a skirt and top ensemble with a skirt that trailed to the ground. It dragged now in the mud. Her efforts to hold it up and do praying hands at the same time were proving unwieldy. In the flurry of last minute preparations, she had forgotten to change into her special gold flip flops with the kitten heel. In the bus she had drawn my attention to the giant boat-like brogues that now spoiled her carefully crafted Mother of the Groom look.

The tables and chairs were set out for us and from the back of the tent came the hiss and fry of food being frantically prepared by about twenty harried women. As soon as we sat down, they plonked plates of what looked like wilted cabbage and gristle in front of us. A man (Sunisa's brother) circled the tables with glasses and a long neck of beer, pouring and placing, pouring and placing. I sat with Jean and Maude and Stan. Hal, Ivan and Greg were on the other side of the table. We could either join their conversation or conduct one of our own. Jean was looking tired and wilted already, her pale skin aglow with sweat.

"I did not sleep a wink," she said wearily as she fanned herself with her hat. "Those beds!"

Hal's eyes lit up with the mention of a bed.

"What's that? The beds you say?" He leaned over toward Jean, a strange glint in his eye.

"They're so uncomfortable," Jean said.

"Yes," Hal agreed. "And no push back." Ivan giggled into his chest. Hal looked toward him to elaborate. "Did you find it hard to get purchase on the nest."

Jean's face remained slightly bewildered. She either had no idea of the gist, or chose to feign ignorance in the interests of common decency. Beside me I heard Maude sigh and Stan 'tsk'.

"Did you find a hose?" I said to Jean, referring to her determination to take an outside shower to avoid the bathrooms.

"I did!" she exclaimed, pleased. "It was right outside our room. I waited until dark and then had an outdoor shower, it was lovely."

"In your swimmers?" I said.

"No, starkers," Jean said proudly. "It was dark, no one could see me."

I admired her attitude. Today Jean had gone formal native. She was wearing a bottle green stiff Thai silk wraparound skirt with a matching fitted top. She smiled kindly at the villagers who were milling around us, as though thoroughly delighted by them and their hospitality. I tried to follow her gracious, good Christian woman lead.

I saw Phan working the room in her leggings, clacky kitten heels and sheer red polyester top. She strutted through the villagers like the Queen Bee, a look of bursting smugness upon her boxy visage. Being associated with the busload of *farangs* was a massive boost in status for her. Whenever she caught me staring at her, she would smile widely and shout out "Hello Nell, you having good time?" like we were best girlfriends forever and went way back. I could only look behind me, bewildered to see who she was addressing.

About half an hour later, Maude, Jean, Stan and I had not moved. While we were sitting there, drinking warm beer and eating fried gristle and cabbage at ten o' clock in the morning, Hal, who had been prowling the vicinity in search of cohorts, came running up and nearly tripped over himself. He stopped in front of Maude and doubled over with his hands on his knees to catch his breath. Maude, Jean and I looked at him and waited. He had on shirtsleeves and a tie that didn't quite make it over the orb of his ample belly down to the top of his pants. His navy slacks were ever-so-imperceptibly too short and sat just above his shiny black dress shoes. He looked like a man who hadn't worn proper Western clothes for years and had now forgotten how to put them together.

"Darling!" he finally puffed out to Maude, "I've just had the most terrible shock!"

"What is it?" Maude put her hand on her chest in horror.

I bored a hole into his head; *I'm watching you* I hoped my eyes said.

Jean just smiled at Hal and said with genuine concern, "Are you alright, Hal?"

It did look like he was about to have a heart attack. His face was bright red and he was still trying to catch his breath. "I need to talk to you privately," he puffed to Maude.

*Like hell you do.* I thought to myself. I was onto him. Maude and I had had him in Coventry for the past two hours. Any time he came near us we Queen of Sheba'd him and looked the other way. It was beginning to unnerve him. He couldn't quite put his finger on what was going on. Was he imagining it? And now he'd decided to step up the tactics a bit. He led her about ten feet away from the table and they stood in the stark sunshine. The villagers moved around them and behind them, a constant moving tableau of giant palm stalks and big silver urns on heads. I watched intently, twisting myself in my chair to keep an eye on them. Hal was speaking frantically, occasionally bending over again as though so exhausted by his news that he had to catch his breath.

At one point, Maude put out a hand to his back to settle him. She looked over at me, took in a deep breath and rolled her eyes. When he stood upright again, he seemed to be trying to drag her away further. *Come and look,* he seemed to be saying. *No, thank you,* she seemed to say back. She put a hand up, palm facing him to stop whatever he was saying. She shook her head. *I'm not listening.*

What the hell was going on?

Finally, Maude came back to the table. She sat down and looked around the table for her glass. When she couldn't find it, she reached for mine. "This yours?" she asked. I nodded. She chugged it back.

"Oh, for *god's* sake!" she exclaimed as she rooted through her handbag for lipstick.

"What's going on?" Jean and I leaned forward.

"Not now. I don't want to talk about it now."

"Are you alright?" I said, sotto voce, when Jean had turned away.

"I'm fine. Honestly Nell, I can't talk about it here. I'll tell you later."

About an hour later we were all standing one kilometre up the dirt road waiting for the signal. Apparently, in keeping with the custom, the groom's family were to dance through the village streets toward the house. The front gates would be locked and Tom was then to request permission to enter the house and marry Sunisa.

Sunisa's nephews Ban and Bon would be the gatekeepers. A group of villagers would be joining us in our quest. They milled around us now and I noted with a shrewd peripheral awareness that there was a gaggle of women forming a posse of admiration around Andy.

They were teaching him how to dance. How to dance, my arse. They were one step away from dragging him before the monks and demanding a quickie wedding. I was onto them. He was laughing and carrying on with them as they posed him this way and that and showed him how to wiggle his hips and applauded him. He was *loving* it.

"I've been asked *three* times," Maude held up three emphatic fingers, "if Andy is married."

"He's very popular, your husband," Stan teased.

"Yes. It must be his dark handsome looks," I said. "Or maybe his fat wallet." Appalling I know, but it was quite galling to be standing three feet away from your own husband and have a virtual pack of vultures swooping on him like he was a prize carcass for the taking.

Afterwards, Andy claimed, with barely concealed pride, to have felt objectified.

Ben had procured a large palm frond to stab in the air as he danced down the street. He was openly thrilled as apparently, this was a big honour to be a palm frond bearer. He was smiling and practising his 'air stabbing' with one of the locals helpfully instructing him on the proper motion.

"What was Hal on about?" I said quietly to Maude, as I kept my eye on the subject. He was standing with Andy, trying to get in on the action with the ladies.

"Oh Nell, honestly. I can't . . . I just don't want to talk about it," she said unconvincingly. I could see she was bursting with it, now that Jean was out of earshot.

I left it at that. But then she put her hand over her mouth and muttered in her faux-teacher-of-the-deaf-no-one-can-hear-me voice, "Apparently, the villagers are all saying that Sunisa has a child."

"Rubbish!" I retorted, if only for Sunisa's sake.

In my head, I was thinking of the small boy who had come on the boat with us. How Sunisa had gone to great pains to explain away the fact that he was calling her Mum.

"According to whom?"

"Hal said Phan told him," Maude said.

"Even if it is true . . . " I said carefully, "what does it matter?"

"It's not the time to talk about it," Maude said "I told him to be quiet and not say anything to anyone. Now is not the time."

"Do we care though?" I said, genuinely non-plussed by this information. "I mean, really, what does it matter? She's obviously just trying to save face."

"Whether it's true or not," Maude said emphatically, "now is not the time."

I could see then that Maude did not share my nonchalance toward this information. She seemed genuinely rattled by the elaborate deception of it. It confirmed all her worst fears about Sunisa; that there was a vast net of lies holding up her overtly wealthy lifestyle.

"He came running up, you saw him, he could hardly get to me fast enough!" Maude scoffed. "And he said, 'Darling, I've just had the most terrible shock! Come and meet your new grandchild!'."

He was talking about Bon.

"It's not Tom's, that kid is six years old."

"Of course not!" Maude dismissed. "He's a fool. Apparently one of the villagers pointed him out to Phan, *that's Sunisa's son*. The little one who's running around, one of the so-called 'twins'. Bot or Bat or whatever their names are."

"Bon and Ban," I corrected. "Why would they do that?"

"I have no idea. But the point is, for Tom's sake, now is not the time."

"Oh, he was so desperate to tell you, wasn't he?" I said remembering Hal tripping over his own feet to get to Maude earlier.

"Oh!" she laughed. "Wasn't he? He could barely speak! He was so delighted! I told him not to say anything to anyone. But then as soon as he walked off, he was telling everybody. It's just *completely* inappropriate, on Tom's wedding day. Imagine how Tom feels."

"Maybe Tom already knows," I said hopefully.

"I doubt it," Maude said. "He's said nothing to me."

Maude seemed strangely adamant that this was something Tom would tell her.

"Phan's been working the crowd all morning," I said, putting it together now. "Tom said she would do that."

The drums started up behind us and we were on. The group started surging forward and we were dancing down the street, en masse as one, towards Tom's wedding day. We looked ahead and saw Stan being spirited forth by a small mob of solicitously giggly village women.

"There we go," Maude said wryly. "Look at him, he's in seventh heaven."

"Ladies," I said, "hang on to your husbands!"

We danced down the dirt road towards the house, a big gaggle of pasty *farangs* amongst the sinewy brown locals. The final insult for the group came when we arrived at the gates. The same villager who had bestowed upon Ben the honour of carrying the largest palm frond, now in one swift dancing manoeuvre, grabbed it from him and carried on through the gates into the front yard, victoriously stabbing it in the air. Like he'd carried it all that way himself. "He stole my moment of glory!" Ben said.

The wedding had begun.

# 35.

The intrigue surrounding Sunisa continued to grow. After we'd been let in through the gates, Sunisa and Tom were spirited inside the house where a ceremonial temple had been set up to conduct the marriage. An orange-robed monk, complete with thick-framed coke bottle glasses and a microphone, stood at the flower-framed entrance like a game show host. He ushered them through with some holy flamboyance and they knelt side by side on the tiled floor. This was the first moment since coming to the village that we had glimpsed Sunisa. Gone was the Bangkok Carrie Bradshaw with her Ralph Lauren handbag, skinny jeans and tank tops and in her place was the full Thai princess.

Her hair was piled on top of her head in a tightly groomed, hair-sprayed-to-within-an-inch-of-its-life bun and her face had been so thoroughly covered in makeup she was barely recognisable: it was a white-powdered look that was slightly geisha. She had a delicate garland of fake flowers in her hair and was wearing a long stiff cream dress of Thai silk, boned and fitted at the corset and with a lace detail across one shoulder. She was dripping in garish yellow gold jewellery. Her smile was blank and pasted on. Occasionally her eyes shifted and blinked evasively around the perimeter as though scoping for the closest exit should she need it.

Tom and Sunisa knelt in front of a makeshift floral covered altar and occasionally, on cue, dipped their upper bodies forward. The monk droned on in a monotone of prayer that was amplified across the yard and village. But the strangest sight was Phan shuffling on her knees around Sunisa; a self-appointed handmaiden, she tied flowers to her wrist, handed her water, solicitously arranged plates of food offerings onto the altar and held Sunisa's ceremonial purse when needed.

"What's she doing?" I whispered to Andy.

"She wants to be associated with Sunisa and her *farangs*."

Outside the house, the party continued on, unhindered by the apparent holiness that was going on inside at the altar. More and more villagers rocked up to partake in the food and booze. One particular man named Dodo was prowling around trying to lure *farangs* over to his house across the lane. Andy (a sucker for adventure) went, and was not seen again for about an hour. He came back breathless with excitement. Dodo had a gun and cockfighting roosters in cages. Once you were in his lair, partaking of his home-brewed rice whisky, he was quite reluctant to let you leave. Andy had asked for a refill and then when Dodo was inside, he had run for his life. Later Sunisa sent around the warning that we were not to go with Dodo as, "He is very bad man." Dodo continued to prowl the party for *farang* buddies and was eventually chased off by Sunisa's father, with an efficient and menacing flick of the hand.

The culmination of the ceremony was the paying of the dowry. Maude who had been charged with guarding the dowry until it was needed carried it in her handbag all day, which she held closely clamped inside her armpit for good measure.

When the time came, she handed the bundle of notes to Tom so that he could offer it up to Sunisa's parents. I was inside the house by this stage, sitting on a plastic chair beside Maude. I'd been quite happy sitting outside by myself until a group of old men began looking and pointing at me and wagering their bet as to how old the waxy-faced cadaver was. When they delightedly told me in broken English that they had come up with the number 52 I convinced myself that they just had their numbers backwards with the language difference. Even so, shortly afterwards I moved inside.

When Tom handed the bundle to Sunisa's parents, they spent about fifteen minutes carefully counting it. Officials were called in to verify the count. Then, once it was established beyond a shadow of a doubt that it was all there, Sunisa's mother placed it carefully inside a large silver urn, (like it was a sleeping baby) and carried it lovingly upstairs to the main bedroom.

"I have *never* seen that woman smile so widely," Maude said slyly to me.

Meanwhile, Phan continued to spread the rumour. I saw her pointing at Bon and brightly telling anyone who would listen as though it were happy news. Happy for her maybe. Hal also could be seen at various moments pointing to Bon and proudly enlightening people. I was beginning to see that Hal and Phan possessed a certain compatibility that bridged all age and cultural divides. Hal, distracted by all the other evil deeds he could get up to in this setting, had all but given up on cornering me for the day.

But you can imagine for yourself his glee when tradition called for a ceremonial consummation simulation. It was a bizarre and thoroughly humiliating tradition where Tom and Sunisa had to lie on her parents' bed for ten minutes with everyone standing around watching on as though waiting for something to happen. Hal's behaviour, goading Tom to 'throw a leg over' and various other schoolboy references to 'humping', made it the most excruciating ten minutes of Tom's life.

When Tom's duties were done and he emerged as a married man, he came over to me and Andy. His wrists were enlaced by a busy tangle of notes and string. Andy applauded him as he approached. We were sitting on chairs and he crouched down between us. He looked around first then spoke softly.

"Apparently, there's a rumour circulating regarding Bon."

"Yes, there is," I confirmed.

"Mate," Andy said reassuringly, "tell Sunisa, it makes no difference to us."

"The thing is, it's not true," Tom said, sounding stressed. "Phan is trying to discredit Sunisa. Hal is making things worse."

He looked around again. Maude was standing with Sunisa's parents having her photo taken.

"Has Mum heard?" Tom said.

"Yes. Hal came running over and told her as soon as he heard it from Phan," I said, glad to drop Hal in it.

"Bastard!" Tom hissed. "Sunisa's freaking out."

He looked longingly at the beer on the table. "That your glass?" he asked Andy.

Andy nodded. Tom stood up and filled the glass with beer. "Jesus I'm fucken racked," he said. "I haven't eaten all day." He rubbed his rumbling stomach. "This whole day has been a fucking nightmare."

"We've had a great time!" Andy assured him brightly. "I met Dodo."

"Dodo?" Tom's eyes widened slightly. "He's Rangsan's standover man."

"Holy crap," I said quietly.

"Shit!" Tom added, mocking my scared white-lady tone.

"Listen," he said, putting a hand each on our shoulders, "I know this has been a difficult day. But the reception later is going to be a big party with a band and dancing girls." He put the cigarette in his mouth and mimed some dancing girls with both arms. "It'll be weird but fun."

Weird but fun. He had at least one adjective right.

# 36.

Later that evening, at the reception, Hal finally got to me.

The reception was at the local high school grounds. A massive stage had been set up in the open air hall, which had about fifty round tables with chairs for the guests. By the time Tom and Sunisa turned up to their own reception, however, all the tables had been filled by uninvited freeloaders and they were forced to wander the hall aimlessly doling out their wedding favours to strange Thai people they'd never laid eyes on. This apparently caused massive small face embarrassment for Sunisa's family as there were family members who'd been invited, only to find their seats taken by smiling villagers in shorts and T-shirts openly enjoying the band and happily partaking of the free food.

Outside the hall, the school grounds were dark and unpatrolled. By nine o'clock, the shabby darkness was liberally scattered with locals in varying degrees of intoxication; from lightly toasted and indiscriminately friendly to passed out in the dirt. Maude claimed to have seen two boys no older than ten stumbling around so drunk they finally collapsed onto their backs and just lay there looking up in wonderment at the starry sky.

When we had first arrived, the reception hall was virtually full. We were unloaded from our bus and sent inside. The same hushed wave of awe and amusement that greeted us everywhere we arrived en masse travelled across the reception hall. Someone had at least had the foresight to reserve us three tables in the centre and as we walked towards them the curiosity peaked to an excited chatter and open laughter that I wondered momentarily if my dress was see-through. Two of Tom's friends carried our booze discretely in front of them and quickly stashed it beneath our table for safekeeping.

I waited until Hal and his posse had sat down and then led Maude and Stan to the next table along. Hal leered at us hopefully as we passed and waved us down to sit at the spare seats on his table. I looked the other way and continued onto the next empty table.

Meanwhile, behind me, Maude cackled with wicked Schadenfreude at my overt cold shouldering of him and moved to sit next to me. I think it was this very public snubbing that set him in a mind to corner me before the night was out. Andy was right, I was completely out of my league in terms of pouring scorn and inviting vengeance in return.

As soon as we took our seats, an army of women emerged from the kitchen carrying plates that were plonked efficiently in front of us. Then just as we were leaning towards each other to say, 'Well, this is nice' the band started up and we were unable to communicate with each other, apart from sign language and shouting directly into ear canals. I had nothing at that point that really needed to be said, so I turned in my chair and busied my focus toward the stage.

A funky young guy came strutting out and did some charismatic, 'Hey how you doin?' banter in Thai before introducing the dancing girls. About fifteen girls filed across the stage in pink sequins with giant pink torpedo-shaped things strapped to their backs. They didn't so much dance, as just sort of move in formation, in almost-unison with bored looks on their faces. Their main trick was that every few songs they'd disappear for a costume change and then re-emerge onto the stage with the same deadpan expressions, in entirely new and increasingly more ridiculous matching outfits. We were treated to pom pom girls, go-go dancers with matching white wigs, slutty school girls and a bordello-style variation on Carmen Miranda, just to name a few.

But the highlight was when the singer came out with a cucumber down his pants and sang some sort of song in Thai that was apparently hilarious and involved some naughty and titillating reference to the cucumber, with a lot of pelvic thrusting. But really, who's judging? Western wedding receptions are just as embarrassing and ridiculous. I'll see your cucumber pants man and raise you the bride dancing in all her white-virgin finery to 'You Give Me Head' by *The Radiators,* while she swings her garter triumphantly in the air, drunk dishevelled men making boorish speeches, a bunch of sad middle-aged people dancing in formation to 'Let's Do the Time Warp Again,' or 'YMCA' and finally the bride and groom earnestly reciting their own homemade vows. Hell, I've even been to a fancy dress wedding where the bride came as Elvira, the groom as Dracula and the rest of us stood around in solemn silence during the ceremony in various ridiculous outfits ranging from the Easter Bunny to a gorilla.

Anyway, by 11pm, I was considering another trip to the toilet, if only to alleviate my boredom. Maude had decided that the only way to combat her own boredom was to slug another glass of beer and dance with the locals.

"That little woman with the underbite is so taken with me," she said with a fond repugnance as she took her seat beside me again.

Andy was outside somewhere, probably smoking his head off and sifting through proposals of marriage from Thai women. I was beyond caring at that point. *Let them have him,* I thought tiredly.

The bus was scheduled to ship us all out en masse at midnight, which was still a good hour away. With nothing left to say to anyone, I excused myself from the table and went for a walk, with the bathroom as my destination. Maude had been pulled up to the dance floor again by her underbite friend so contrary to Tom's warnings, I ventured out into the darkness alone.

Ironically, the warnings to not go alone were more to do with Thai locals. No one considered that an encounter with my own father-in-law could be just as perilous. I stepped out into the darkness and headed along the dusty path to the shed. As I passed the trailer where the dancing girls changed their outfits, the darkness fell deeper around me. I could see the shape of the tin shed in the distance. There were people loitering in dark corners all over the place.

As I was walking, I heard footsteps behind me. I stepped up the pace instinctively, only to find the footsteps behind matching my increased pace.

"Just getting some air, darling?" Hal said, falling into step with me. I tried to outpace him but he virtually skipped to keep up with me.

"Need the loo," I said.

"Shouldn't be out here alone, did anyone tell you that?"

"Yes."

"I'll walk you, if you like."

"I'm okay, thanks."

"It's just a bit dangerous out here, for a *farang* lady," Hal said. "They think you're loose women, that you like the rumpy pumpy, that you're up for it, you know."

I ignored this. We walked in silence. Then he sighed conversationally and said, "Pity all this nastiness about Sunisa, quite deceitful really."

"No one cares," I said.

"You know what I'm talking about?" he said, as though surprised I wouldn't weigh in on it. "This business with the bastard child and all that."

"No one cares," I said again.

"Well, Phan says it's a fraud issue, given the dowry that was paid and all. It can mean that Tom has paid too much, that's all. It's a bit sinister really if you think about it. She's hiding all this stuff from him. Phan says Sunisa's got three other humpers on the go."

The dowry issue was a moot point, as Sunisa had essentially paid her own. The only people committing fraud were her own parents and for a split second I thought to warn Hal about who he was accusing of fraud, given the ready presence of Dodo and his gun and the seven disappeared people buried in the corn fields. However, I decided this would be misconstrued by Hal as me being concerned for his safety. Hal was moving his hands around to emphasise his point. I stopped walking.

"Why don't you shut up," I said as evenly as I could manage.

"Gee, quite waxy," he reeled back as though hurt.

"Seriously, shut your trap," I said again.

In the darkness, I saw his eyes measuring me up. He was surprised that I would take him on like this. Then his face closed over and he said something softly to himself, just ever so audibly so I could hear it.

"Frigid cunt."

My stomach dropped away. Andy was right, I was completely out of my depth here. Who *says* things like that?

"Nell?" I heard Tom's voice. He was standing behind one of the sheds smoking. He materialised from the darkness in his cream Nehru suit like some sort of spy.

"I was just walking her to the bathroom, trying to be chivalrous and she starts getting stuck into me," Hal said. "She's gone on the attack. She's poisoned my son against me and now she's attacking me personally. She's *attacked* me, she's just *gone* me."

"*You* poisoned your own son against you," I said, wishing suddenly I could have put that more eloquently. In the heat of the moment it was hard to put in a nutshell everything that had happened over the years and I found myself frustratingly at a loss for words.

"Just . . . " Tom put his hands up toward us both in a 'settle down everyone' gesture. "Just be nice boys and girls. Hal perhaps you could go back to the party, I'll walk Nell to the toilet."

"I'm just worried about you, son," Hal said. "I'm worried for you, this business, it's terrible, it's a real shock."

"Hal, just go back to the party," Tom said in a low, dangerous voice.

"Why are you turning on me?" Hal started shouting. "It's Andy and Nell who are talking about you behind your back."

"What?" I said, my heart hammering with shock. I thought then of all the gossiping I'd been doing with Maude, the conjecture about Sunisa, the mistrust, the completely racist assumptions I'd made aloud and inside my head. For someone who appeared to have an extremely low emotional intelligence, Hal had an uncannily well-pitched sense for the undercurrents of relationships; all that stuff that rushes along beneath us as we tread water and try to get along with each other. He seemed determined to have us all thrashing around trying to drown each other.

"Hal, just piss off," Tom said, his own voice rising in pitch.

"I'm on your side, son. I'm on your side," Hal was grasping. "You need to watch your back."

"Why do you do this?" Tom said.

"Do what?" Hal said. "I'm just trying to warn you. Sunisa's got this bastard child she's hiding from you and three other humpers . . . "

"I told you to shut up about that," Tom said and as he said it he reached out with both hands and shoved Hal in the chest. Hal wasn't expecting it. He fell back into the corrugated wall of a shed behind and the wall gave a little to make a small Hal indent. The low, metallic thumping noise shocked both Tom and me. Tom seemed surprised by his momentary loss of control. Still he didn't move toward Hal to help him. He just watched as Hal righted himself.

"Seriously Dad, why do you do that?"

Hal was making small 'arrgh fuck' noises as he prised himself out of the wall. When he was upright again, he said, as though completely bewildered, "Do what, son? What have I done?"

"Why do you have to try to turn us all against each other?" Tom asked, exasperated. "Why can't you just be supportive? I just want to be part of a family that supports each other, instead of all this ripping in."

"No. Not me," Hal was saying. "It's Andy and Nell who are calling you a dunce."

"Bullshit!" I said.

"Just go back to the party, Dad." Tom flicked his hand at him dismissively, then he turned to me, "Come on, let's go."

I fell into step beside Tom and we walked away. Tom was repellently silent. He lit another cigarette and heaved the smoke into his lungs with some desperation.

"Really?" Hal called after us. "You'll side with this bitch over me, your own father?"

Tom turned then and called out into the darkness. "Just fuck off, Dad. I don't want to know you." Then he turned and kept walking.

"Evil prick," he muttered, not to me, but to himself.

I sensed then that this whole encounter had gone beyond me and my experience of Hal. It went deep into the family history and Tom's stony silent mood told me not to even try to empathise. We walked side by side, inches apart, without connecting in any way.

Tom stood outside the toilet shed while I weed. Then we walked silently back to the party together.

## 37.

It was Sunisa who exacted the sweetest form of revenge. When Tom and I returned to the reception hall, the dance floor was still in full swing. Without a word, we went our separate ways, still stinging from the encounter with Hal and the unsettling bits of truth dust he had kicked into our faces. As I approached our table I saw an unlikely scene being played out on the dance floor.

Hal was in the midst of an old white man's wet dream; a bevy of young local girls were dancing around him provocatively and he was in their centre, his face alive with lascivious glee. He threw his arms in the air and let them have their wicked way with him. And as they moved toward him and stroked him from all angles, his eyes were aglow with a blind 'I can't believe my luck' euphoria. There was something vain in the way he preened about in the middle of this unlikely tableau, as though it made perfect sense that a group of young Thai girls would gather around him and essentially give him a stand-up lap dance for free. He seemed to think it merely his due as a handsome *farang* man on the prowl.

He continued to enjoy himself until, mysteriously, the girls melted away into the crowd. And as the circle of dreams dissolved around him, there stood Phan. He was given not a moment of reflection on his fantasy before she moved in and swiped him cleanly across the face with her open palm. The slapping noise was lost in the volume of the band but the violent leeward throw of his head was not. The crowd parted and moved out to watch from a safer circumference. Hal stood holding his cheek, but the respite was brief. Phan pulled back her fist and shot it forward. It connected bluntly with his mouth and jacked his head backward. As Hal disbelievingly touched his fingertips to his lower lip to check for blood, she struck again and finally brought her knee up into his groin. He doubled over then, finished.

Phan, her fury beyond English, shouted in Thai, her face was red with passionate rage. Then she took her seat again at the table and crossed her stout little legs in an unashamedly righteous 'well that's dealt with now' fashion. The crowd surged forward around Hal. Mostly it was locals reclaiming their dance floor positions, but Jean, Ivan and Greg rushed to his aid.

It wasn't until later, back at the accommodation, that we found out who had set Hal up with the posse of lap-dancing beauties in full view of Phan. It was Sunisa's carefully plotted revenge; the harem of girls led by her sister. In some ways, the sight of Hal holding his bloody, split lip, bewildered and unawares that the final blow to his groin was yet to come, made me realise definitively that whatever paradise he had sought, whatever easy option he had chased so single-mindedly to Thailand, now more closely resembled hell. If my wish for Hal was rot in hell, it seemed likely that's how he would live out his days, with a stronger, younger and more volatile wife who was prepared to strike back physically. In addition to that, he now had no choice financially but to work until he collapsed in a heap of old age, at which point, Phan would probably drag him into a dark corner and march down to the bank every second week to collect his pension and spend it for herself. He'd made his bed carelessly and now he was well and truly lying in it.

Back at the resort after the reception, Andy and I aligned ourselves with the young people and stayed up with Tom's mates for one last nightcap. There was a sense of divide with us at the bridging point; we stepped either side of it depending on our mood. The older generation, Maude, Stan, Jean, Greg, Ivan (still being trailed hopefully by Jeng) and Hal (thoroughly castigated and practically dragged by his hair back to the room by Phan) had retired to their rooms and the rest of us enjoyed the time without the adults like a bunch of adolescents who'd been on their best behaviour all night.

Ben found an old karaoke machine and proceeded to sing the available selection of Thai pop songs in a racist way. In our drunken, tired and emotionally exhausted states, we let go of any remaining semblance of cross-cultural decorum and guffawed like a repulsive bunch of colonial buffoons. It was a moment of pure, unchecked racism to which we all surrendered gleefully until the door to the supply cupboard flew open and Granny waddled bow-leggedly out in her nightie. She went straight to the machine and shut it off, taking the power cord back into her cupboard with her for good measure.

"Is that her bedroom?" Ben spluttered disbelieving. "I thought it was the pantry."

Even I didn't want to go to bed by that stage and Andy refilled everyone's glasses as we resolved to finish off the last of the beer before morning. By the time Sunisa and Tom pulled up in their car to spend their last night with us, we were all royally tanked and cheered them in. As Tom came up the steps towards us, I wondered how we would resolve what had gone on out in the darkness at the reception. He heralded himself, Hal-style, with applause over his head and we all joined in.

Then he came over to me and knelt down beside my chair. "How you going there, Nell?" he said softly.

"I'm tanked," I said with uncharacteristic enthusiasm for the theme.

"Good-good." He touched me lightly on the back. I took this as some form of acknowledgement that we were still on the same side. Then he turned to Andy,

"Good sport, mate?" he said simply.

"We're having a great time!" Andy said. "What an amazing day."

Tom took a seat and accepted a glass of beer. Sunisa drew up a chair beside him and rested her head on his shoulder. They both looked, like any newly anointed bride and groom; slightly shell-shocked. The party continued on around them but I noticed a faraway look on Tom's face. He smiled and laughed but he wasn't all there. Andy noticed it too because I heard him say, "You right mate?"

"Evil weed?" Tom said proffering his smokes as enticement.

Without a word, they got up and walked out of the hall into the darkness to smoke in brotherly privacy.

At that moment, sitting in the open air dining hall with the dark balmy night spread out around me, I was at peace. I had let go of my bugbears and my grudges, I no longer concentrated on holding them carefully in both hands. I had set them loose into the remote Thai wilderness. I was ready to go home without them.

But Hal, he just couldn't let things be.

# 38.

The waterfall was Sunisa's idea. In one last gesture of hostessness, she wanted to show us the countryside surrounding her village. The drivers had told her there was a waterfall with a swimming hole nearby that was worth visiting. Sunisa organised for them to take us there the next morning, after which we would head back to Bangkok at noon. I was tempted to give the waterfall a miss, but Andy said Sunisa was still trying to save face and it would be rude not to partake of her tourist activity. Besides, it was stinkingly, clingingly hot and the thought of swimming in a water hole with a waterfall gushing into it was appealing. Added to that, the rumour was that Hal, in the aftermath of his big night, would not be joining us.

The night before, after lights out, Andy had returned to our room after a long talk (and about fifty million cigarettes by the smell of him) with Tom. He told me Tom was pretty deeply torn up by the things Hal had said, all the stuff about me and Andy calling him a dunce.

Tom still held in his mind a gilded idea of Hal that did not match the reality. And every time the reality crashed through, Tom felt it as the hard blows of life knocking him around. He refused to see it as the shortcoming of his own father.

Hal had also informed Tom that Andy had given his marriage five years. This was eerily similar to what Hal had said about our marriage. It was unlike Hal to recycle his own bile and reattribute it. Andy and I agreed that Hal was losing his edge.

"I told him that wasn't true," Andy said, upset. "I'm not sure he even believed me."

"He doesn't seem to have reached the point of enlightenment that you have," I said thoughtfully. "Where you just keep Hal at an arm's length."

"I told him," Andy said, "I told him to just stay calm and not bite."

"What does Tom expect from Hal?" I said, still bewildered that Tom had moved to a foreign country where his only family contact was Hal.

"I think he expects him to be a father."

"Well that's sad," I said. "Because that will never happen."

"I know. See, I know that now. And I'm much better for it."

Andy's eyes were bright and sharp with fight. He had the look of a runner who was out in front, but still saw a long road stretching out ahead. Despite his bravado, he did not seem to me to be at peace. He was still fighting to stay ahead of his history, still trying to outrun it.

By the time we had all piled into the bus (sans Hal and Phan) it was already nine o'clock. We all had towels slung hopefully over our shoulders, sunhats and sunscreen, shorts and sundresses like we were on a jolly trip to the seashore. (Except for Sunisa, who was wearing her requisite skinny jeans and tank top.) Jean, unable to find her swimming top, nudged me from the seat behind and asked me if I thought she could get away with wearing her black bra instead. She flashed it to me from beneath her sarong and, given Hal would not be joining us, I assured her it was fine. Maude had brought her book and was planning to sit in the shade somewhere and read.

Just as the bus was revving up to reverse out and pull away, Hal appeared on the rise that led to the bungalows, trailed happily by Phan, like they were the endearingly crazy couple of the tour we all couldn't help but love. They both ran clumsily in their flip flops toward the bus, waving their arms, *Wait for us!*

I may have imagined it, but I'm almost sure that an audible groan of disappointment moved through the bus at that point. Hal and Phan climbed in and took the two seats left without complaint. Perhaps it was Hal's tacit acknowledgement of his own bad behaviour. Even so, I turned my face to the window and went on with pretending he did not exist. My fury had settled into a bone deep sadness for Tom, Andy and Maude. Their family history was so blighted by this man that they could not look back on themselves, as every family needs to, without being confronted by uncomfortable memories from which they had to avert their eyes.

And even when they tried to change their history, to reimagine things as harmless, crazy times, here he was, reminding them of the reality.

We bumped along the dirt roads of the village for about forty minutes and then finally the bus pulled in to a tourist spot with parking and picnic tables. There was a small weir rushing water across a concrete plinth and then a stagnant pond. We looked around and couldn't see any other evidence of running water. The disappointment was palpable as we all assumed this was the 'waterfall'. We climbed out of the bus and stood on the grass, slightly bewildered. Then Sunisa took charge in her shiny-soled court shoes and led the way across the flat grass plain towards a steep, jungle-covered hill in the near distance.

We followed and saw then that there was a river trickling slowly down the hill, over rocks and tree roots. It was a shallow river, about ankle deep and it pooled here and there in shallow puddles that didn't seem satisfactory for a swim.

We followed Sunisa up the hill. There were signs in Thai and English, *Swimming hole this way*. When the path got steeper and we were stepping over slippery rocks, Maude, Stan and Greg fell out of the procession and decided to stay put on the gentle rise where the river ran coolly over a large rock. Maude got out her book and Stan sat, knees apart on a rock, catching his breath and mopping the back of his neck with a hankie dipped in the cool water. Greg lay on some grass and shut his eyes to the sky. Brittany decided, too, that this was enough for her. She fished a book out of her canvas bag and sat cross-legged by herself in the grass beneath the wide brim of her hat. The rest of us walked on. With Stan, Maude and Greg out of the running, there was only Jean between me and Hal. I stepped up my pace a bit, trying to get as far from him as possible.

We walked up and the river got wider, and a little deeper with bigger leachy pools between the flows. At a cool, shaded platform where there was a log on a rise looking back over the river, Jean sat down on the log to catch her breath.

"Is it much further, Sunisa?"

Sunisa nodded unconvincingly, indicating that as far as she knew it wasn't much further but that what she knew wasn't really much at all. She looked a bit stressed at this point, no doubt worrying about how this excursion was going to turn out now that she had dragged us all up this hill into the jungle where there appeared to be no sound or sign of a significant waterfall nor the deep cool plunge of an accompanying swimming hole.

The incline was quite steep and we had to stop to help each other clamber up rocks and over tree stumps. The tree canopy was dense and the sound of trickling water was cooling in the thick muggy air. At a point where the track forked away from the river and disappeared up an even steeper incline into deep jungle growth, Jean decided to call it quits. It was a good enough spot, the river cascaded down into a rock platform forming a waist deep pool. She threw down her towel and untied the sarong from around her neck.

"Well," she said, "this'll do me." Then she waded into the rock pool with her bra and swimmers and squatted down to submerge herself. Phan, Jeng, Ivan and Hal decided then that this would be their limit too. Phan set her towel down in the grass for her and Jeng to sit on. Ivan took up roost on a rise behind them, looking out evasively to the horizon. Hal squeezed himself onto Phan's towel. He sat with one leg crooked up, his elbow rested on it in what I imagined *he* imagined was a handsome manly pose. Then he reached up and untied the neck of Phan's bikini top. She grabbed it just in time to preserve her modesty and playfully slapped him.

"You very bad."

They had obviously patched up their differences overnight. Or perhaps Phan considered her public pummelling of Hal on the dance floor a satisfactory resolution in itself.

"Come on, tops off, in you go." Hal cupped his hands around his mouth then and shouted. "Tops off, Jean!"

Jean, to her credit just smiled and said, "Oh, I don't think anyone wants to see what's inside *my* bra, Hal," and then sunk herself deeper into the cool water pool.

I looked down at this scene and decided that, in spite of the fact that I did not want to venture any further into the leachy jungle, I had no other choice but to keep going upward. I did not fancy sitting on the rocks with Hal and Phan, even with Jean there as a buffer.

And it was too late to go back down to where Maude was sitting. So onwards and upwards I went. At this point, Ben, Joe, Andy, Tom and Sunisa had forged ahead with some determination. I turned to follow them, about ten feet behind. Then fifteen as I had to stop to catch my breath.

It was a steep incline, the track was narrow and virtually non-existent. I heard Andy and Tom, at one point Andy called out, "Cooee!"

I stopped to catch my breath and that's when I heard footsteps from below, making their way up the track toward me. I prayed that it was Jean. My heart sank when I saw that it was Hal, huffing and puffing to catch up and not miss out. He stopped about three feet from me, cupped his hands around his mouth and went, "Cooee!"

At which point, both Tom and Andy returned the call. I turned and kept walking, away from Hal, up the mountain into the jungle where I could not see anything but thick growth ahead of me. To the right of the track, the hill fell sharply away to the river below. Hal, out of breath, was mercifully rendered unable to speak. But he managed to move himself into position just behind me, so that the only way I could go was up.

Somewhere in there, I lost my footing and stumbled backwards slightly. And that was when he reached forward and seized the moment. He stretched out a hand to steady me and cupped it just neatly onto my left bum cheek. I felt my flesh jiggle in his grasp. His hand lingered then squeezed.

It was a knee-jerk reaction on my part. I spun around and I shoved him away from me.

He reeled backwards and on the steep incline, where he expected to step, there was only air. His foot searched for ground that wasn't there. It landed heavily about a foot below where he expected and his ankle buckled beneath his weight. Hal went over sideways where the track dropped steeply to the river. He landed heavily with his shoulder downhill, followed by his head which snapped his neck with the weight of his body following over. His body contorted over itself like that, a sickening series of plunges through the undergrowth before gravity took over and unfurled his body into a more streamlined, faster, sideways roll.

I heard a small movement behind me. I looked around and saw Sunisa standing uphill on the overgrown track that led to the top of the waterfall. From the look on her face, I knew she had seen exactly what had happened.

Hal, who had been standing directly below me on the track, was simply no longer there. He'd gone over the edge without uttering a word and was still rolling, silently now, through the dank, leachy undergrowth down the steep incline toward the river. There was a small splash, (really a more benign 'plip' sound) as he slipped into the water below. A few seconds later, we heard the others screaming.

Sunisa and I stared at each other. Her hand went up to her mouth. Tom and Andy came rushing down, sideways side-stepping down the hill.

"What the fuck happened?" Tom said, hearing the wailing and panicked shouting that was coming from below.

I was speechless. My body was prickly with adrenaline, I felt all the blood drain from my face and I thought for a moment I might faint. My knees went to jelly. I lowered myself slowly and carefully onto the damp ground and dipped my head down to redistribute the blood to my brain. I had not kept calm. I had snapped and now Hal was floating lifelessly down the river like a rag doll.

It was Sunisa who spoke. "He fall, he trip," she said. "Hal, he fall down there." She pointed towards the sheer drop that fell away to the river.

Andy and Tom moved quickly down toward the clearing. Sunisa came and sat beside me on the ground. She placed her palm gently on my back and left it there.

# 39.

Death in Thailand is as perfunctory and as ad hoc as life. The ambulance, when it came, was a mini van. Something about the lack of proper authority attached to this terrible event made me suddenly wonder if it was happening at all.

Hal's lifeless body was lifted by two small Thai paramedics in white shirts. Tom and Andy stood by at first, then stepped forward instinctively when Hal's unsupported head lolled down between his shoulder blades. Andy was quick thinking enough to get himself and Tom into the back of the ambulance just as the doors were shutting, nimbly excluding Phan at the last strategic moment.

She was shut out and left behind as his two sons delivered him through to the official bureaucracy that would mark the ending of Hal Straw. There was no siren as they drove him away. Just the keening sound of Phan, wailing like a banshee, like she'd just lost the love of her life.

A police car arrived and Sunisa's father stepped out. He was wearing his uniform, his pants pulled high, nipped and belted around his tiny waist, the mirrored aviator sunnies; a miniature tough-guy cop from Thai central casting. Sunisa stood up and walked towards him. They stood in the middle of the picnic ground, their heads bowed together conspiratorially talking in Thai.

I don't know what she said, but she kept me out of it.

IV

# Hal's last request

**pen·ance** [**pen**-uhns] *–noun*
a punishment undergone in token of penitence for sin

# 40.

In the two years since, no one has ever questioned Sunisa's eye-witness account of what happened to Hal; it is widely accepted that he simply fell. In fact, because they are so confident that this is the truth, it has become a macabre family 'joke' that I pushed Hal to his death. Each time this joke is referenced in a familial shorthand way, my heart surges momentarily with fear and I arrange my face in a way that I hope is inscrutable.

Apart from Sunisa, no one knows what really happened and she continues to be a reliable and unflinching alibi. Indeed, she has proved to be a master of deception herself. On travelling back to Sydney for the funeral, she was required to fill out a visa application. One section of the application called for the declaration of any known 'dependents'.

It was not until Tom wrenched the visa application from her hands that he saw the box ticked with the name Ariyanuntaka Boon-mee beside it. As we said all along, it's not a big deal. But still Tom has instructed us never to mention it in front of her. It is culturally telling that she is more shamed by the truth, than by the act of having lied about it.

According to the death certificate, Hal Straw's death was caused by a fractured vertebrae; a broken neck that resulted from an accidental fall. And while I am not claiming I did them all a favour, Hal's death, and with it the absence of his malicious personality coursing through the present, has allowed them a reinterpretation of their history. Death brings out the best in people and when someone is gone, it is all the sweet stuff that floats to the top.

Andy remembers his father with beach towel wings. They are on a beach somewhere up the coast and Hal is a pterodactyl. He is chasing the boys around the sand, flapping his wings and making a wild 'arrk arrrk!' sound in the soft light of a summery afternoon. Eventually, he captures Andy and holds him there, folded inside his wings for just a moment before setting him free.

Tom remembers a camping trip, just him and Hal. Tom is eleven and the fact that Hal takes him alone thrills him. They build a campfire and toast marshmallows, Tom is allowed to have as many as he wants and he scoffs the entire packet before teatime. They cook sausages on the fire and eat them with their fingers like wild cave men. When it is time for bed, Tom begs to sleep outside the tent beneath the stars. At dawn, Tom wakes to the smell of the charred burnt-out fire and realises he is now inside the tent. Hal must have carried him in while he slept.

For some memories, they have colluded and recreated them anew. Once told to me as an example of Hal's unpredictability, his wild temper, this memory has now been repackaged as a funny memory. A Chinese restaurant. The meal is finished and the table is covered with dishes. The waitress is taking too long to clear it and is nowhere to be seen. Hal stands up, gathers the corners of the tablecloth around the uncleared dishes, bundles it all into a package, carries it across to a nearby window and drops it out.

It's funny now. Because he is gone.

Some years before Hal went to live in Thailand, in the period when Hal and Helen had just separated and were squabbling over their assets, I had received a terse phone call from a hospital matron.

"Can I speak to Andrew Straw please?" The woman already sounded fed up.

"I'm sorry he's not here, can I take a message?"

"It's St Vincent's Hospital, his father's been admitted, he's had a heart attack. Tell him to call us as soon as possible please."

Her tone had been curt and officious, completely lacking in the sort of empathy I would expect were my own father to be alone and near death in a hospital somewhere on the other side of the city. Probably, Hal had long ago used up any ounce of patience and empathy the poor woman possessed. When Andy had gone to the hospital, he had found Hal lying in a hospital bed with an oxygen mask across his face and a pastor sitting dutifully by the bed.

"So, what do I have to do . . . " Hal was grilling the priest. ". . . for absolution, Father. Tell me; pray? Repent? What do I have to do?"

"Well Harold," the priest had replied tiredly, "I've already told you, there are no guarantees, you just have to put your faith in God and ask him forgiveness."

"But what do I have to *do*?" Hal had asked again.

It appeared to Andy that this exchange had been going on for some time. Even the priest, a man of god, showed signs of compassion fatigue when faced with Hal Straw. And it was typical and telling that as he looked death in the face, Hal had been thinking not of the life he had led and how he could have done it better, or of the people he loved and how he could have loved them better, but rather he had been thinking only of himself. He had been desperately seeking a last minute 'get out of jail free' card to ensure him a spot in heaven.

Hal had recovered, but not before he had grasped Andy's hand one day and rasped at him from beneath his oxygen mask, "Son, we should've been closer."

"It was like talking to Darth Vader," Andy had said to me later, completely unmoved by what he saw as too little, too late.

"What a pity he didn't cark it," Maude's best friend Beverley had sighed.

The point is, in the aftermath of this earlier brush with death, Hal had put his life effects in order. Before he left for Thailand, he handed Andy an envelope containing his will and a handwritten note regarding his preferred funereal arrangements in the future event of his untimely death. In the will, he left to Andy his stamp collection and whatever motor vehicle 'I may possess at the time of my death'. To Tom, he left his collection of contemporary music and pornographic videos. What remained of his estate was then to be divided evenly between the two of them.

For the funeral arrangements, Hal's one emphatic demand was for a traditional burial rather than cremation. To ensure this was carried out to his liking, he had gone to the trouble of booking a burial plot on the eastern hillside of Rookwood Cemetery, beneath the canopy of a large fig tree.

> Refer to attached receipts for exact plot number and location, (don't burn me, son!) My preferred hymn is 'Amazing Grace' and I would like an Anglican service at the Rookwood chapel with a top line mahogany coffin (life insurance policy should cover this and all funeral costs). Afterwards, a small wake with closest friends and family. Nell to serve tea and sandwiches.

Galling to the last, Hal had paid the deposit on his plot but not the balance. When Tom and Andy went to make the burial arrangements, they were presented with the remaining bill. Andy says they did not exchange a word between them and I believe him. Their final decision regarding Hal Straw's life was mutual, unspoken and resolute.

At the funeral, Maude wept elegantly without smudging her mascara. She lifted her glasses gently and dabbed at her eyes with a tissue when Andy delivered a eulogy in which he remembered his father as a 'larger than life character whose sole purpose was to have fun'.

Daniel and Elizabeth remained preoccupied with Hal's dead body inside the coffin. *Is he really in there?* and Albert spent most of his time terrorising the carefully manicured hedging in the courtyard outside with Stan watching over him.

Greg, Jean and Ivan were a sombre presence in the third row, a grim trio and a reminder of the fateful trip we had all taken together to arrive here at Hal Straw's funeral. Phan remained in Thailand, choosing to arrange her own version of a funeral in which she could take centre stage as the grieving widow. She also ensured any benefits would be paid to her. You had to admire her extensive knowledge of death and the financial bureaucracy of its aftermath.

An old woman played a halting, dirgey version of *Amazing Grace* on the electric organ and we all stood and sang in that embarrassed sort of way, without opening our mouths properly; occasionally just humming through our noses and glancing around to check no one was looking at us. All except for Maude, who opened her mouth and caterwauled tunelessly without shame. It seemed some sort of catharsis and I just left her to it, without once glancing in her direction lest she feel suddenly self-conscious and stop.

When the final prayer had been said, we sat down and waited. The funeral director stood by the coffin (the easily combustible kind) with his hands held down at his crotch for a respectful moment. Then as the standard goodbye music played, he reached up and pushed a button on the wall. The coffin shunted forward, gliding slowly towards the maroon velvet curtains, which parted automatically and then swallowed Hal Straw and his coffin whole.

Hal was being sent straight to the furnace.

With this in mind, you'll probably be surprised to learn that as requested by Hal, I did serve tea and sandwiches. If the punishment is to fit the crime, I consider it a worthy penance.

As for the truth. I have not yet told Andy. I can't see what good would come from him knowing. And while I haven't ruled out telling him the truth some time in the future, experience has taught me that, for the sake of marital harmony, there are some things a husband simply does not need to know.

## Acknowledgements

Taking the time to read an unpublished manuscript is the most immense favour you can grant a writer. The following people took the time to read this manuscript in its raw unpublished form and gave invaluable feedback: Tohby Riddle, Catherine Drayton, Cassie Cale, John and Leonie Flanagan and most importantly my sister, Katie Flanagan—whose opinion I value so highly. Kylie Matthews provided much-needed writer's counsel at a crucial point in the process. My cheerleaders Joan Flanagan and Barbara McKee provided regular bolstering—reminding me to take my writing self seriously—and Jane Johnson provided critical advice on all things architectural. Most importantly, I would like to thank Ed Wright and all those at Puncher & Wattmann for accepting unsolicited manuscripts and bravely committing their imprint to publishing contemporary Australian fiction.

## About the author

Penny Flanagan was born in Sydney in 1970 and grew up on the northern beaches. She spent her early twenties as a musician. Her debut solo single, *Lap It Up,* reached number 58 in the 1994 triple j's Hottest 100. Her debut novel, *Changing The Sky* (written for children), was released in 1994 by Hodder & Stoughton and her first adult fiction, *Sing To Me,* was published by Penguin Books in 1998. Her short stories have been published in *Meanjin, Imago* and *Picador New Writing.* Penny lives in Sydney with her three children and is a regular contributor to parenting and lifestyle websites *kidspot.com.au, babyology.com* and *news.com.au.*

www.ingramcontent.com/pod-product-compliance
Lightning Source LLC
Chambersburg PA
CBHW022000010726
47494CB00003B/817

*9781925780000*